Bennett & Company

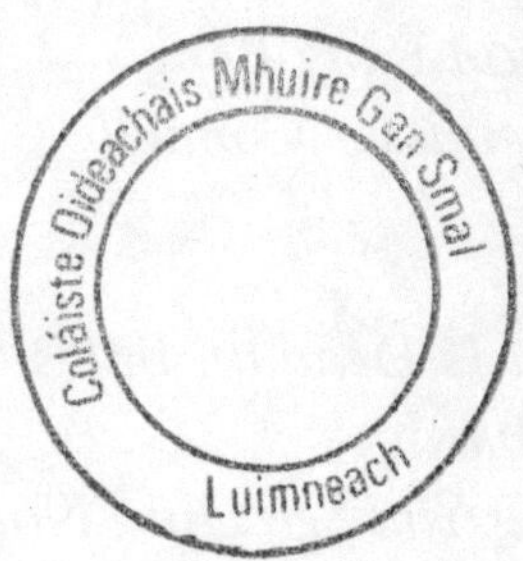

Also by J. M. O'Neill

Novels
Open Cut
Duffy Is Dead
Canon Bang Bang
Commissar Connell

Plays
God Is Dead on Ball's Pond Road
Diehards
Now You See Him, Now You Don't

A NOVEL OF LIMERICK IN 1928

BENNETT & COMPANY

J. M. O'NEILL

MOUNT EAGLE

First published in 1998 by
Mount Eagle Publications Ltd.,
Dingle, Co. Kerry, Ireland

ISBN 1 902011 06 6
(Original paperback)

Published with the assistance of the
Arts Council/An Chomhairle Ealaíonn

Typesetting by Red Barn Publishing, Skeagh, Skibbereen
Cover design by the Public Communications Centre, Dublin
Printed by ColourBooks Ltd, Dublin

To Jim Kemmy

CHAPTER ONE

EDWARD BURKE, PRINCIPAL of the Hugh Latimer School, was still a young man, a person of ability and fair talent who was progressing well enough in life.

This was his native town – called a city, it had an ancient charter – of perhaps thirty-five thousand souls. It spanned a great river that flowed on for sixty miles in a wide magnificent estuary to meet the North Atlantic Ocean, and it had a fine stretch of granite and limestone quayside where coal boats from Swansea Bay and Whitehaven came to discharge their loose cargo in thunderous noise and dust and grime. At high tide they floated on twenty feet of water, and at the ebb their keels sat on a hard, gravelled bottom. For the bigger ships that brought maize and timber, there was a floating dock that captured high water and held it behind swivel gates to keep them afloat and free from the strain of grounding.

The Latimer School, a school of primary education, sat on high ground above the river. Edward Burke, walking through empty classrooms, could look down over rooftops and warehouses and steep, falling streets, along the sweep of dockland to the graceful bridge that spanned the river and, at a distance, a more ancient bridge and the impressive ruins of a defending castle. The river's navigable range ended at the first bridge, where only tiny craft could move beyond rocks and white water.

He turned his gaze from the view and walked the corridors. The walls were covered with a cream gloss oil paint, and a black line separated it from the deep brown of the wainscot that dropped to the skirting. Pupils came here in school uniform, polished shoes, gartered stockings, shirts and ties. He looked in at the blackboard and desks and inkwells of sixth form. That was the final year of tuition before they went, almost without exception, to the advanced curricula of boarding schools.

The pupils of Hugh Latimer Primary were the sons of professional men or city merchants, being groomed to inherit responsibility.

The year was 1928, a changing world, and a lot of the old certainties that had been been the bricks and mortar of Latimer's lifetime of almost two hundred years were showing cracks and fissures. Pupils and their progenitors were growing fewer on the ground.

Latimer was a Church of Ireland school, a Protestant school of quality.

Edward Burke closed doors and checked windows. He had come down from Trinity in 1919, a distinguished pupil and graduate, when the country was in the travail of rebirth. He had been in Dublin on that Easter morning when a squad of men marched from Liberty Hall through Sackville Street. Those days of engagement and fighting seemed momentary now, but he remembered the aftermath. They were a protracted infliction of horror on a population that had hardly been aware of a rebellion. He remembered with anger the lorry-loads of troops, the searchings, the beatings, the killings. He remembered two friends of his father, men of substance and integrity, taken out and shot on their doorsteps. The strand walls looking out on the river would be their memorial for ever.

He remembered the truce and the treaty and the tragedy of northern counties. He remembered the savagery of civil war. It was all in the past now. Except for the loyal enclave of a new-cobbled northern territory, Edward stood on the holy ground of the Irish Free State, member of the British Commonwealth of Nations.

October 1928. He had been nine years at Latimer and he was headmaster at the age of thirty-one. His predecessor, an ageing man, had held the fort with stand-in teachers during the war years and enjoyed hardly a year of retirement. The staff of 1914 was buried in France without grave markers, and the stand-ins had gone back to their drawing-rooms. The old order changeth. There were fewer pupils now, and only five teachers.

It was a Church of Ireland school, a Protestant school, but Edward Burke was a Catholic. The only Catholic. The board of governors of this small but important place judged a schoolmaster on the excellence he could impart to their diminishing numbers. They had lost so many fine young men in so many useless wars. Catholics, too, had been lost, fighting blind fights for a remote monarchy across a separating channel of water.

Except for a diehard few, they were Irish, Protestant Irish. They were part of this country, part of this city.

Pupils, like years, were arriving, moving on; curricula were changing, history being refocused, priorities rearranged.

Edward Burke was of average height and there was friendliness in his face, but hardness, too; he was upright, light on his feet. In the staff cloakroom, he donned a navy blue topcoat with a velvet collar and a pearl grey felt hat with just the faintest trace of blue and a band of darker shade. He carried in his hand dark brown leather gloves. There would be a slight chilliness in the air.

In the entrance foyer there were notice boards and a well-carved presentation of the school title sitting above the armorial shield of the city: "The Hugh Latimer School of Primary Education", and below it, the twin crenellated towers flanking a domed barbican. The armorial inscription read *Urbs antiqua fuit studiisque asperima belli:* this was an ancient city skilled by the hardships of war.

Storan, the school janitor, wearing dungarees with yellow dusters showing from pockets, emerged from the main corridor. He had served as a regular in the British army, a light infantry regiment, and he still walked with a short quick pace and seemed to come to attention before he spoke. A man who seemed short in stature for regular army service, but perhaps it was his stockiness that gave the illusion, he had survived two wars. He had a cute, weathered face.

"The end of another day, sir."

"Yes, Storan."

He saw that Storan was carrying a newspaper.

"Have you seen the new coins, sir? There's a picture."

"New coins?"

"Everything with the king's head is to be filtered out and this new stuff brought in. A farmyard in our pockets, someone said. A horse, a fish, a bullock, a rabbit, a hare, a hen with her clutch, a pig and its litter and a woodcock. That's it, from half-crown to farthing. Near enough to a farmyard, I suppose. Bank notes are going, too."

Edward Burke looked at the picture: the images were good, he thought, finely worked. "It'll take some time," he said. "Perhaps a long time. We'll be enriched with two currencies for a while."

Storan grimaced. His army service, he thought, had given him rank above the gunmen politicians who sat in Dublin. "Two currencies. We'll have diehards who won't take English money, and people of breeding who'll have doubts about horses and bullocks. I'd have doubts myself."

Edward Burke said, "Shopkeepers and banks will take everything."

He didn't care very much for Storan. An ex-soldier, son of

a British soldier, pensioned, employed because of his references and loyalties, he wore his army slang like a badge.

"Blimey," he said with bowdlerised politeness, "it'll be a proper old brew-up in a dixey, won't it?"

Edward Burke said, "You've seen the world and its money, Storan. Rands in South Africa, francs and kroner and dollar bills in France. You'll cope with it very well. What rank had you in the Durham's?"

"Lance sergeant, sir."

"Sergeant without pay?"

"It was an honour to serve, sir."

Edward Burke was moving towards the door. "Good man," he said.

Storan halted in his pursuit, watching the moving figure of Burke. Burke was a bloody papish bastard playing with himself in Dublin University until the war was over, till the bullets had stopped flying. And he had married into Protestantism and money. His wife's Protestantism had found him a place in a Protestant school, Storan thought, and pushed him to the top of the ladder. She was a fine piece of game, but she had been well past thirty-five, ready to sit on the shelf, when Burke had smiled at her. Burke wouldn't be wearing the schoolmaster's hat if Protestant fighting men had been spared the bullets and shellfire of the bloody battle against the Hun. He moved quickly forward and held open the door.

"I was polishing up the old gongs yesterday, sir."

"Gongs?"

"Medals, sir. Six service medals. Only a short spell now to November 11th. Remembrance Day." A time to get together, to stand in silence, hear speeches in honour of the dead. To offer prayers for them.

Edward Burke tried to imagine Storan's prayers. Churches praying on opposite sides of the trenches for the defeat of an enemy hadn't stopped the war.

"It should be a fine gathering," he said.

"You'll be there, sir?"

"I'll turn out to see it."

"You should participate, sir. Your two brothers gave their lives. Fighting men would be honoured to have them represented, to walk beside you."

"Only Francis, my eldest brother, was killed. 1917. Buillycourt, France. The other had volunteered, but been rejected. He worked with the postal service at Mountpleasant in London. Died in 1922."

"But he volunteered?"

"Yes, yes."

Edward crossed the quadrangle and looked up at the weather vane. The breeze was blowing off-shore. Wars and flag-waving he didn't understand. He thought about the first day of July 1916, only months after a revolutionary march from Liberty Hall near the Liffey, when twenty thousand men had perished in a single day on the Somme; he thought of bodies buried in prison yards with a covering of quicklime, and the millions in France, and beyond, suppurating, dissolving into the soil and mud. He thought about his brother's unknown grave. Yes, he feared pain and death; everyone did. Standing against a prison wall, waiting for the metallic cocking of rifles and the explosion of mind for ever; or the last moments of climbing out of trenches to run across pocked bogland, tumbling into wire, falling, rising, waiting until the rattle of the machine-guns reached you and you lay to die in the mud, listening to the groans and screams that seemed loud as the thunder of gunfire. God was too fond of war-games, and now Edward's prayers were in the privacy of his study to some shapeless, amorphous creator. He prayed for understanding. Yes, he thought, you could call me an apostate.

He walked a distance to the steep hill that ran down to Dock Road and the quaysides. Two ugly, rusted coal boats, monster crafts really, were discharging cargo farther ahead. There was a tall stone wall and, at a distance from the water, a footway where Burke walked. The stone of the wall was dressed, pointed and crowned on top with broken glass set in concrete. There was a gargoyled niche with a drinking spout and a cast-iron drinking vessel heavily chained in the stonework. Children, some of them barefoot, drank from it, played a game. He looked at their patched knee-length trousers and buttoned ganseys. Underfed bodies but noisy and restless with life. Slaves or freemen, it meant little to them.

He passed the turmoil of the work area. Great hawsers held the vessels tight against the quayside. Aboard, a man sat behind a donkey engine and fed down the huge skip to the black dusty pile that had been chiselled from the deep earth across the water. Four men with broad shovels filled it; they were stripped to the waist, black, except for a tiny ring at the eyes and mouth, like ghostly singing minstrels. The piled skip rose up, away from them, and was swung ashore on the jib to sway above the loading-hopper. A man on a gantry, with a sledge, sprung the latches and the skip upended to empty itself. Horses and carts and drivers waited in line. Dust, like smoke, rose up from the hold and the hopper and was blown away across five hundred feet of river from bank to bank.

A car-man in working clothes with a cap and a tight scarf raised a finger, a salutation to Edward Burke, who nodded.

"A dirty job, isn't it?"

The man said, "We're the toffs here. We own a horse and cart, make a few shillings. But it takes a lot of drink to wash down filth and coal dust." He coughed, excused himself, and spat on the roadway. "That's what coal dust does. You can wash it out of your throat but it sticks in your pipes."

"You can leave it."

"Ten years spent on it. Five years coughing."

A strong man, clean, well-covered, passed them; he glanced at Edward; traffic and confusion seemed to make way for him. And then he shouted instructions, and his voice rang like a bell through the bedlam of movement and machinery; it had the ring of a hammer blow on metal.

"A foreman?" Edward asked.

"That's Carmody."

"Carmody?"

"Carmody, a stevedore. He hires and fires. Boards the boats when they dock, looks at the cargo and gear, makes a price."

Edward Burke watched the hopper filling the coarse, almost rigid gunny sacks that were swung on the shoulders and carried at a trot to the carts. Time was money. The carts pulled out and thundered away on iron-shod wheels to the city coal yards of importers. That was the retail point where money was made.

Burke looked at the ridged stained skin of the man before him. "Take care of yourself," he said.

The man nodded his thanks, and as he walked on, Edward could hear him coughing again. He turned away from the river towards the city streets, moving past warehouses, open spaces, licenced premises painted and sharp. The main streets were alive; horse traffic was common, but petrol-driven cars, vans and flat trucks were creeping in. Great high-sided wagons, chain driven, groaned under their loads of maize from the floating dock to the mills for grinding. Pedestrians were plentiful: men tatterdemalion or in varying degrees of correct dress, from cheap nondescript cloth to expensive serge; caps, a plethora of hats, even a silk stovepipe of distinction peeping above the crowd here and there; women were workhorses in hat, blouse and apron; or fashion plates of colour and elegance. Skirts were worn to the ankle or calf; only the cheap or daring showed an inch or two higher. Times were changing, Edward Burke thought again.

He went down the hill of the market street and turned left towards one of the city's four parish churches. Narrow busy streets where poverty and small commerce mixed. The Burkes had been a comfortable family. Like his dead siblings he had walked from here to the school of the Christian Brothers, good men, with a few remembered exceptions, who taught literacy and numeracy and left you well equipped at the crossroads.

The family dwelling was a corner house, but a substantial edifice of three storeys with a tall wall enclosing the place of business: Roderick Burke, City Cooperage. Roderick Burke, his father, had died after a short illness, a little more than five years past, at the age of sixty-eight. He had been fighting a losing battle to keep an old trade alive. A tall man, bespectacled, educated, an only child, he had been heir to the cooperage. He had stuck with it and died in it, leaving a great deal of money to his widow, Catherine.

Catherine Burke had been a governess; she could draw, paint and play daintily on the piano once. She had come from a minor genteel family, undowried, overbearing, apparently without capacity for even fleeting love or affection. Coopering was "trade" and she loathed even the precise skills of her husband and his workers. Edward could never remember her arms embracing him or the touch of her lips. He had been a small boy in the care of a nursemaid, even estranged from his brothers by a space of years. His father had loved him. Catherine Burke, if she could love, had loved only her eldest son, a boy of great brilliance, who was in a lost grave somewhere in Europe.

On the day following her husband's funeral she had closed the cooperage and shut herself in the dwelling-house. Daily, each evening, at almost precisely the same minute, she left her house. Except for the tight, pallid skin of her face, she was sheathed in black: good cloth, leather, lisle, millinery always draped with the tulle of mourning. She walked for an hour and a half through the fashionable streets, crossing the bridge to the northern bank and turning left to meet the open fields and the track along the raised dyke to the turn of the river stream. For a few moments she stood, erect and still, with both hands on her umbrella, looking across at the distant Snuff Box shipping-light, and then the return to her silent bastion.

Edward Burke raised the knocker and rapped lightly on the six-panelled door with heavy cast-iron furnishings. She would move about slowly, leaving him waiting, he knew. He looked up at the weathered brickwork, and at the blinds which had been drawn on every window since 1917, when the news of the death of her eldest boy, her only loved one, had arrived. The death of her husband, Roderick, had been a small sorrow. She had given him a more than adequate funeral-display and sat, distantly, in her private mourning carriage while his peers lowered down his coffin beneath a towering family memorial. Edward had returned with her to the twilight dwelling of drawn blinds.

"Don't let me keep you," she had said. "You must have work to do with your schoolmastering or something."

"You didn't come to my father's graveside."

"Women should not be at gravesides displaying grief."

"Grief?"

"Or whatever is displayed at gravesides."

"My father . . .," he had begun.

"He is dead and buried. I don't lack for anything."

Edward Burke stood now on the pavement. The corner house stood at the junction of a broad market street and a narrower uphill passage to a main thoroughfare. Greyness had crept into the light, and the lamplighter was on his rounds. There was a lamp-post at the corner and a great ornate iron-framed glass shade mounted on it. It seemed a magic feat: the lamplighter raised up a hooked rod and tipped the mains valve, the gas jet ignited, grew in intensity, and became a warm island of light between long spaces of crepuscle.

Suddenly the door was opened. Catherine Burke, even in age, had a strange theatrical presence. Her swept-up grey hair had substance and style. Years had sharpened her features, but there was good bone structure and she must have been a young woman of great beauty. She wore a black gown and a delicate shawl, black of course, carelessly draped on her shoulders. Her hands were loosely clasped. The sound of the knocker might have been her cue, and she might have come from her stage dressing-room to the wings. Edward looked at her eyes; their intensity could pierce and wound.

"Mother," he said.

"Don't loiter on the pavement," she told him. "These visits aren't necessary, you know."

The dull outer shell of the house and the surrounding work sheds of the cooperage belied the tasteful adornment of the dwelling. Catherine Burke lived in comfort. The fading light, filtering through the blinds and curtains, was reduced almost to darkness. There were gas pendants with ornate shades, but they were unlit. They walked silently on soft pile.

She occupied only the ground floor: a drawing-room, a dining-room, a spacious bedroom, a spotless tiled kitchen of coppers and cupboards, of delph and a modern gas cooker, blue and white enamelled, with a grill and a dish-warmer. There were expensive portable paraffin heaters in dining-room and bedroom, but the drawing-room had an impressive fireplace of black flecked marble with inlaid strips, ornate fluted pilasters rising from their bases to plain cornices supporting the overmantel; there was a polished brass fender about the hearthstone, fire-irons and a coal scuttle. The fire was a glowing pyramid of warmth.

She tightened the curtains, stifling even the small leakage of dimness from the outside. The coal fire made spears of light and shadow about the room. There was an armchair where she sat with a little delicate side-table that held books, a fountain-pen and a pad. He avoided it, and the armchair facing it. There was an ample cushioned sofa facing the grate, and he sat uneasily there. She took a taper to the fire and from it lighted three wax candles on a curved candelabrum of embellished silver. There was a single candlestick on her fireside table that she would perhaps use for reading or sketching. She left it unlighted.

She sat down slowly, gracefully.

"As you can see, you find me giving an appearance of health."

"You look very well."

"That will give you reassurance."

"I call on you once a month, that's all. I feel I should call more often."

"My staff come here every day. A cook, a maid, a skivvy. If I am dead, they will find me."

"Yes."

"They shop for my groceries, fruits, greens, whatever I need. You don't need to come more often. You don't need to come at all." A shadowy amusement. "You understand?"

"My wife sends her good wishes."

"I don't know her."

"I could bring her."

"Never."

"Our marriage in London was a private affair. But there was a reception on our arrival home. You didn't come."

"Years ago. I hardly remember."

"Only three years."

"Public displays are vulgar."

"My father would have come. He had dignity."

"I don't remember his dignity. I married him, you know."

"A public display?"

From a sideboard she brought a small slender glass of sherry and placed it on the table beside her. She sat and raised her chin and studied him.

"You came more often when your father was alive."

"He liked me to come."

"Now he's dead there's hardly need."

After a long silence he said, "I like to come and see you. It's my duty to come."

She showed her dislike, almost disgust. "Don't talk penny-dreadful rubbish. You're a grown man, reaching middle-age."

"Thirty-one."

"And your wife ten years your senior. Forty-one. An ageing woman."

"And a Protestant."

"Churches are just political parties," she said. "You made a bad choice, I suppose. She's dry and barren. No children."

"No."

"A blessing indeed."

The candlelight was a soft glow in the shadowy room, with sudden small flickers from the burning coal and little escapes of gas. He knew every contour since childhood; he had seen every change that she had imposed on it. The books, the encyclopaedias, the bound collections of art prints: Goya, Rembrandt, Vermeer, even the starkness of Hogarth and Munch. And the Impressionists were there; undisciplined, she called them: "Looking at the world through squinting eyes." Her own easel stood in its accustomed place. In this world that daylight never pierced, she painted from memory. She had some skill and talent. Some of her drawings, he thought, were fine. He had become adjusted to the gloom. Her piano, of beautiful rosewood with hinged candle holders and a fretted music rack, was open, as if during her day she might feel a need for music and whatever emotion it might bring. It had been silent since 1917. A piece of music had sat there, open, all these years. She was aware of its banality, but it was an act of humility she imposed on herself for her lost beloved son. The candles had always been half-burned with black curled wicks. The music was a piece of Victorian drawing-room sentiment, loaded with Tennysonian sweet sadness, titled "Absent".

He remembered the words that had sat exposed for eleven years as her tribute, her memorial:

Oft times between long shadows on the grass,
The tall trees whisper, whisper heart to heart,
From my fond lips the eager answers fall,
Thinking I hear thee, thinking I hear thee call.

He had been looking into the dancing flames of the fire when he saw her sip her sherry and, effortlessly, with a slow grace, stand erect. She was unaware of him. She lit the single candle and held it shoulder high, seemed to move ghostlike from the room. Her eyes, suddenly quiet and softened, disturbed him. He stood and followed her. She left doors open behind her; they moved soundlessly to her bedroom. The candlelight flowed into the darkness, exposing a spacious room, spotless, almost bare of furniture. It held a bed, a chair, a washstand. Not even a picture, a mirror, a statuette or a crucifix adorned it. The bed was of metal and brass.

He saw the garments hanging on the end-rail: a uniform tunic, untorn, but stiff with dried blood, the breast pocket open and a bloodstained notebook showing, a Sam Browne belt and a hat. The remains of the dead, the loved, the unforgotten.

Facing them like a priest, she was intoning, "I'm here, my loved one. You called me. I know you are at peace, there's peace in your voice. Missing you is a burning pain. Let me embrace you, feel the touch of your body." She moved, opened her arms and embraced her ghost. Her fingers seemed to clasp his flesh, pull him close to her; her head might be resting on his shoulder. She was breathing hard as if she were caught in a grinding passion.

Edward Burke felt a coldness that might be fear.

He watched her hands wander over the invisible, insubstantial body, the movement of her hips and groin. And then, suddenly, her face seemed to be held between other hands. He saw the movement of flesh pressed and fondled, the gentle stirring of her hair.

He was trembling. He sidled out of the room, hurried back on to the silence of the floor covering to the coal fire, the armchairs, the sofa, the open piano and its silent music. He was shivering with cold that pierced into his body. He stooped close to the fire and let warmth restore him. Even the sweat on his forehead was cold. Slowly life returned. He sat on the sofa and waited.

In a few minutes her voice reached him, a trembling, almost sobbing happiness. And then stillness.

Edward Burke remembered the house of two grown boys and a child. She had slept apart from his father ever since he could remember.

Edward had held his father, an industrious man of good temper and a generous, loving parent, in admiration. Did he know that his wife had left his bed to cuckold with his eldest son? Of course, he knew, Edward Burke thought. He thought of all the years of estrangement, and the shame his father must have felt. He was glad that he was at rest in his grave.

He looked at the blazing fire before him and hardened. Now she was demented, finding a relief in a charade of passion. He thought about her spartan bedroom again, the uniform and the battlefield blood. But had he seen her flesh move beneath caressing fingers and a gentle hand smoothing her hair? He was filled with confusion. Did the dead come back seeking their loved ones? Or did she call him forth, her heroic bloodied incubus? The family was cursed: his father and two brothers dead in the short space of eleven years; and the hidden unspeakable coupling of mother and son. He felt the shiver of cold again. The dead were living here in this evil house.

The small sound of the closing door roused him. She had returned, cold, unruffled. She blew out the candle, placed it in its stick on the overmantel. A thread of smoke wound upwards from it and he smelt the wax odour of churches and sacrifices.

She sipped her sherry again. "I thought you might have gone. Doesn't your wife get impatient?"

"No."

"Convenient."

"I wanted to say good-night."

"Good-night."

He paused. "He comes to see you, does he?"

Her long piercing stare again. "Every night. His batman wrote to me from London, a cheap little man but decent. I asked him to bring his things. He told the story. My dear boy's head was shattered, blown away in pieces into the mud and slime and dirt. The blood from his neck congealed and caked in his uniform, stuck the pages of his notebook together. In retreat, this batman person brought his tunic, his belt and hat. Left his body. It was never found. No known grave. But his name will be engraved when tablets are erected: Captain Francis Burke, Duke of Wellington's Regiment. They will write to me."

"You'll go to see it?"

"A piece of stone with a thousand names on it!" She dismissed it.

Edward looked up at the pendant gas fitting, its expensive shade, the mantle fragile as gossamer. And at the pale candles.

"Don't you use your gaslights?"

"Candles and the smell of wax are more spiritual."

He looked at the immobility of her face, her eyes; a mask of indifference. She had created this nether world and conjured up her own image of pleasure. He remembered the chilling sounds of her voice.

He said quickly, "Gas will be outdated soon. Electricity, electric lighting, is almost here. It will mean employment for hundreds of men."

"We chose idiots to rule us, we must expect chaos."

"It's a fine project," he told her. "Overseas engineers, people of great skill. We can learn from them."

She was standing, her voice very soft in a heat of anger. "Germans! They have soaked Europe in blood. They have taken sons and husbands. Blood, blood. And we employ them!"

"Yes, yes," he said, but there wasn't need to appease her. She was calm, ice-cold. "The people have chosen a government," he said.

"People? Prognathous sub-humans from the pages of *Punch*."

"I'm sorry I mentioned it," he said. "I'm going now. Is there anything I can do? Do you find it difficult getting to the church? I could call on Sunday mornings."

"The church is fifty yards from here. I walk three miles a day. The church comes to *me* once a month. I requested them."

He felt a moment of confusion and puzzlement. "With the Host?"

"Yes, with the Sacred Host, the body and blood of Christ that was pierced and ripped like my son's."

"Here?"

"In this house, close to other precious blood."

He tried to visualise the cleric, in surplice and stole, holding before him the white disc of unleavened bread. *Hoc est enim corpus meum* . . . for this is my body.

"You kneel before him?"

"I kneel before my son."

"The priest who ministers to you, he is a friend?"

"A friend? I pay him and give him whiskey to drink. He is a tosspot, a sot. I gave him a silver pyx for his 'holy companion'. You could say he works for me."

"You are being disrespectful."

"I am being honest. He was the celebrant at my marriage. He was a drunken sot then."

"Your marriage?"

"Yes."

Edward moved, stood behind the sofa. "A public display?"

"A private ceremony, here is this room where you are standing. He brought a curate and a young sister from the convent to stand beside us. They were lovers, I knew."

Edward was still for a few moments; he said, "I think you need help. You are ill."

"An illness of my mind?" she asked.

"All this mockery and perversion . . . ."

"Isn't your brother-in-law a doctor? Have you discussed it with him?"

Edward said, "Sometimes I think perhaps I should. He's not a fool; he can see the distance between us."

"Does he think I am mad?"

"I don't know what he thinks."

"Be careful, Edward. I could hurt him. Remember that."

He went out to the hall and took his coat, hat and gloves from the stand. She passed him and opened the hall door.

Silently, as he stepped on to the pavement, she shut the door behind him. He heard the noise of the heavy chain and the snap of the bolts.

CHAPTER TWO

Edward Burke walked up the narrow gaslit hill that he had known from early childhood. Theirs was the only dwelling-house in the confined street. Here was a world of grain and corn stores – they were scattered all over the city – and the market area and the market streets surrounded it. The old constricted passage climbed up from the parish church of St Michael to a main business street. Nothing had changed since his school-day journeys. He could remember shops open at all hours – fine Protestant shops, well-fed, well-dressed men in supervision. He was teaching their children now. Hardware stores, grocers and vintners, pharmacists, saddlers, photographic studios, specialist bakers and confectioners; and there were Catholic entrepreneurs in growing numbers: millers, building contractors, painters, decorators, shopkeepers, hucksters in the race to keep abreast. There was the barracks of what had been the Royal Irish Constabulary, of course, with its archway and courtyard: Catholics hadn't moved beyond the rank of sergeant.

Edward Burke was looking back over two and a half decades, but things had changed in the last ten years. Civic Guards in flat peaked caps manned the station now; the helmeted constables were gone.

He crossed the busy thoroughfare of people and horse carts and a growing bustle of motor-cars. To his right, the highway went on to cross the city's main street and over the lighted bridge, through an enclave of small secluded mansions, into the countryside. To his left, you passed the places of captivity, despair and final rest before you left the gaslit world: the prison of stone, the asylum of stone, and the cemetery of stones.

Edward walked along the back streets now that were still busy with their small shops and hucksters and street traders. Gas lamps were more distantly spaced, dim beacons in the darkness. A big shapeless woman with an infant suckling her bare breast, a huge pendulous udder, stood before him, barring his way. He could smell her uncleanliness.

"May Jesus and his Holy Mother bless you, sir. A little gift to keep hunger from myself and the child?"

He gave her two pennies.

"God will put your name in his golden book. There's a place close to him in heaven for you."

Her hard weathered face smiled a toothless smile, and he was glad when she moved and took the foul body smell with her. The child was a dressing, a stage property; in a day they passed it from one to another. The money was for drink, an escape.

Edward Burke understood.

He remembered his hall door again, the rattle of chain, the noise of bolts, the streets he raced along as a child. The world of stone-built, tall-storied bastions of storage, six rows of four-foot-square windows, shuttered but without glass; each floor loaded with loose grain and men with broad wooden shovels turning it, airing it, preventing it from heating.

He remembered his small bedroom at the front of the

house, the comfort of sheets and heavy blankets. Often there were nights of storm. You could hear the wind buffeting the naked gas flames about, and the interminable slamming of wooden shutters on warehouses: slam, slam, slam, all night, sometimes in unison but mostly in confusion. Sometimes there was the crash and shatter of slates on cobbles.

He thought about it and felt he should be older; it seemed such a long time in the past. There had been a war and a rebellion, executions, murders, burning and pillaging. And there had been an exodus. Many of the Protestant Irish had left. They had always been held apart, and now they were subsumed in distant colonies and protectorates. Good people, too, many of them; they would be missed.

A small boy, he remembered them well: their industry, the crowded shelves of their special shops, the huge stone towers of grain and flapping shutters.

In wintertime, when weird, frightening wind howled through these stone castles and he hid beneath the comforting bedclothes, sometimes he heard the heavy steps of the Night Watch, who would be wrapped in black frieze overcoats and carrying small oil lanterns on leather belts. He remembered the whistles and lanyards, the heavy iron-shod staffs, their great bulky watches, the constabulary helmets. They brought reassurance on wild stormy nights when there must be spectres and witches abroad. They were night workers of law enforcement, from ten o' clock to eight each morning. As they walked their beats they called out, at intervals, that time and place was in good hands. He had heard them often beneath his window: "One o'clock and all is well." Then there was the measured pace as they moved away. They banished the ghosts and goblins of darkness. All is well, all is well. Good friends, gone for ever now.

They handled brawls and brawlers, too. If it was a losing battle, they struck on the pavements with their iron-shod stakes and blasted on whistles to bring Watchers from other beats. They won their battles, stuck prisoners in the clink, the temporary lock-up down where the street narrowed at the approach to the river and the Customs House. In the morning the brawlers would be hauled to the main station that he had passed only moments before. He looked back at it; nothing had changed and everything had changed.

A long time ago; he smiled. The rare horse-drawn vehicle on iron-rimmed wheels that might come down their narrow street after midnight always brought terror with it. The Headless Coach: the driver headless, the horses black and thundering on the cobblestones, and the coach flying past, forewarned the death of someone close at hand. The wind and slates and banging shutters. Times of innocence.

He remembered suddenly the candle-lit house he had left, the bloodied tunic, the act of love or lust. He shivered.

He walked on more briskly on the flagstone pavements. Shops, darker inside even than the gaslit streets, might be open until eleven o'clock. It was still early evening; Catholic church bells rang out, close at hand or distant, to announce rosaries, the ceremony of benediction, perpetual novenas, the impending arrival of a corpse that would spend its last night on earth in the house of God. People were shabby or in working clothes; wild, smeared children ran in small groups to jeer or cheer or pilfer.

A newspaper-boy trotted beside him for fifty yards. "Paper, mister, paper, paper. Paper lastedishoon."

"No."

"Lastedishoon."

It was another way of begging; the thin bony hands held a single paper, creased, stained. Paper, last edition.

"Paper, mister. If you can't read, you can look at the pictures."

An old paper, an old joke. He looked down at the blackened bare feet, the dirt lodged between the toes, then up at the bright eyes. Admiring his persistence, he gave him a penny.

The street noises had become a little less raucous. A funeral was approaching. As the cortège came near, people stopped and stood silent. The undertaker, in a black, cutaway coat and tall hat, led the way. Tired horses pulled the glass-case hearse and a couple of closed mourning carriages; men walked behind the hearse. Some onlookers made the sign of the cross, and there were murmurs of "God rest the dead . . . called away . . . rest in peace."

When it had passed, Edward Burke could see his destination ahead. It was a formerly vacant shop, with a small counter and a long narrow space behind where there were tables and seating-forms. Two paraffin lamps barely pierced the gloom. Brown paper had been pasted on the inside of the thin glass, holding three wooden mullions, for privacy and protection. There was a furtiveness about the people who came and went. A sandwich board at the doorway said, "Everyone Is Welcome."

Edward entered and smiled to the woman at the counter, saying, "Good evening, Miss Langford."

"Good evening, Mr Burke."

She was a middle-aged woman, confident, well-dressed, wearing a brown warehouseman's loose coat over her tweed costume. She wore a plain, unobtrusive hat, and from a cauldron on a low gas ring, she ladled soup into pint-size tin mugs. When there was space at tables, she handed out the steaming brew and a wedge of bread. The bread was two days old but fresh enough for soup and hungry mouths. A younger woman supervised the tables, wiping them down, and waiting for mugs to wash and leave draining. Mugs had a small value, were portable, needed surveillance.

"Mr Burke," the woman at the cauldron said, "your wife is in the kitchen, just through the glass door."

Lillian Burke didn't look forty-one. She was a beautiful woman, not very tall in stature, but slim as a young girl, with piled-up auburn hair and good skin. She looked at Edward Burke and loved him with her eyes. He took her hand and pressed it.

"I thought I'd call," he said.

"I'm glad, but I can't kiss or hug you now," she said. "That's the trouble with glass doors."

Although she also donated money to many other causes, this soup kitchen was her brainchild. You should give to people, she felt, person to person. They should see that the giver wanted to give and that the one in need only paid for it with, perhaps, a softening of features, maybe a smile. She had rented the shop, opened up its back room, bought cheap tables at a half dozen auctions and the tin mugs that hung in clusters outside every ironmonger's. From her churchgoers came the bread, meat, meat bones and scrag ends and discarded vegetables, too shrivelled for rich tables. She had also bought the three cast-iron cauldrons, with broad looping handles for two persons to grip and carry.

She stood now before a small Stanley range with a tea chest of coal and a shovel next to it. She and her helpers worked three hours every evening from four until seven.

"I feel useless," Edward Burke said, looking out at the ragged street. "Sometimes there are loiterers out there. A lot of whispering sometimes. There could be danger, I feel."

"These are bad times for the poor, Edward. Time to give a helping hand."

"I called to see my mother."

"I wish I could visit her."

"Oh, leave her in her own world," he said.

Standing before this busy young woman who had married him, he was overcome with the shameful thought of close family lust. It was a heinous act of abomination. The thought of their grasping, struggling, turning, was overpowering.

He, Edward Burke, had been the runt of the litter. Perhaps not the runt; he had been an afterthought. His brothers, dead and buried, had been respectively fourteen and twelve years his senior. He had never thought much about it, but when he was still a small boy, they were reaching manhood. Why had she given birth to him? She had been thirty-six when she was carrying him; not an unusual age at a time of large families and high infant mortality, but for twelve years, since the birth of his second brother, her years of child bearing seemed over. And then *he* had arrived.

He remembered his second brother, Michael, wild, but clever, too, with his skill at sketching and painting. But he was distant from him. He had left school with a record of distinction and was almost immediately in demand for his art work. Travelling theatre, music-halls and operettas needed posters, and he immediately grasped the garish flamboyant style that pulled in crowds. She was scathing: the stuff of erotic hacks and comic-cuts. He became silent and withdrawn at home. Edward, still a small boy, listened to her poisonous tirades: loose living, rubbing shoulders with stage persons who were given to drink and licentiousness, a fine return for the education that was handed to him. He was compared with Francis, a junior law partner before he had gone to fight in France, a person of repute in the city. He was nothing. A drinking womaniser.

He had left, made the journey to London to join the fighting forces, to keep pace with the paragon sibling who had preceded him, but he was rejected for army service. However, posters were needed in London, too, and moving pictures had arrived. He drank heavily and picked classless women off the shelf. His health failed and he died, emaciated, friendless, in a mental hospital in the London home counties. He had surpassed the chosen offspring only in age. It was a year before word had reached his father. He had made the journey to a paupers' corner in a Surrey graveyard, a wild lumpy acre of coarse grass and tussocks, without a single marker.

A grave-digger had said, "Impossible to say where anyone is, guv." He had looked about the stretch of fertilised ground, the tall grass. "We put them down here in blocks of ten or twelve. The office might have a record, but most of them don't have a name."

The office had a burial record of Michael Burke, buried in common ground in the autumn of 1922. His father had travelled back and was greeted in his own house with silence. That same year he had walked with Edward to the cemetery at the city's northern edge, and stood before a four-sided plinth recording a hundred and fifty years of family death: the fresh engraving said, "In Memory of Michael Burke, aged 37, 1885–1922." Above it, more prominent, *she* had had inscribed, "Capt. Francis Burke MC, killed in France, 1917, aged 34."

"My sons," was all he had said.

It was the beginning of his decline; he had died within a year, in 1923. He had been young once, in love, so eager, Edward Burke supposed, to wed his adorable Catherine.

Edward Burke looked at his wife Lillian, who was chopping ends of meat, fat and scrag and arranging a mound of bones on a bare scrubbed table. She turned and looked at him.

"You're so quiet, Edward. Are you feeling well?" she whispered.

"Yes, I'm fine."

"You look pale."

"No, no."

"You allowed yourself to be upset again," she said. "She is a good woman, Edward, but it is difficult to cease grieving. Grief is a dreadful thing. Two sons dead, remember. And then her husband. She is alone."

Yes, alone, Edward thought.

"You call but she isn't ready to meet you yet. It takes patience."

"Yes."

"I'll be home before eight. Hannah will have dinner ready. We'll freshen up and there'll be time to talk. And we can sit at our own fire."

Edward looked around the soup kitchen – the tables, the long seating-forms, the noise, the faces of hunger – and then he looked at her face.

She looked at the half-hunter watch she carried in her

pocket. "Go and have a drink," she said. "You'll feel better. It'll drive away that paleness."

He nodded. "Yes," he said. "I'll enjoy a drink."

"Good."

He waved, pushed out through the crowded dining-space; it was murky in a bad light, but the warm smell of food filled the room. The pavement, he thought, seemed a little more busy. Or were people gathering? He crossed to the opposite side and stood at the entrance to an alleyway leading to a church fire exit. The alleyway, in the dark spot between gaslights, had a single light mounted on the wall, distant from him. He felt uneasy.

The noise alerted him. He saw the approach of marching men: young men, mature men, some of them in Sunday best, some of them striving, with little, for respectability, some ragged. They had taken the centre of the road. Rosary beads were evident, and some carried small crucifixes. An enemy would call them a mob, but the zealotry of set faces and eyes would leave him in doubt. These were crusaders, purifiers. The street was crammed. As they halted before the soup kitchen, Edward was crowded, isolated. They dragged a table from inside and blocked the doorway, raised up a lion-hearted champion to stand surveying his believers and the faint-hearted on-lookers of the streets.

The man was in his thirties, maybe older; a navy blue suit, a shirt and tie, polished shoes. His cap was pulled low; he wore glasses and a scarf. He held out his hands, waited until there was almost silence.

"You are Catholics," he thundered; a great, rousing, metallic voice. "First we pray."

He held up glittering rosary beads, made the sign of the cross, recited the Pater Noster while he looked up at the rooftops and the black low-lying clouds that shielded earth from heaven. He called out the Ave Maria ten times and orchestrated the volume of their response. He paused for stillness; the road was blocked, the small traffic was detouring.

He held up his rosary chain of glass beads, and a shiny crucifix that had been dipped in pinchbeck.

"Good friends were in Rome last year," he began, "and Christ's Vicar on Earth walked among them, raising his hand in blessing. He blessed these holy beads that are a hymn of prayer to the Mother of God. We call out, 'Hail Mary, full of grace, the Lord is with thee.' Our humble words of homage. Our faith has survived dungeon, fire and sword. This land, our land, newly recaptured from repression and slavery, is still the Island of Saints and Scholars; and it has been decided, I'm told on good authority, that within the short span of three or four years His Holiness, Pius XI, will come to walk among us. He will walk on the same Irish ground as we, poor banished children of Eve, have walked.

"He will say mass and sanctify the Host, and ask God to bless our nation, to make us worthy of the blessings he has showered on us."

He was silent and the crowd was silent. He was gathering breath and power for his attack. He flung up his hands as if he had been stricken, shouted at heaven beyond the blackness. He was a raging, hysterical demagogue.

"Are we worthy? Do we deserve that the Vicar of Christ should come to visit us? Do we? Do we? Answer me! You stand there like cattle. But cattle have dignity. Answer, answer! Are we worthy? Are we worthy that Christ's Vicar on Earth should come to walk among us? Are we worthy of God's love, or deserving of his contempt?"

Silence again.

Now his voice was heavy with sadness. "I am waiting." He kissed the pinchbeck cross of his rosary beads, held up his hands.

A great shout came from his little army. "No!"

"We are not worthy?"

"No!"

The entire gathering was enmeshed now; they were chanting, beating their hands together. He stood before them, head bowed, the rosary beads wound about his hands. The voice, Edward thought: a hammer on steel.

Suddenly he was upright, a hand raised for silence. It came slowly, unevenly, possessed them.

"Why are we not worthy?"

A shuffling uneasiness everywhere.

"Will I tell you?"

"Yes!"

"Louder!"

"Yes!"

He rolled his words at them like great crushing orbs of stone; he paused, studied them, was unhurried.

"You have allowed your city, a tabernacle of Christ, to be invaded, desecrated, by *apostates*! Those who forsook the infallibility of Rome to proclaim a lewd, sensuous, diseased, lustful, royal dissolute to be head of our Church! Who spurned the holy commands of the papacy. Who live only awaiting eternal damnation."

Silence.

"Who are they? Where are they?"

Silence.

"They are here behind me feeding soup and bread to your brothers and sisters in Christ. And for what? I ask you, why are they feeding your brothers and sisters in Christ?"

A great pause for silence again.

Then almost a whisper. "To take hold of their immortal souls! To win them over. To cast them into damnation." He waited. "Apostates must be crushed, destroyed, driven out!"

There was a thunderous cheer; he was lifted down from his humble rostrum.

Edward Burke watched. He didn't fear for himself; he was a person of courage, caught in the crowd, tossed about in the heave and sway. He saw the table raised up and flung against the window. The thin glass shattered, the crude peeling mullions snapped. He was trapped tight in the crushes. The vanguard was already at the work of clearance. War cries were in the air, and the hungry were bloodied, beaten and pummelled, chastised for sinful greed. There was the crash of cast-iron. The pendant paraffin lamps were flung against the walls and there was smoke and licks of flame. The crowd was tossed like gravel in a sieve. Edward, in the alleyway, caught a small boy, gave him a shilling, and sent for fire brigade and ambulance.

There were residents and small shopkeepers, and the passing few, too, trapped, crushed, left to stand and stare.

A place buying souls for soup. It would be sinful to touch it. Charity was only for the *very* poor, the totally incompetent, the wretches of society who came down through every generation. The Church and Catholic people, their committees and societies, looked after them.

Edward Burke roared at them. "There are people in there!" He was fighting his way through, past little groups that might be in shock as they stood in gaping wonder at the sudden explosion of violence. Now they were coming to life, moving again.

He saw Lillian, his wife, and the younger supervisor from the tables. They had tied wet towels to cover mouths and noses and were dragging the few remaining staggering bodies to the space outside the doorway where the air was clearing. Lucy Langford, the dispenser of soup, was lying on the floor, blood smearing her face, distressed with smoke inhalation. Then everything was clear: bodies on the pavement breathing air again, being tended. Lillian Burke and her helper wiped away the blood from the face of Lucy Langford, propped her to sit up and breathe. But she was ill. The bell of the fire brigade was only a block away.

The gathering flames lit up the smoky room and kitchen: tables had been ripped asunder, the legs used to beat the ragged clientele, the huge soup cauldrons were toppled, the chest of coal scattered.

The fire brigade had arrived. The ambulance, old-fashioned but clean, efficient, functional, was a legacy from the

British army garrison that had left hardly seven years ago. Both were manned by city crews who had learnt their trade in the days of military occupation.

Lillian Burke came to Edward, gripped his hand. "You're safe and sound?" she asked.

"You?" was all he could say.

"I'm fine, not a scratch," she told him, "but Lucy Langford is shaken. The window, and the table that smashed it, caught her. The bleeding is nothing much, but she may have fallen heavily, and her legs were scalded when the cauldron was toppled."

The ambulance men passed carrying Lucy Langford, loosely strapped to a stretcher and covered in a red blanket.

Lillian Burke said, "I must go with her to the hospital."

"Barrington's?"

"Yes. Taddy will be there, and the matron is a good friend."

Taddy, Thaddeus Bennett, was her brother. He had attended at College of Surgeons in Dublin and then returned to his home town.

Lillian said, "I'll go then. We'll meet later at home. The day had a lot of trouble hidden for us. Whenever you arrive Hannah will have dinner ready for you. I'm sorry, Edward."

"I'm glad you're all right," he told her.

He watched as she and her supervisor of tables were helped on the step of the ambulance, the doors closed, and it growled away into the distance.

Steam and smoke coloured the soiled air; firemen in belted tunics and traditional helmets were flattening and rolling up their hoses, removing stand-pipes, sealing off valves. They examined the burnt-out shell of the shop. A job finished, they took their regal seats on the fire engine and drove away from the combat like gladiators.

The smell of the fire would last for days. Edward pondered the speech-maker, hearing the ring of metal in his voice.

CHAPTER THREE

EDWARD BURKE WALKED slowly away from the scene of such recent confusion. The strange threatening power of the rabble-rouser, the power to arouse hatred, to set his troops to pillaging and burning, to the administering of punishment on the hungry, even to the endangering of life, was a step too far in freedom. Edward was angry. The Church would look after its own was the speech-maker's message. Apostates must be crushed. His face had been shrouded, but Edward Burke would remember his voice.

Yes, there were rich Catholic families in the city who had country estates and town houses, had motor-cars to supplement horse carriages, lived in admirable style, sent children to boarding schools at an early age and travelled frequently abroad without plan or restriction. They moved in the city's circle of society.

The Catholic Church was proud of them, and they, not entirely proud of *it*, kept it at a respectful distance. They accepted the Church's exclusive invitations, for occasions lent it their splendour. They would have been happier to have affairs of state decided in London; but their money and status allowed them to sit outside the arena and watch the performance from afar.

A great middle class of Catholics existed, too, a hierarchical middle class of myriad strata and importances, from professional, intellectual, all down the ladder of trade and wealth from merchant to shopkeeper.

And there was the working class. They eked out a precarious existence with a flimsy solidarity. They earned and spent. Some of them would be on the streets at night-time or in the bar-rooms. Edward, walking, passed them by. Never with more than a few shillings between them and beggary, freedom had brought them nothing. When he heard them singing in a pub, he was glad for them.

Edward Burke remembered his disillusionment when, hardly more than a year past, he had attended a meeting of a city Catholic Benevolent Fellowship, a group of comfortable men who, it would appear, felt that the sacrifice of giving a small weekly space of time to the abject, the poorer classes, the irredeemable, would gain them some plenary indulgence in numinous account books. Edward Burke was unhappy at their round table. Like objective physicians and surgeons they looked at sick bodies, nameless beings, assessed them, decided how many grains of food or shreds of clothing would sustain their misery and leave the donors comfortable in their piety. Meetings opened with a prayer from the chairman for the foundering homeless, the hopeless, the hapless.

Edward wondered what was the will of God. He visited hovels, brought away the awful picture of their squalor, the fecklessness and savagery it fostered. He had given up his corporal works of mercy. He had only gone there for Lillian's sake: it was his duty, as it was hers, to offer some daily sustenance, she had said. He should attend his church, too; they were praying to the same God. Lillian was a gentle person, but only an hour ago she had met street-life face to face.

He thanked the Deity, whoever he might be, for her safety.

He walked down to the broad main thoroughfare, named to honour a German monarch on an English throne: 'By the grace of God, of the United Kingdom of Great Britain and Ireland, King, Defender of the Faith.' Those days were gone, we were free, we could manage our own affairs. Our members of state took only an oath of allegiance to the reigning monarch now. Change was important. They were christening, or had rechristened, the squares and streets and bridges. But to Edward Burke this would always be the George's Street of his youth, and the bridge, with its statue to honour the death of Fitzgibbon at Balaclava, belonged to Wellesley, Marquis Wellesley.

Horse traffic was no longer abroad, except the cabs of jarveys with their vertical whips like spears, but motor traffic was flowing. Cars were becoming smarter every day, with distinctive radiators and hoods and spare wheels like an embellishment on running boards or screwed on rear luggage racks, and drivers wearing caps and silk scarves.

Lillian said they should buy a car. Edward, however, liked to walk the streets of his small city, this town, to see its gloss and its dross. George's Street was a majestic sweep of thoroughfare with its four-storey houses of brick and the shops at street level, shining with paintwork and care. Or the great emporia of fashion and cloths, serges and millinery. The fine presiding clock tower, distinctive as a church spire, was a landmark. There were not many Irish names on the fascia boards of stores on this broad fashionable parade. The smaller shops in smaller streets were for a rising native generation.

He walked on past the obtruding, raised podium of the County Club. With four disproportionate pillars propping the timbers and pediment of its roof, it encroached on the adequate footway, leaving only four of its sixteen feet for the pedestrians. Two men, in Burberrys and tweed plus-fours, stood there in lazy conversation. A few paces beyond was a friary church that had been a music-hall. Except for the glow of a sanctuary lamp, the serried pews, church trappings and confessionals, it had changed little. It still had its parterre and balcony seats, and the remnants of dressing-rooms and back-stage survived. Near by were a book binder and a vendor of bicycles and, across the street, an imposing pharmacy and druggist. When Edward reached the 3d and 6d Stores, he crossed the street to the Royal George Hotel. It had a raised forecourt and the façade was tiled in white.

He climbed the steps, the doorman held open the brass filleted door for him, and he walked into the soft carpeted world. The bar was restful as a drawing-room. There were tables and comfortable chairs. People sat at the counter with its heated footrest of polished brass.

Close to him a voice spoke softly. "Ed?"

It was Lillian's brother, Arnold. A strong, confident, smiling man of forty-seven, with hair receding a little, Arnold dressed in good serge; a gold watch-chain and fob spanned a barely sprouting archway of stomach.

The first Bennett, a merchant, had come when Napoleonic wars were raging and when the governors of Ireland had been wedded and bedded with Westminster. He had brought money and prospered. The family business was now in Arnold's care.

"You're alone?" Edward asked.

"Just arrived. I drove to Castleconnell to see the old folks, my father and mother, you know."

"They're well?"

"They're getting old, Ed, but they'll last a while yet. I brought him out a case of malt and a bottle of port for my mother. Keeps the circulation at a decent speed."

He raised a hand for the waiter and ordered a glass of Irish for Edward. "The old man likes Scotch malt. My mother remembers to sip a glass of port once a week. What the hell, have a drink, I tell them. Something gets us all in the end."

Arnie was a clever businessman; he prospered, the family prospered. Two older brothers had died in 1900: the South

African War. Thaddeus, his surviving brother, was seven years his senior.

"How's Lillian?" he asked.

"She's fine." He raised his glass and drank more than half its contents. The whiskey brought new life. "Good whiskey," he said as he finished it and nodded to the waiter.

Arnie smiled. "You needed that, Ed, I'd say. I needed one, too. Sixteen miles on a rocky road round-trip to the Castleconnell riverside earns a couple of stiffeners. You look pale. What happened? Did the school burn down?"

"Lillian's kitchen burned down."

Arnie paused, looked at him. "That soup place?"

"Yes. A mob of brothers-in-religion marched to the attack. Wrecked the place; set it alight." Edward calmed him with a gesture. "Lillian is untouched, not a scratch."

"The others?"

"Only Lucy Langford. She took a tumble. Might have scalds. The ambulance took her to Barrington's. The girls went with her."

When the waiter brought the drinks, Arnie took his with him to the office where there was a telephone.

Edward sat and waited, sipping his drink. Everything would be all right, he hoped. The comfort of the bar-lounge was a bastion. Edward liked the discreet privacy of hotels. His father had used Cruise's Hotel. It was only a short walk for him and, Edward suddenly thought, it was an escape from his captivity. He remembered his returning late at night, the sound of his passing through the hallway, climbing the stairs to his room. He would be drunk enough to sleep, to be insulated from the night. He had said to Edward once, "Public houses are too public for me. In hotels I'm hardly visible."

Edward thought of his loneliness, the ignomy that he carried about with him, the shame, the anger he must have felt. He drank back his second drink and collected one from the counter. When Arnie returned he was sitting at the table again.

Arnie said, "Everyone's fine except Lucy Langford. She lost consciousness. Cause for a little concern, Taddy thought. He's down there. Perhaps a stroke or an embolism. However, early days, it may pass off quickly. Oh, and Lillian's fine."

Edward nodded. "Lillian has strength."

Arnie raised his glass. "You make a good pair. I worry about her when I have time. Do-gooding and soup ladles, and all that kind of thing, well it's Christian. But stir in a little religion and you get high explosive. I know you understand what I mean, Ed."

"Yes, I understand. We talked about it. You can't stand by and watch people in hunger, she said."

"Let their own people do it. No offence, Ed. A lot of them have wealth and comfortable homes; they could do it. Our crowd would chip in to parish funds, anonymously, of course."

Edward laughed. "The same money in size and shape."

Arnie caught the humour. "No, I don't suppose they can smell the difference. I explained it to Lillian once. We're lucky, I told her. Unemployment and too many people is the world's problem. When I cross the water to England – Liverpool, Bristol, London – it's the same story. Awful poverty. And always the wealthy guarding their share. You can't blame them. It's a small rapid slip to the bottom. It's the shape of the world, Ed. I'm importing stuff here now that we manufactured not many decades ago. English factories and machines can make it at a fraction of the cost. And English factories and machines leave industrial waste. They call it unemployment, poverty."

Edward nodded. "The city's breweries and distilleries have gone, too," he said. "Canal boats from Dublin bring our porter and liquor now. My mother lives in a good house, on the fringes of Irishtown and Pery, but the business is gone. And people have been stampeding for a century to the west, to the east. Still there are whole acres of hovels teeming with hungry newborns. The Church blesses them at baptism, smiles, and launches them on the world like paper boats."

"Soup kitchens won't cure it."

"My father employed a lot of men," Edward said. "Where are they now?"

"They vanish, move out of sight."

In the hotel lounge, there were two dozen or more people about now, hardly noticeable behind the mirrored pillars and little allotments of palm and shrub. The waiter in white shirt, black tie and waistcoat was busy.

Edward looked towards the entrance. Lillian was here! Behind the gladness at seeing her, there was a sudden anxiety: they dined out together occasionally, a drink, a glass of wine, but Lillian didn't arrive alone at public places.

Arnie said in surprise, "It's Lillian."

"Yes."

Arnie said, "Something's gone bloody wrong, I'd say."

She arrived and smiled at them as Edward held a chair for her to be seated. It was a brave smile for whoever might see it.

Arnie said, "The news isn't good, is it?"

"No."

"Lucy Langford?"

She put her hand on Edward's. "Yes. Lucy Langford is dead."

"From injury?" Edward asked.

"The fall, the slight scalding might have contributed. Taddy said it was an embolism." She shook her head at Arnie when he offered her a drink. "I am going to visit the Langfords. Taddy will telephone them later, but I'm going alone," she told them. "It's a task for one person only. I thought I'd find Edward here to tell him. I'm glad you're here, too, Arnie."

"I'll call you a hackney cab."

"I have a cab from the hospital. It's waiting outside. And Taddy should notify the Gardaí."

"The what?"

"The Gardaí, the police. There will be a post mortem tomorrow. Taddy says it will verify that embolism was the cause of death. But the affray, the burning must be mentioned, I suppose."

They stood and watched her go. She had hidden her distress, Edward knew. Lucy Langford had been a friend. He thought of the feverish shouting and exhortations of the navy-blue suited evangelist and was filled with rage and shame. He watched the fading image of Lillian until the door closed and she was gone.

He had been distracted; Arnie had beckoned the waiter to bring them fresh drinks.

"She wasn't married," Arnie said. "A spinster."

"Lucy Langford? I know, but there was a family who cherished her. Brothers, sisters, nieces, nephews, all of them. She was Lillian's friend." Edward Burke sipped at his whiskey. After a little silence he said, "Her death was an act of murder. I was there."

Arnie looked at him. "Yes, it was a foul piece of work. It deserves to be punished, but one moves carefully in these times. How many hands lifted up the table and launched it? A face, faces, in a crowd. Manslaughter perhaps, but by whom? Did the police arrive to disperse it?"

Edward thought. There had been no police. The station was out on the main business thoroughfare that he had crossed at the beginning of his journey. It was out of sight of the mêlée, but hardly three hundred yards distant. They should have heard the uproar, noticed the disturbed stream of traffic. Yes, it was possible, they had washed their hands of it. He felt anger and uncertainty.

He said to Arnie, "The headquarters was a stone's throw from us. The soup had the wrong religion, the wrong politics."

Arnie stilled him with a hand on his. "Stand back from it, Ed," he said. "Let matters take their course. Stay calm. There are good and bad police, but a policeman has a good job and wants to keep it. He doesn't want to be a lone crusader. There can be enemies in his own house."

"Enemy? The Church?"

"Or the state. Some priests should be politicians. Some politicians should be priests. This is a new country; give it time to settle." Arnie dropped his voice, held his hard, sincere face close to Edward's. "These are dangerous times, Ed. The shooting still goes on between themselves. Give it time to settle."

"Lucy Langford is dead."

"My brothers and yours are dead in other ways. Millions are dead. Only twelve years ago poets and philosophers were put to death. Executed. Remember them." Arnie raised his glass and looked at it. "Don't be too honest, Ed."

Edward nodded, drank a little.

"Yes," he said.

"I'm forty-seven," Arnie said. "You're thirty-one. You learn a lot in sixteen years. When I was thirty-one I had a young son, a daughter, a lot of hopes. And my wife, Ethel. She was a picture. Harry hadn't left school when he was kicking over the traces. Harry, when he was fourteen, got at a little kitchen maid and left her carrying his seed. She was afraid of being handed over to the Laundry Home for fallen women. She came to me for money. I gave her a generous hand-out, Ed, and she hooked it for Dublin. She has a boarding house somewhere there, clean and strict, I'm told. I think of it all with regret."

"The child?"

"I don't know. No trace. Probably a back-street, kitchen-table job."

Edward drank and was silent. He knew some of Harry's history.

"You're thinking about Harry, aren't you?" Arnie asked.

"Yes."

"You never met him then. He was a charmer, of course."

"I saw him often."

"Everyone saw Harry. I didn't know it then, but he was syphilitic when he was eighteen. Yes, eighteen. When he was seventeen he had a body rash, but it passed. Taddy looked at it. Wait and see, he had said. We did and it vanished. Syphilis can mimic a dozen rashes, he told us later. Ethel nursed him through rashes, aches, pains, fevers. But in the end Taddy told us. Hard facts are best. Later, we found a home for ageing people, our own religion of course, where he could be kept in isolation. Ulcers running inside and outside his body, awful. But you go to see him, Ed."

"Once a month. I just sit there and watch him for an hour."

"Good. The women can't go, of course. We've all agreed on that."

"I know."

Harry's sister, Dorcas, was in London now, recently commissioned in the Queen Alexandra Nursing Corps. She and Ethel had left together. Arnold was glad that she was away from it all.

"I'm back where I started, alone in a great empty house. The housekeeper and staff are my family." Arnie had beckoned the waiter. "We'll have a nightcap and get in motion again, Ed. I'm glad I met you. There seem to be fewer people to talk to."

They tipped glasses and drained them. They parted on the pavement. Arnie had a Daimler, black, impressive, with its shining radiator; he cranked it and the pistons fired. He drove away along uncluttered George's Street towards the Crescent.

Edward turned back on his tracks, left George's Street and passed the gutted shell of Lillian's soup kitchen; the smell of ageing burnt timber, the black mess of crumbled lath and plaster, hung like a pall. Where the firemen had swept away the rubbish was the only clean patch of pavement on the street. At this late hour, only a little traffic remained on pavements and streets. Shops had closed at last. The public houses had officially closed, but the tipplers would be inside, crouched in the darkness, gripping their thick pint glasses.

The street narrowed and Edward passed into the broader shopping area, and crossed the street to the Garda station. It was still the same place where the Royal Irish Constabulary had held sway. A lot of them had been shot in so many battles, the residue paid-off. England paid their pensions. They had been almost an army. Their children, too, were doing well, disciplined, their heads down over their books. They were Irish, children of Irish, and they would find a place in a new society. But Edward knew that bitterness would die hard.

He walked under the broad archway looking at the expanse of cobbled yard, and turned left into the day-room. There were three uniformed men there, two of them on some clerical duty. The third came to him and opened a window in a glass partition mounted on a high counter. He wore a navy-blue belted jacket with a high tight collar encircling his neck. Flat peaked caps hung on a rack. There were no guns in sight. Edward nodded his salutation.

This strong, hardy young man was younger then Edward, perhaps twenty-eight. Too young to have come through a lot of ambush and hit-and-run battles to take up a position of authority. He assessed Edward, his appearance, his importance, and waited.

Edward said, "Good-night." Did one add constable or officer; hardly Garda?

He was asked, "Can we do something for you?" in a voice that might be from somewhere in the midland counties.

"Yes. I have some information I'd like to offer."

All three faces were looking towards him now.

"Information?"

"Yes."

"Of a criminal nature, is it?"

"It could be."

Long moments of silent waiting.

The uniformed man raised his eyebrows. "What is it?"

Edward Burke could be a hard man, too. He looked about him.

"This is hardly the place," he said. "'I need some privacy."

"Privacy?"

"Yes."

"Very important, is it?"

"It might be."

"Wait." He was studied for a few moments.

He watched this young officer knock on a door and enter an adjoining office. In a few moments, Edward was escorted to this private sanctum and asked politely by its occupant to be seated.

"I am the district inspector," he was told.

"My name is Edward Burke. I'm a schoolmaster at the Latimer."

"A Church of Ireland School, isn't it?" The inspector was quiet, circumspect. "If I can be of any assistance?"

"I'm grateful," Edward said. "It concerns a disturbance at a soup kitchen tonight. Not very far from here. A dangerous crowd marched on it. A speech was made that inflamed them, I think." Edward paused. "At any rate, the place was wrecked, set alight, gutted."

The inspector had probably turned forty; he was fit and strong but his face showed wear and tear. He was in plain clothes, a good three-piece suit, a white shirt and tie. The office was a neat orderly place with crowded notice boards and gloss oil painted walls. There were two swivel gas fittings glowing from the ceiling. A telephone rang in the outer office; a single burst of sound.

"I'm just back in my office," he said. "I was travelling today. I have a lot of outlying stations to cover. My sergeant reported a minor disturbance. He did mention some damage."

"Your sergeant?"

"You just met him."

"I was caught in the crowd," Edward said. "Very difficult to see anyone. No doubt your men were there."

The inspector paused. "Yes, I would expect so."

"The damage and burning are very extensive. These men came marching like an army. A table was dragged out and a speech was made."

"You remember the speech-maker?"

"Not very distinctly."

"You can't name him?"

"No."

"Difficult. A lot of faces in poor lighting. There is a lot of bias, you know, collaboration; so many blind men in a crowd. There have been a lot of burnings in the past six years. Shops, warehouses, country houses. Bitterness and some blackguardism, too. That's the smouldering end of rebellion. There are no names."

"I understand," Edward said. He liked the inspector. He was different, with the appearance of inherent discipline. There had been no police and he was probably becoming aware of it. Edward had a strain of good sense. Let sleeping dogs lie, he thought. When he had left, they could settle their differences.

"I'll do whatever I can," the inspector said.

Edward nodded his thanks. The faceless rabble were in pubs or their homes now, and the inspector could only probe about in an endless futile investigation. And how good was his sergeant? Edward Burke felt angry with the world.

"There were three women working in the burnt-out premises," he said. "My wife was one. There were two others. I sent for the fire brigade and ambulance."

"Garda officers?"

"Probably in the crowd with their hands full."

The inspector paused. "I see," he said. "The ambulance was necessary?"

"Yes, a Miss Lucy Langford was knocked over. A heavy fall. And she had some scald marks, I'm told. They took her to Barrington's. She lapsed into coma and died about an hour ago."

Another pause. "Dead?"

"An embolism, in Dr Bennett's opinion. He is my wife's brother. He will carry out a post mortem tomorrow. The disturbance at the soup kitchen, the heaviness of Miss Langford's fall, might have contributed to the movement of the embolism. That's why I mention it."

"Yes," the inspector said; he had stood up and was pacing about.

Edward reiterated, "Cause of death will probably be attributed to embolism."

"The movement of the embolism is another question."

"I was a witness," Edward Burke said. "I thought it my duty to come forward."

"Of course."

The inspector sat at his table again and tapped two or three times on a percussion bell. The young sergeant knocked and presented himself.

Edward Burke looked at his expressionless face.

"Sir?" he said with just a little deference.

"This street brawl that was reported involved destruction of property and arson, didn't it?"

There was a pause. "The men on duty considered it a faction fight. The same old tale. Anti-soupers versus soupers. It appears the escaping soupers broke tables and chairs. And an oil lamp was knocked over. Everything is very confused."

"A woman had a heavy fall. She was taken to Barrington's. She's dead."

"We just had a telephone call, sir."

"Who telephoned?"

"The matron. A Miss Langford, one of the soup kitchen organisers, is dead. From natural causes, it would appear. There will be a post mortem in the morning."

"Thank you, sergeant."

When he had gone, the inspector sat, arms on the table, gazing at the closed door. He had learnt the lessons of law and order down the years. Eventually he turned his gaze on Edward Burke.

He said, "You see, you could find yourself in a very dangerous position. This firebrand who inflamed the situation, you would have to lay charges and be prepared to meet him face to face, put a hand on his shoulder and say, 'This is the man.'"

"I can't do that."

"And at the drop of a hat he could have twenty witnesses to place him elsewhere." The inspector shook his head. "The Church and state are close friends, Mr Burke. If you want my advice, I'll give it. Or I can be silent. But you have my sympathy. And I admire your courage. It has been a bad night."

"Manslaughter?"

"Close to it."

Edward sat, head bowed, for a long time. He thought of the grief of gentle Lillian, Arnie's tragedy and empty house, even Thaddeus with his mixed fortunes.

Arnie had said, "One needs to move carefully in these times." The Bennetts were his family now; his anger shouldn't endanger them.

He said, "I'll take your advice, inspector. And I should mention I'm a Catholic."

The inspector said, "Yes, stay out of it. Your marriage or your place of work doesn't endear you to the statesmen or the Hierarchy. The verdict will probably be a regrettable accident suffered in the course of a street affray."

The inspector rang his bell again.

The confident young sergeant arrived, silent and expressionless, held open the doors and saw Edward Burke to the pavement.

Edward thanked him and crossed the prosperous trading street with its shops closed and shuttered now. When he glanced back, the sergeant still stood in the archway.

Edward didn't walk through George's Street to his home but followed the untidy street that ran parallel to it, through the dim night-time glimmer of gaslight. There were still a few people abroad, little groups that might be from crowded dwellings that had no lure, even in tiredness; people of the streets.

It had been a long difficult evening: the visit to the darkened house where he knew he had seen evil; the street riot, the wrecking, the burning, the death, the inspired holy rabble-rouser; the lesson in the dispensation of justice.

He had drunk his share tonight and he was still sober. When he arrived home, Lillian would be there. She would have sent Hannah to bed and be sitting before the fire in their drawing-room. She liked to read, but tonight she would be in thought; tonight Lucy Langford would be very real. He should be with Lillian tonight. Dinner would be spoilt, but Lillian would have sliced cold meats and home-baked wheaten bread and butter. She loved him and treated him with love.

Like her brothers, Edward and Lillian lived in a Georgian house of four storeys and a railed-off area for kitchen work and staff. Hannah cooked for them and an upstairs maid kept fine, shining rooms. Two reception rooms at ground floor were for Lillian's use, where there was a fire burning and she and her friends could gossip or plan their church festivals, or school prize-givings, their lectures, their charities. The drawing-room, with folding doors to the dining-room, was on the next floor; on the street-windows was a wrought-iron balcony. On a storey above were bedrooms and Edward's study, which he called his library. The attic was for staff.

He was walking smartly now, nearing home. At the end of this long street he would turn right, from where he could see George's Street and his house almost on the corner. The Bennett family lived within easy reach of each other.

Suddenly Edward was accosted.

Out of the darkness of an alleyway, once a busy mews of stabling and staff, came a limping beggar-man.

"The price of a drink, your honour," he said.

Edward saw the weather-slimed hat and a face below it blackened, smeared with soot. It was an attack, he knew. He crouched. He was struck from behind with a heavy stave, across the kidneys. He was flung against the iron rails of an area and held there by a practised man of bravo. There were three of them, all blackened.

The square man said, "We don't need Luther's food for our poor. The Church sees to it that they are fed. And the grace of God is food for their souls. And remember this! The Guards don't give ear to soupers who share a bed in damnation with foreign seed!"

He took a beating on his ribs, his stomach, his groin. They left him on his knees. He could only remember black minstrel faces, feel the pain that each driven fist had inflicted; and, on his knees, he remembered a polished square-toed boot in his stomach. God had brave soldiers in his army. He knelt and rested for a while, slowly got to his feet and rested again. The steps of the portico of the Savings Bank were in view, with its columns and capitals and the ornate corniced pediment. A stone reality. He stared blindly at it while he recovered. They had been careful. His face was unmarked. The harsh metallic voice, he had recognised. He remembered, "The Guards don't give ear to soupers." The figure of the sergeant standing in the archway came suddenly to mind.

He gathered strength and moved, erect, but dragging each footstep. Home seemed a great distance; he could barely tolerate the pain in muscle and bone. He moved on. As he turned away he glimpsed the Mechanic's Institute, the "sinking" church, and the railing of the People's Park. He reached the steps of his home. Climbing them was a great effort. He rested, leaning against his door.

Finally he entered the hallway. Lillian was rushing towards him. Hannah was standing farther back, raising the strength of the gaslight. Surroundings of home comforted him: carpet, pictures, wallpaper. He held out hands to ward off Lillian.

"I had a fall," he said. "I feel sore."

Lillian could see the pain in his eyes and the paleness, the set sober mass of his face.

"But you were with Arnie," she said. "And it's a short walk from the hotel to our doorstep. Didn't Arnie have a car?"

He nodded. "I had a call to make."

Lillian looked at him for a moment; she took his arm and they climbed the stairs to the drawing-room.

"Nothing broken," he told her.

She took him in her arms and held him; she was trembling.

"Soreness, that's all."

Lillian had pulled the bell-handle at the fireplace. Hannah entered. She stood, hands clasped, silent as a grave-mourner.

Lillian said, "Mr Edward will be fine, Hannah. Some food, you'll know what to bring."

"Yes, ma'am."

When she had gone, Edward said, "Arnie and I had a few drinks, but not too many. Lucy Langford's death was a shock. I'm sorry, Lillian. She was your good friend. And bringing bad news to a family takes courage." He could see traces of tears in her eyes. "Sit and rest."

"I'll bring you a drink," she said. "You look pale as paper, Edward." She brought a tray with a squat crystal glass, a soda siphon and a bulky bottle of Redbreast whiskey. She put them beside him on a coffee table.

He poured whiskey and soda and drank a little.

"Are you cut, bleeding?"

"No, just soreness."

"You went back to the kitchen?"

Edward paused. "I went to the police station."

She was silent for moments. "Edward, it was good but foolhardy. There were two hundred people on the street. You're different, you know that, don't you? You married *me*. You're different. You placed yourself in danger."

"The police weren't at the burning, were they? I met a decent man. He offered an opinion."

"Stay out of sight, let things run their course?"

Lillian pulled over a stool with fine leatherwork, that had come from abroad. She sat before him.

"In so many words."

"You didn't *fall*, did you, Edward?"

"I refused to give money to a beggar. He had friends. They came out of an alleyway. I took a beating."

Lillian knew he was lightening the blow. "I'll send a note to the school tomorrow. You'll take a few days rest. Taddy has a post mortem, but we'll go to see him after that.."

Hannah arrived with food.

CHAPTER FOUR

DR THADDEUS BENNETT had an allocation of beds at Barrington's and he had access to its operating theatre and surgical equipment. He was reputed to be a good surgeon and physician. If he felt something was beyond the scope of his personal ability, or beyond the range of the hospital's resources, he sought the help of his peers; he had earned their goodwill and friendship. Taddy would admit he had some ability, but it was mostly common sense, he said, that pulled him through.

He was fifty-four, seven years Arnie's senior, and cast in a very different physical mould. He was tall, rakish, with good features and greying hair. He smoked heavily and, like most of his profession, he took a little alcohol every day.

He stood at the metal table of the mortuary examination room in the hospital basement. He wore a long waterproof gown, rubber gloves, high rubber boots. A nurse attended him. He laid down his scalpel and sat smoking; he said, "Yes, embolism, respiratory and cardiac failure . . ."

Corpses didn't bleed, but there was always blood; his gown and gloves were smeared with it. He had covered Lucy Langford's face and her torso with sheets. Her chest wall was open and expanded. The body's organs were like blobs of colour waiting to be mixed.

It wasn't an ideal situation to know your patient well; but they had shared so many defeats and survivals, moments of celebration and laughter when she came to visit with Lillian, that it seemed fitting that this ignominious chapter of death should also be shared. The nurse pulled off his gloves and robe and he scrubbed at the hand basin. He sat and she pulled off the rubber boots.

Dressed again, ready to leave, he put a cigarette in an amber holder and held a petrol lighter to it. The smoke rested like cirrus streaks on the cool stillness of this basement. Refrigeration was hardly adequate. Verdicts were nearly always foregone conclusions. It was the law, a medical procedure, a statute. He could remember only a single instance when they had sent a waterproofed cadaver, packed in ice, to the Dublin vaults. A foreman, or someone of rank in the construction industry, had been killed a few miles from the city on the vast sprawl of the new hydroelectric scheme. There could be a hanging in retribution.

He looked back at the opened body of Lucy Langford. The cause of death, he knew, had been aggravated. The shock of the break-in, the frenzied crowd, the destruction and her tumbling fall to the floor had decided her moment of death. A shock of sudden bad news or a slithering crash on icy pavements could have ended her, or she might have lived in her peaceful environment for thirty, forty years. She had been a gentle person.

He bowed his thanks to the nurse, saying, "You can do the closing now. Do a tidy job. She was a tidy person. Talk to the undertaker, mention my name. I want her to look very peaceful in her coffin."

"Yes, Doctor."

"And thank you.'

Taddy Bennett went up the stone steps from the basement to the glittering linoleum of the corridors. He had two male patients in a general ward. A staff nurse met and escorted him.

"How are my patients?" he asked.

"Collins. Up and down."

"No plunges?"

"No."

"If he holds on we might send him home for a while. He could see the winter out."

The corridor was perfection in its cleanliness, the walls and floor shining. Nurses and probationers passed in their calf-length uniforms, hair almost totally hidden in gleaming starched caps. Taddy Bennett nodded to them. An army of devotion, he called them, for the spans of time they gave, day in day out, and for so little. Probationers paid for their uniforms and training! Qualified, many sailed away to become the proud mainstay of Britain's hospitals.

Thaddeus asked, "Old Pettigrew?"

"Holding on."

"Keep him comfortable, if you can."

Taddy entered the ward and stood by their beds. He looked calm, said all the usual things that might restore confidence and hope. He felt guilty at times, but dishonesty was part of medicine, too. They walked back along the corridor.

He handed two theatre tickets to the nurse. "I won't be using them," he said. "The local group. 'The Mikado' this year. You'll enjoy it."

She thanked him. He walked on to the matron's office. She was a small welcoming woman, having nothing of dread or dragon about her. He had known her for years, since she had been staff nurse, theatre sister, sister-tutor. She had always been clever, bound for the top.

"Maggie," he said, "you don't look well, you look perfection."

"I used to believe that once," she said.

"Good days," he said, remembering. "Even with garrisons, Crossleys and curfews. Rebels from Irishtown and Englishtown, and the Munsters were marching to Flanders. The city has become a stagnant old pool."

"Not stagnant here, Taddy. Beds never empty for more than half a day. Poverty and sickness are thriving and God is burning down soup kitchens." She paused and looked at him. The death certificate was on her blotter and she held a fountain pen. "I'm sorry about Lucy Langford."

"Yes."

She waited for a few moments. "Cause?"

"Embolism, cardiac, respiratory – the usual."

She completed the certificate and he signed it.

"How is your wife?" she asked.

"She's dying, Maggie. We don't know how to cure tuberculosis yet. We're just dabbling about. I have a big house, you know. I've made her a little sanatorium there. Abigail talks to her, reads to her, and she has a night nurse to attend to her. And myself. She's isolated, but not alone."

"How long?"

"I don't know. I ordered a wireless set and loud speaker from Dublin. They're to send a man down to set it up for me at her bedside. It needs an aerial on the roof, and an earth wire going to ground. But good music, news, drama, comedy, coming all the way from Daventry in England." He paused. "I should cancel it, I think, Maggie. She's very low." He paced about a little and said, apropos of nothing. "Daventry is in Northampshire, I seem to remember."

"Yes, I understand, Taddy," she said.

"Lying in bed all day is a punishment."

"Remember me to her. And to Abigail."

"Of course."

He was on his way to the door when she called out to him. "There's something else. More bad news, I'm afraid."

"What?"

"Three cases of diphtheria since yesterday in Irishtown."

"Oh, my God," he said. "October, November. The bad time of year. It might last till April. Our own private epidemic. If the dispensary staff is overloaded, call on me. I must go, Maggie. So many things to do."

"The police rang. About Lucy Langford."

"Send them a copy of the certificate. By hand, Maggie."

Taddy drove away from the hospital along the Abbey River. The war years and the rebellion years had left a mark on the city. In times of strife everything was neglected. Except for the hospital building, the housing and small businesses had a downcast look. He crossed the river at the Customs House, its black and gold clock-face measuring the moments of life, and drove past the Town Hall and what had been the clink, and where once there had been a roadblock; past the towering landmark clock that gave stature to three great commercial houses. He passed Cruise's Hotel and the County Club, where he had membership and never visited, and passed the fine houses and shops of the new city of Pery and his entrepreneurs. He turned left to the stately terrace of his home and private consulting rooms. He had a fine house, one of the many built during the reign of the Hanoverian Georges, looking across the People's Park at the tall column raised to honour an adopted citizen, Baron Monteagle of Brandon, a man of great ability and compassion who had devoted his life to the alleviation of the people's poverty a century ago.

A housekeeper in her tunic and apron, anticipating him, opened back the panelled front door with its polished furniture. A brass plate said, "Dr Thaddeus Bennett MD BCh BAO." The housekeeper was close on fifty; he hadn't been long married to Matilda when she had come to serve. The management of the house and staff was safe in her hands, he knew.

"Thank you, Brigid," he said.

She took his coat and hat, hung them on a hallstand and gestured towards an appointments book.

"Nothing till half-past three, Doctor. Then only two patients. Mr and Mrs Burke are in the drawing-room with Abigail. And Mr Arnold. Mr Arnold brought them in his car."

"Almost a family gathering," Taddy said. "I was expecting them, Brigid. Mr Burke had a fall, might have sprained something or other, I expect."

"Yes, he limps a bit. I can arrange luncheon for you all. A half an hour, no more."

"Oh, just some sandwiches and a pot of tea, Brigid."

"Yes, Doctor."

When she had gone he looked at his reflection in the hall-stand mirror. A little pale and drawn, he thought. He was thankful that autopsies were infrequent. There was some intangible reward in carrying out surgery on the living; life was precious, it needed care. But opening up the dead, even though he tried to give it dignity and respect, was a sordid business; motionless organs, just an ooze of blood, cutting through flesh and bone to satisfy civil and medical jurisprudence. Necessary, of course, but without reward or hope of restoration of life. And then, he had known Lucy Langford, the sound of her voice, her laughter. That didn't help. He arranged himself before the mirror. Pathology wouldn't have been his calling, he thought.

There were two rooms to the left from the hallway. His consulting-room looked out across the broad street and the park railings. The back room, perfectly furnished and maintained, was the waiting-room.

Taddy Bennett looked at his pocket watch; it had been his father's, a conferring-day present at the College of Surgeons so many years ago. It was still early. Long expensive curtains, light as tulle, draped the glasswork, and heavy lined brocade could shut off the world when it was time for gaslight and privacy. It was a functional room, but it had good taste, even beauty. Illness, too, needed reassurance. There was a blazing coal fire, a rolltop desk and a swivel chair, two upright chairs for patients, a leather upholstered *chaise-longue*, a flat examination table with spotless woollen blankets, a weighing scales, a height chart. The walls sported certificates and photographs of football teams with their trophies. There was warmth in the floor, the ceiling, even from the metal and glass that caught the erratic dance of the fire flames.

From a cabinet he took a whiskey decanter, poured himself a drink and sat in his swivel chair for ten minutes. He closed his eyes, emptied his mind and slowly sipped his drink. It was a little self-devised routine to shake off tension.

Feeling better, he moved out to the hallway, where Brigid met him, saying, "Everything will be ready in five minutes." He climbed the stairs and entered the drawing-room, a fine room of colour and light. Beyond the open folding doors lay the polished wood of table, chairs, sideboard and serving-tables of the dining-room. The company greeted him.

Lillian said what was foremost in her mind. "Lucy's body. You arranged everything, Taddy? Were the police in touch?"

"Police? Oh nothing like that. Just a routine perusal by me and I signed the certificate."

"Dear Lucy. The old people tried to be brave about it. A full church service before the funeral tomorrow. I'm so relieved. Police, a coroner's court, questions: it would have been dreadful."

"Yes," Taddy said, raising his hand to Edward and Arnie. And to Abigail. Matilda was always in his thoughts. "Everything all right upstairs?" he asked.

Abigail said, "She's sleeping, comfortable. Brigid will tell me if she rings."

Abigail, an attractive girl of twenty-two, was tall and slight with tied-back fair hair, good eyes and skin.

Taddy smiled at her.

He turned and said, "How are you, Edward?"

"Just bruises, Taddy."

Lillian smiled. "I'm the worried parent. He didn't want to come, but I insisted."

"Morning-after stiffness," Edward said. "Garryowen days revisited. There's a fair chance of survival."

Taddy laughed; he had seen Edward dish it out himself in the rucks and mauls of recent years. "We'll see to it later, Ed. You were on the fringes of the street scene last night?"

Everyone was seated now.

Edward said, "I heard the speech, saw it all. I sent for the ambulance and the fire brigade."

Taddy said, "Nothing could have saved Lucy. Any of us might have an embolism sleeping in the system. Anything or nothing could see it in motion. That's the end." He paused: "No police there?"

Edward shook his head. "I went to the police. It was an impulse. The mob, the destruction and a death I thought might be connected with it. I thought it was relevant. I was wrong, of course. The law doesn't deal in surmise."

Arnie said, "It was the proper thing to do."

Lillian looked at Edward, relieved that he was in one piece. She had never seen him out of temper; a faintly smiling calmness was always in his face. Edward could fight his own battles.

"I met an inspector," Edward said. "He was helpful. There was a sergeant, too. Ambitious, I thought. He didn't miss much. I wondered about him."

Taddy asked, "His loyalty?"

Arnie smiled. "When jobs and promotion are in the air, loyalty takes flight."

Silence settled for a few moments; all the men were smoking. Edward said, "I was coming from the police station. It was late, of course. No blood, just bruises."

Arnie asked, "No idea who?"

Edward was remembering the metallic voice, but it was hardly worth mentioning it now. "No," he said. "A dark night, blackened faces. It was too sudden."

"They were waiting for you?"

"It seemed like that."

Edward left the details of the story untold. "The usual aching and stiffness," he said to Taddy.

Taddy nodded. "I'll get something to ease that."

Brigid and a parlour-maid had arrived and were setting out food. The table-cloth and cutlery, the glass and china gleamed.

Brigid came in to announce. "Everything is ready, Mr Taddy. You can stand or sit." She ushered away her junior maid and followed her, closing the door almost without a sound.

They sat casually around the table, and Lillian tended to them. It was only sandwiches and sauces, scones and a few sweet things.

Arnie broke the silence. "Yes, Edward, there might have been a conspiracy to waylay you."

Taddy nodded. "Blackened faces, fists and boots. Some secret militia. Finding the middle of the road these days is difficult."

"Men of the Church, I thought, might be taking a hand in the game, too." Edward paused and considered his words; eventually he said, "My marriage to Lillian. I know it has importance."

"It was mentioned?"

"Yes."

Arnie said, "There was the fiery speech of holiness at the burning, too."

"Yes," Edward nodded, "and visiting the police station might have been an indiscretion."

Arnie was quiet in tone, at ease. "We know there are republican legions out there, some of them still at war. Some of them want us out. We've always had enemies. We can live with that. I'll work till they shoot me down," Arnie said. "There's no cure for people, is there, Taddy?"

"I don't think so."

"No more soup kitchens, Lillian," he warned.

Taddy said, "I send anonymous hand-outs to the workhouse. The City Home, they call it now, but it's still the

workhouse. Or the Vincent de Paul Committee. They do good work."

Lillian had been sending donations for years; she felt that little private moments of charity were personal secrets. Lucy Langford had been generous and anonymous, too. She thought suddenly of Lucy's voice and laughter silenced for ever, and of bringing the news of the death to the ageing Langford parents in a home where they were alone now. Lucy, unmarried, had tended them, cared for them.

Old Mrs Langford was a querulous, impatient woman; but she was ailing, hardly ever without pain.

"It's about Lucy, Mrs Langford."

"Yes, yes. What is it?"

"I'm sorry, Mrs Langford. There's bad news."

"What are you talking about?"

"Lucy is dead."

There was an awful shocked silence; pale gaping faces; not a single word spoken. They had good servants, ageing side by side with them. Lillian had advised, instructed them. There were relatives in the city, burial arrangements to be made. Leaving that house of stillness had been an awful moment.

She could see the outline of Edward seated beside her and wanted to reach out and grip his hand. Without him, she felt, she would have been in tears. Edward had walked to the police station to put the facts on record, to offer himself as a witness. Regard welled up like tears. It was good to have Edward, to have a home of comfort, to shut out the world.

As she talked with Abigail and Taddy, Arnie and Edward stood by the window. Like conspirators, she thought.

CHAPTER FIVE

TADDY STOOD FOR a few moments on the doorstep and looked across at the People's Park, the banks and parterres of late flowers, paler green grass and tended pathways, shrubs and tall trees and the rising centre point of ground that was a further plinth for Monteagle's column.

Brigid would be shocked: one didn't stand on doorsteps. Even servants, when there was sweeping or polishing to be done, didn't look or stare, but kept their eyes on their work.

It was very still and peaceful here. Daimler engines made only a little noise, but he could still hear the faint powerful stroke of Arnie's car that must be close to George's Street now.

When he re-entered the house, Taddy took a thick quarto notebook from his consulting-room desk, closed the door and began to climb the stairs to Matilda's sanatorium. He had been born in 1874 when Victoria still had more than a quarter of a century to sit on her throne, in strange seclusion, for ever in mourning for her cherished Albert and leaning on the shoulder of reliable John Brown. He remembered wars, rebellions, strikes, murders, executions, tales of indiscretions at the card-tables and in bedrooms. He remembered the death of the deathless queen, and the death of Edward, too, belatedly proclaimed a statesman in funeral orations.

Matilda and Taddy had been young then. He had seen her at the Royal Dublin Society in a flowing summer gown with a parasol and a picture hat. She had been very beautiful . He was instantly smitten and had found a way to meet her and marry her. He stood on a landing of his house now and remembered it. He had been a not impecunious houseman at the Rotunda, finishing his studies and missing the South African War where his two older brothers had perished. Matilda had a considerable dowry and she loved Thaddeus Bennett. Love and marriage and ample means: it had all been so simple.

In 1919 she had contracted a poisonous influenza and survived the awful death toll of the pandemic. But it had left a weakness.

After six years of indifferent health came the short dry cough that had alerted him. It might be nothing; a cold or a throat irritation. Honey and glycerine would be soothing. It passed. Then suddenly night sweating plagued her: intense sweating without fever or apparent cause. And it, too, had abated. He was alarmed but waited patiently. The coughing and discharge of mucus eventually came. And blood.

The phlegm analysis was telephoned to him from Dublin: "Koch's bacillus. Immediate treatment." Tuberculosis.

Matilda was too intelligent to hoodwink with calming stories of passing infections that were doing the rounds.

She made the opportunity for him. He had returned from his hospital calls and found her sitting in the drawing-room.

She said, "I had nodded off, Taddy. I don't seem to have any energy these days. Should I have a tonic, something to pick me up?"

He sat before her. "You have a cough, too, and sputum."

"Yes, it comes and goes."

He sat for moments in silence, looking at her face that had grown older, but where he could see all the beauty of his first glimpse of her. There was no cure for tuberculosis; you merely waged a war of attrition against it. He had sent two dozen cases to isolation hospitals in a few months; a tidal wave of it was rolling in, ready to sweep the country. It might take decades to find a cure, but he had money and space and he could fight it from day to day.

He said, "I sent sputum to Dublin for analysis."

She reached out and took his hand. "What is it? You can tell me, Taddy. I think I know."

"Tuberculosis," he said.

"Yes."

"But we've caught it early. I have space and time to treat it. And you can change your life, Matty."

"I'll do whatever you say."

"Two, three years, perhaps, may get it in recession. Isolation, of course, and someone to nurse you."

"Abigail will nurse me."

Taddy thought of Abigail: nineteen years old, young men looking at her already. It was a big sacrifice. He said, "We can afford a nurse. Money isn't a problem. It will be a demanding job." Taddy paused for a moment. "Even a risky job."

"We discussed it days ago. I knew I was ill, Taddy. Abigail knew it. You don't live in a medical house for almost thirty years and not become a kind of shadow physician. Coughing, night sweats, fatigue. She is determined, Taddy, and she's devoted to us."

"All right," he said. "Just a night nurse with Abigail will be adequate."

That was three years in the past. There had been weeks of work: two rooms on the top floor had been stripped and converted into one. A new floor of seasoned wood, tongued and grooved, was laid, primed and sealed. The walls had been laid bare, made good, and painted with gloss oil paint; the ceiling was treated. The furnishing was spartan: no window curtains, waterproof blinds, the chairs of bare wood, a cabinet and a table. Everything could be cleaned and purged. There was a wash hand basin and a large sink for soaking clothes and utensils. Two gaslight pendants had opaque glass shades. The windows now swung like doorways to admit light and air, warm or growing cold. And sunshine when it came. Sunshine might shorten the life of this deadly bacillus. Exit doors to the house were fitted tight to the threshold, lintel and jambs.

Abigail had a separate room on the same floor. She could throw off her long protective gown, calf-length rubber waders and her mob-cap, and leave them behind before she crossed the landing to rest or sleep. Taddy had left her antiseptics and mouthwashes. Once a week her room was sprayed and cleansed, and twenty-five paraform tablets and formaldehyde were left vaporising over a burner for ten hours to complete fumigation.

It was probably useless, Taddy knew, but perhaps it was a small deterrent. Koch's bacillus was transmitted by contact and it travelled like wildfire. Isolation, air and sunshine were the only weapons to fight it.

Poverty, overcrowding and malnutrition opened the door for it, too. Sometimes whole families were wiped out. And now, another habitual killer was coming to spend the season: diphtheria. Three cases, Maggie Norris at Barrington's had said. From autumn to spring it could hover like a threat, and sometimes descend with swollen, choking throats. They were experimenting with serums: journals trotted out the story from time to time. How long?

Taddy climbed to the top floor, left his notebook on the landing table and knocked on the door. Abigail opened it and handed him a long robe that reached to the ground. She closed the door on the healthy world. Taddy held her hand for a moment before he went to the bed.

Matty, well wrapped up, was propped up on spotless pillows. The bare floor, the bare walls, the scrubbed furniture, the big tall windows open wide to the sky made Matilda's home seem a barren world. Matty lay there, eyes closed, perhaps in the great lethargy that was enveloping her, the line of her face wasted, pulled tight against the jutting bones. It was a peaceful face but wasted. Years of battle had shrunk face and body. Her hands, always long and graceful, now were pale, sculpted, with a fresh beauty. But there was effort in her dragging in breath slowly and releasing it in weakness.

On a table behind her was a mound of paper towels and covered containers for sputum. Taddy took a paper towel and lifted the lid to see the contents. Hardly anything there. Once he might have seen that as a step towards improvement; now it was deterioration. The early winter air blowing through the open windows had a chill. Matty was covered and warm, but Abigail's hands were cold.

In the open diary on the table, he read Abigail's notes of an infinitely slow progress towards death.

Abigail was watching him; he looked at her and smiled. These years of living with illness had enhanced her beauty, given her strength. Her fair hair was just showing from beneath the mob-cap; she had good features and eyes and a determined mould of chin.

"She sleeps a lot of the time now."

"The night nurse is good?"

"I get days off, and evenings. I go to Castleconnell when I can. That old house and the trees and the river. So much beauty and life. I can sit for hours and watch men holding their boats in the currents and casting for salmon. Have you ever listened to the sound of the river at night-time?"

"I grew up there, remember. And Arnie and Lillian. Father and mother spoil you, I'm sure of that."

"I make them laugh," she said. "I call them grand-père and grand-mère. I like to be with them."

He paused. "They're both healthy people. Just ageing, that's all. Close to their eighties now."

"Yes."

Looking at her, it suddenly occurred to him. "What plans have you?" he asked. "For your future, you know, all that?"

"I'll think about it."

He paced about, stood at the open window, watched a park attendant sweeping leaves. He had worried once about Abigail's health, but whatever strengths were needed to ward off the illness that was surrounding her all this time, she had in abundance. There were some who toppled over at the first breath of contagion, and others who were untouched even by the blackest of plagues. In the Bennett family only Matilda had contracted the Spanish flu, and now this.

He went and stood close to Abigail. "There isn't much time left now. Weeks, maybe only days." She had been close to pneumonic for some time, and there could be sudden acceleration.

"When it's over . . . ." He looked at Abigail. "It's difficult to speak of parting with people we love, isn't it?"

He looked at the bare walls, the open windows, the floor clean from its daily swabbing. "When your work here is finished," he asked again, "have you any plans?"

"Nursing. I'd like to train at Barrington's. And the city is our home, isn't it? I told grand-mère all about it. She didn't mention it?"

He wondered if his face showed his emotions. "No," he said. "I think you could be a good nurse."

"I hope so."

"A hard life."

"Yes, I've watched you," she said. She smiled. "You would have liked me to follow in your footsteps, wouldn't you? Your practice?"

"Nursing, you will be following in my footsteps."

"You're pleased? This will be my home."

"I'm pleased," he said. "I brought my notebook from the consulting-room. It's on the landing table. You might find it interesting." He held her hand in both of his for a moment.

Then he washed and disinfected, rinsed his mouth. He

went and stood by Matilda's bed, head bowed in thought, or prayer. He didn't pray very much; he had seen too much poverty and death to believe in providence, guiding forces, other-world rewards. He probably spoke to some great healing entity, more harassed than himself, who had the world in his waiting-room.

He moved to the door and, leaving, raised a hand to her. She could see just a trace of tears. She listened to his footsteps, soft on the carpet, all the journey down to the hallway. She and Brigid would take good care of him.

Matilda slept for long periods now, deeply at times, breath always laboured, almost comatose. Abigail washed and rinsed like Taddy, stepped out of her waders, hung her gown and mob-cap on the door and, on the landing, took Taddy's notebook from the table.

Beneath the table were Abigail's slippers; she stepped into them and entered her private room. Even her comforts, which she kept at a minimum, had almost a lavish welcome after the scraped bareness next door. Brigid had lit and stoked a fire, and Abigail sat before it, enjoying the warmth. The coal burned and released its hissing gas to send a fresh brightness into the corona of flame. With window closed, she could hear the rhythm of burning, a tiny flapping sound. She was thinking of age; her mother was fifty-four.

The last time Abigail had visited Castleconnell, the first enquiry had been, "How is your mother progressing? Is she eating plenty of beef and vegetables? And milk? Milk is a nourishment against all diseases."

"She was never a big eater."

"Taddy is advising her?"

"He sees her two or three times a day."

"Then she's in safe hands. Taddy knows how to deal with these things. He could have made a brilliant career in Dublin, but he had to come back to his 'dear old city', as he calls it. He works too hard."

Abigail said, "He's known it all his life. The dear old city."

"How old are you, child?"

"Grand-mère! You don't ask a young lady her age."

"Yes, I do."

Abigail laughed. "I'm twenty-two."

"A grandchild of twenty-two! Father, we are getting very old. Abigail is twenty-two."

John and Alexandra Bennett were still lively, but showing signs of age. John Bennett, in his time, had enlarged the business, had travelled to England and Europe. He had always been in motion. He had taken Alexandra abroad and they had travelled the tourist tracks to Baden and Nice, down to Rome and Naples and to Greece and Constantinople. He was reading the London *Times* now.

Alexandra pierced his concentration at last. "Are you listening, John? Abigail is twenty-two."

"Oh, happy birthday, Abby. Twenty-two, I see. Did we get her a birthday present, my dear?"

Alexandra nodded at the hopelessness of it. "Not her *birthday*. Her age is twenty-two."

"Ah, I see."

Alexandra liked sometimes to talk of family relationships, marriages, good and bad connections, ages. Like a priestess, she sat back in concentration, dredging a great pool of memory.

"What age is your mother now?"

"Fifty-four."

John Bennett said suddenly, "A dangerous age."

Alexandra stared at him. "Dangerous? We seem to have escaped serious injury, you and I. Some superstitious nonsense, I suppose. Fifty-four meant we were at our prime."

He nodded. "Yes, we seem to have come through without a scratch. Life is divided into nine-year spans, they say. The whole body changes in nine years. Eighteen, twenty-seven, thirty-six, and so on. Absolute fact, I'm sure."

Abigail said, "Six nines makes fifty-four. And five and four make another nine."

"That's it, Abby! It's a kind of grand climacteric. Seventy-two is another."

"Go back to your newspaper, John. I'm sorry I disturbed you. I've never heard such rubbish. Like some fortune-teller in a fairground."

"Yes, yes." He was already hidden behind the broadsheet. "That young Prince of Wales fellow moves about a bit, stops and chats with the miners in Wales. The working man's friend, they call him. A good move. Keeps the pot from boiling over."

Alexandra said, "He's a grown man. Born in 1894. He's thirty-four years of age. Should be married. Probably following in his grandfather's footsteps."

Tea was always a break, with light-as-air buttered scones and chocolate biscuits and confections. There would be silences and desultory talk. They both enjoyed their food.

Alexandra conducted the ritual with an unhurried tempo. "You're not eating, Abigail."

"I've finished."

"What!"

"Two buttered scones and a chocolate biscuit."

Alexandra sighed. "I know you don't change your mind. You inherited that stubborn streak from your grandfather."

Grandfather was eating and reading, in his own world.

Alexandra dropped her voice. "Does that nice boy of the Connick's still write to you from Dublin?"

"Sometimes."

"A very good family. They want for nothing. Your Uncle Arnold does business with them. Your grandfather knew them very well. Nursing your mother is a noble thing, but it has taken precious years. Taddy could get full-time nurses in there overnight. You should be enjoying life."

"I have a good life. Sitting here is good. We have concerts and recitals in town, you know. And there are house parties with lots of people."

"Young men?"

"I meet them at parties."

"No one special?"

"Everyone is special."

Alexandra smiled. "You're saving yourself for young Connick, I think. A good choice. You say he writes to you?"

"I reply occasionally."

"Occasionally?"

"Oh, eventually he will tire."

"But your future, Abigail!"

"He wants to put me in a gilded cage. I wouldn't like that. I'm going to train at Barrington's. And I'll be at home in our 'dear old city'."

Alexandra was dumbfounded. "Nursing?"

"Yes, nursing."

"Well, it isn't marvellous, is it?"

"Life isn't always marvellous, grand-mère."

"You should reconsider, Abigail. You need substance. A husband, a family, an excellent home. But, above all, substance."

"I have substance and an excellent home. And father. But I must do something worthwhile. Marriage might fit into the scheme of things. I'm twenty-two. Lillian was thirty-eight when she found Edward. So, you see, there's hope for me."

Alexandra looked out across the gardens at the tumbling white water of the river in full flow over the scarred rock-bed. Yes, she thought, the world was changing, and people were pushing out of closed doors.

Abigail asked, "You're not cross with me, grand-mère?"

Alexandra smiled. "Of course not. Whatever you do, I know you'll do it well. I've often wondered how a young girl could live in a sick room all this time. Strength, character, I suppose."

Abigail had looked towards the newspaper, saw John Bennett's eyes over the rim, smiling; he was nodding . . . .

Sitting before her glowing fire now she remembered them both with love. Alexandra could rise late from her bed, instruct servants, arrange her day; there was no rush or strain. She had been born and lived in another age.

Abigail opened Taddy's notebook – a case book of his skirmishes with disease and death – to where he had left a marker.

She read: "Tuberculosis – pulmonary tuberculosis or consumption." It was a diary of Matilda's illness. Recently he had written, "I feel that her illness took root following the 1919 influenza epidemic; that inflammation of chest and lungs had permanently weakened her, left her predisposed to the tubercular bacillus."

Abigail fixed her marker and put the book beside her. This was Thaddeus' story of Matilda. Abigail knew the depth of pain that had prompted it: Thaddeus wondering how he had sat unaware of the illness for so long; or whether he brought it with him – however much he had scrubbed – to pass it innocently to her with his hands or his lips. He was blameless and he was reaching for straws. The influenza pandemic? A predisposition? The will of God?

Abigail sat before her fire and rested. Her mother would soon be dead, absent for evermore. But her father was a person of great strength; and she had two healthy brothers at business in Dublin. She thought of Edward and Lillian with affection; they were people of strength, too. You counted your blessings. Arnold had a great store of wealth and security, but an empty house and a shattered family: Harry, her own age, locked away in his final syphilitic struggles, and Dorcas and Ethel who had fled from it all.

There was a soft rapping on the door. That would be Brigid with Matilda's special food. Abigail stood and prepared for work.

CHAPTER SIX

EDWARD'S BRUISES HAD healed; he was limber again, at ease. He came quickly across the drawing-room floor to sit beside Lillian.

"You look fine," he said.

"I feel better," Lillian said. "Normal. The upheaval that night was like warfare, but now it seems unreal. I remember standing at the kitchen stove and hearing that man preaching to people in the street. I had turned to stare when the window came crashing in and struck poor Lucy." Lillian was silent for a long while; eventually she said, "Now she's at rest."

It was approaching evening; darkness was setting in. The folding doors to the dining-room had been shut; the drawing-room with its coal fire, the softness of gaslight, was a place of comfort. Sometimes they dined sitting close to each other at a small table in the drawing-room.

Hannah brought dishes and arranged them. A retainer of years' standing, she had watched Lillian Bennett grow and, when it seemed she was dedicated to her spinsterhood, suddenly marry Edward Burke from a substantial Catholic trading family.

Hannah was proud of Edward: he was a Catholic who behaved well, walked a straight line. Like most people in service, Hannah was a Catholic, but in living close to more temperate religious practices, she had diluted hellfire, damnation, awful punishments of everlasting pain to a more gentle catharsis. She had a contented face. A parlour-maid assisted her and drifted away.

"Everything is ready now, ma'am," she announced.

"Thank you, Hannah."

They sat and Lillian poured wine.

"You can talk about it again," Edward said. "That's good."

"For days I couldn't even think about it."

Edward put an arm about her.

She said, "The burial, I'm told, had a certain peace about it. A clear day, a lot of fallen leaves."

The burial had been private, with no women present. That was their custom. The small group of women would sit at the home of the bereaved and wait.

"Lucy would have liked it," he said.

Their meal was simple, carefully prepared by Hannah, and the wine was good. When Lillian rang a small hand-bell for the changing of courses, Hannah brought light pastry and fruit. And tea. Tea was a lazy hour by the fire.

Lillian said, "You were angry, Edward, weren't you? When I left on the ambulance with Lucy, I was worried."

"Yes, I was angry, but I allowed myself to be silenced," he said.

"Has that angered you?"

Edward took her hand, sat close to her. "There's no anger," he told her, "but I feel lessened, a little ashamed, I suppose."

She turned on the seat of the couch and looked into his face. There were times when she was glad to be older in years, perhaps occasionally in wisdom, too. She kissed him very softly on the lips, and his hands held her head there for moments. She lay against him and his arm embraced her shoulders.

She said, "Aren't you a better man than those who silenced you?"

"I don't know."

"I know. We had our turn as masters. Now it's their turn. It isn't an easy job. An Ascendancy class, they called us. We had our differences but we resolved them, kept our excesses in check when we could, but they never saw us as fellow citizens. We were a united other people. That's what we were. That's what we are. But are we different? Am I different, Edward?"

"Yes," he said, "and I love you for being different."

"And you're different and I love you."

Edward embraced her, let his hands feel her body through the smooth satin of her dress, they kissed; and felt each other's breath on their faces. They felt the excitement of the thought that in a few hours they would be lying together naked in their bedroom.

She said, "But are we different?"

Edward smiled. "I don't think so," he said.

Lillian laughed aloud, began to pour fresh cups of tea. He listened to her laughter. Laughter was often a mannerism, a punctuation, but hers had a sound of devilment in it.

"I'm glad I married you, Edward!"

"And I'm glad."

"I know why you agreed to be silent. You were thinking of the Bennetts. You thought you might have damaged us."

He paused. "Arnie's business would be a prize for someone," he said.

"They wouldn't seize it?"

"No. Damage it."

"We all hold shares in the company."

"Frighten us out."

"Who would trade with them? England, Rotterdam, Paris?

Surely not, Edward."

"Politicians dabble in business, too." Edward picked up his teacup, drank a little. "We must sit it out, that's all. Things will calm."

Lillian was silent for a little while, then she said, "From time to time we all have to step off the path, give right of way, Edward. Avoid confrontation. I've done it myself. All the Bennetts have done it. We survive. That's our way of life."

"I'm learning," he said.

"Don't be cross, Edward. You're an honourable man."

He took her hand again. "Not cross. Just little ripples of anger still there. The Garda sergeant was so cocksure."

"Shouldn't he be?"

"He should be vigilant. They could have heard the voice of that crossroads evangelist in full cry. I spoke to the district inspector; he seemed a good man. I'm sure he knew my life story. He knew Latimer was a Protestant school. He had done a lot of fighting and sniping down the years, I thought. He seemed tired. We were in his private office, but I think the sergeant might have been listening. I think he knew it, too."

"Is it important?"

Lillian stood and took the tray away; she rang the wall-bell by the fireplace for Hannah, who came and went.

Lillian stirred up the fire, sending flames licking high. The shape and litheness of her body hadn't changed in twenty years. She was an attractive woman whose face had matured but hadn't aged. Edward thought she was beautiful. She wore a floral, calf-length gown, high collared, and tied at the waist.

She sat close to him again. "You didn't answer. The cocksure man with sergeant's stripes? Is it important?"

"Not very, I suppose."

"He was courteous?"

"He walked me to the pavement, hardly in courtesy, I thought. He watched me out of sight."

Lillian was sitting upright again, looking at him, waiting. A little shadow fell on her brightness.

"In twenty minutes I was cornered," Edward said. "They were well placed to catch me."

Lillian looked at him in silence for moments.

"The sergeant had arranged it?"

"He saw me to the pavement, watched me out of sight. A phone call to some sodality panjandrum with holy soldiers in his command. A little reception could have been arranged."

"Holy soldiers?"

"Members of church sodalities, thousands of them, troop weekly or monthly to services, to be reformed, instructed, menaced with hellfire. Every section has a prefect, a headman."

"They believe so deeply?"

"You only need a hundred zealots, and the rest will follow."

They sat in silence, side by side, for a long time. Here, on the fringes of George's Street, they could hear the noise of evening traffic. This was the "new" city, a hundred, a hundred and fifty years old. The ancient town and fortress was down by the old bridge and castle, and a raised stone on which a dishonoured treaty had been signed. The island in the river had been the first stockade of invaders from the northern and western skirts of the continent. This was an ancient city, well studied in the hardships of war. It had been razed by sieges, and blood and flesh had been litter on the streets. Armies and adventurers, all of them with the steel of tyranny, had ringed its walls with men and cannon. It had made heroes of substance and myth. Fragments of the great walls still survived, and a new uncertain people was emerging from centuries of warfare, suppression, famine, flight, disease.

Lillian laughed wryly as she stood up. "I'll bring you a drink," she said. "These have been weeks to forget. Lucy is gone now. I could blame myself, but I don't. We wanted to do something for the very poor. There are tides of poor people on the streets every day, but the very poor are hidden away. Only the few come to soup kitchens. They have rags to wear and shoes without soles. Was it worth it, Edward?"

Edward stood and crossed to her, took the glass from her hand and put it on the sideboard. He held her in his arms for a few moments. She seemed so strong and alive and yet seemingly weightless.

"Yes," he said, "it was worth it. Only the holy warriors are to blame. And their ghostly commanders."

She kissed him.

Edward remembered his charitable evenings of pious endeavour, and his tiring of it. Comfortable men – there were no women – about a long polished table. It was a hopeless pursuit.

A committee man had taken him aside before long, with arm on shoulder friendliness. "As you know, delighted to have you among our workers, Edward. I know your family. But, I think, any mention of your place of work would be inadvisable. Charitable work is by its very nature ecumenical, of course, but Latimer, as you must certainly know, was a heretic. He was burnt at the stake. And we are a Catholic committee . . . ."

Edward remembered the four-storey and basement tenements, once prime residences, looking out across the river at the British barracks, the perishing quay of small boats and traders. They were crammed neglected middens now, crumbling towards danger. And down beyond them, in view of the Customs House, was another line of forgotten grandeur that had once merited a great open space stretching to the lesser stream of the Abbey River and its bridge. Another midden. The city was poxed with them.

There were the tiny hovels and laneways of Irishtown and Englishtown. Fringing the "new" city, from a street passing a church to which Domingo de Guzman, of noble family, author of the terrible Inquisition, had given his sainted name, there ran two lanes to a street of aged neglected housing, and to the steps of the railway station. The lanes were scarcely three paces wide, with a half-pipe channel, lying open, a tip for house-filth and human waste. The stench was of everything that rotted.

Edward Burke had walked them, through fetid rancid air: hovels that might house fifteen bodies, from adults to crawling infants. Death was everywhere.

He had drifted away from it. He had always been distanced, he felt, by his Latimer connection. He had married Lillian . . . .

Lilian and he had spent four weeks in London: they had been married there in springtime weather in a Marylebone registry office. The parks, Hyde, St James's, had been fresh green and with sudden bursts of daffodil gold; the Serpentine was a calm shoreline. They had sat side by side on a smart pleasure boat, moving through the Pool and past Barking and Deptford to the Isle of Dogs and Greenwich. Tower Bridge was behind them. The lazy words of conversation.

"Deptford. Kit Marlowe was murdered there."

"A pub brawl."

"Murdered, they say."

"And the Isle of Dogs?"

"The king's dogs. Brought across from Greenwich."

A time of great happiness, Edward remembered. Theatres, dinners, Poets' Corner, shopping at Liberty's, Fortnum's, Harrods; and then home to Lillian's own house within sight of the movement and style of George's Street. Edward was happy with his lot.

Lillian said, "Are you back?"

He smiled. "Yes." The fireglow and soft gaslight coloured the room and its furnishings.

"You were deep in thought."

"Yes."

He stood and walked across to the sideboard, carried his drink back. He looked at the room, and the barrier of comfort it represented seemed to glow in the soft gaslight. That world of laneways and naked children, excrement, broken boxwood on the hearth, the sameness of days and years, was an unpleasant memory, but it was still out there, suppurating every day.

"That soap-box orator," he said, "I won't forget him. He led the ambush, too. They were disguised, but voices are more difficult to hide. I won't forget his voice." Suddenly he remembered the docks, the stevedore. Yes, he thought, Carmody; that was the name.

"He spoke?" Lillian asked.

"He preached a short sermon."

Lillian was in doubt. "You know the speech-maker?"

Edward paused. "I know his voice," was all he said.

"Will he come again?"

Edward smiled. "This is our private whispering," he said, "for no other ears. We leave sleeping dogs lie. These little sudden whirlwinds pass. Lucy Langford's death was a random shot, haphazard. That will suffice for now. No one is secure. Even the district inspector looks over his shoulder."

"But he's in charge."

"He's in charge but he's being watched, and he knows it. It's an old trick! Get the watchers to watch each other."

For moments Lillian wished for the return of old times, of smart troops on the streets, of uniformed officers standing on the stage of the County Club, of helmeted policemen. Pre-war times. She had been in her early twenties then. On fine days, with a parasol, you could walk across the Wellesley Bridge, stand and watch the beauty of the river at high tide. Distantly, on the northern bank, the big factory stood like a prison; and on the south, great looped hawsers held cargo ships against the quaysides. Men still raised their hats, doormen held open shop doors, and you could count the motor-cars on George's Street. There was a security, or so it seemed.

But now, in retrospect, she knew that the horrendous war had been about to burst upon them. She had been paid court by British officers, but they had seemed a different race. She was Irish. She had organised food and clothing packages for the troops in France, and watched the city's young men, even from hovels and tenements, go marching off to the railway station with soldiers' coats. Escape for a while, or for ever.

She said to Edward, "Things can only get better. Do you know who this young sergeant is?"

"Not even his name," Edward said. "He's still in his twenties, too young to have done much fighting. Maybe he is what he was. A listening post. A messenger boy. Rewarded for good services."

Edward poured himself another drink and came and sat beside her at the fire.

"I remember the Great War," she said, smiling. "I was twenty-six then. You were sixteen."

Edward nodded. "My brother Francis went out to fight and die. It was called a war for freedom of small nations, I remember. Men of integrity called on us to take up arms." Edward paused.

Lillian said, "Your brother fought in France. The Garda sergeant at home."

"The same battle. The same freedom."

"One has his sergeant's stripes. The other hasn't even got a grave. I'm glad you didn't fight, Edward."

"I was twenty and at Trinity when my brother was killed. I was glad to miss it. In fourteen years all the heroes are forgotten."

Lillian said, "Your family is almost gone, Edward."

"I never knew them. Only my father. He was the protective one."

"Protective?"

"That was how he showed affection for me, I felt. The rest were strangers. All my mother's devotion was for Francis, the eldest, the brilliant one. She couldn't part with him. With a doctorate, he could have travelled, but she was immovable. She would have been ill, he thought. He stayed with us, was sought after by local gentry for tuitions. But in 1914 he answered the call, died somewhere in France." Edward paused. "He was escaping from her at last."

Lillian said, "We won't remember it any more; it hurts. We'll just sit here together. I'll always be here, Edward, you know that."

There were lulls in the street noises now, even periods of total silence. The only horse traffic would be the clop of cabbies' growlers on private calls, or to the railway station; or keeping a watch for fares at hotels and better public houses. Growlers, hackney cabs. English soldiers had brought the slang from London. Even motor traffic was resting now.

The fire spread its circle of light at the hearth, cast a shadow of the brass fender and scuttle along the paleness of the rug. A tall beautiful clock, mounted on a plinth, three sides of it glass, rising to a dome, its frame beautiful rope-patterned woodwork, ticked from a corner, a pendant polished weight driving its mechanism, its mercury-filled pendulum swinging lazily. A clockmaker's clock, Lillian called it.

"It's a beautiful room," Edward said aloud. "So many beautiful things. And you."

Lillian laughed; humour was returning. "You came from a fine house, too. I've never crossed its threshold but I know every room. And I know your mother."

"She is a cold woman, Lillian. Her taste is austere or vindictive. She prefers Bosch and Bruegel. She tolerated the modernity of Munch. As a child I was haunted by Munch's faces."

She took his hand. "Caught in a screaming nightmare."

He looked at the happiness in her face. He had never told her of what must be perversion; the coldness and the corruption that she seemed to carry with her from room to room. He pushed it from his mind now. Lillian was beautiful, slim as a schoolgirl, happy. He pulled her close to him, let his hands move over her soft clothing, feel her breasts and hips and thighs beneath. Her mouth was slightly open and he kissed it, let their lips embrace each other, too. She locked the door and closed the shutters.

She whispered, "Let's love each other here, Edward."

He slipped off his jacket and they stood on the hearth rug.

"It's exciting here, almost as if it were stolen," she said.

"Then we'll steal it."

She put her arm about him, let her lips brush against his neck.

Edward's hands caressed her stockinged legs, felt the softness of flesh. She lay on the hearth rug and pulled up the silk fabric of her gown along her thighs.

CHAPTER SEVEN

CARMODY, THE STEVEDORE, had forty in sight. On the dockside you didn't get to the top of your class without a lot of brawn and the readiness to use it. You met the captains and mates of merchant tramps. You talked figures and made deals; you knew the car-men – those who owned a horse and a flat cart and others who worked for a coal yard.

Carmody stuck with coal: he had worked in the holds in dust and dirt, filling skips; he had worked at bagging it and loading it on carts; and with his own horse and cart he had hauled it. He knew coal and coal men. He knew retailers and their minions and their coal yards.

He didn't get within reach of the big men – the merchants, the consignees who bought by the shipload – but he met their managers, well-dressed, aware of their importance, and he doffed his cap.

They wanted coal distributed to a dozen retailers. Carmody made a price with them, took their consignment sheets, stood over the ordered chaos of unloading day by day, book in hand, saw the orders filled. Saw that there was a small residue in the holds for himself at the end of the day, a ton, maybe more. That was his custom. That was his due, and he earned well.

He had a fairly respectable house, not far from the cathedral and the rugby ground. It had a big adjoining yard. That was his stockyard where he sold coal by the bucket, the half-sack, the sack. Customers knocked at his private door, and his wife, a plain, well-dressed woman, gave them admittance by a wicket gate. Residue coal, sold by the bucket, made steady money.

Carmody was on the road to success. They had a single teenage boy: a difficult birth and incompetent surgery had ended Mrs Carmody's child-bearing. The boy attended at school with the Christian Brothers teaching order, ten minutes walk from his door. He moved between the discipline of home and the discipline of school. He was a quiet, uncertain child.

Carmody stood on the quayside now, watching the empty carts arriving, the loaded ones pulling out. The wind swept from behind him to carry away the interminable cloud of loading dust. This shipload was the property of Bennett Importers & Company Ltd, and Carmody had contracted to deliver its contents as instructed. Bennetts were Protestant, of course.

He had never met Arnold Bennett, but knew him by sight, although he was hardly visible behind an army of managers and clerks. He was a business person in the city hierarchy, living quietly but very well. Carmody knew he had a wife and daughter, living apart from him in London, and a son Harry who had been a bad lot even in his school days. Now, he had vanished; he was somewhere in a special hospital, it was whispered about.

The Bennetts had been a long time in the city – bleeding it, Carmody would say – and had a strong grip on their property.

There was a doctor who made small gestures to the poor and was held by them in high esteem. And there was a sister who with her sweetness of charity, and bread and soup, had been venturing to proselytise.

She had married a Catholic.

Carmody held his jaws tight, his eyes always watching the skips rising up from the holds, the bag-filling, the carts and their drivers. He didn't wear a top coat or hat, but he wore a suit, a coloured shirt and a white scarf at his neck. The scarf was some strange protection of his chest and lungs from coal dust. His shoes were reasonably polished and he wore a tweed cap. He was the stevedore: he must look different.

The days of the Bennett soup kitchen were over. Carmody's face tightened, his lips spreading. And the Bennett woman had married the apostate Catholic, Burke, who still attended mass, paid all his dues to Rome, but lived like a Protestant. And was schoolmaster to Protestant children. The Latimer School!

There was a lot of clearance to be done yet.

Carmody saw a cart and driver arriving, watched it for a moment, and then leafed through his check-sheets. This was a new driver, he knew, for a coal yard not far distant, a big, hard young fellow, blackened with coal dust. Twenty-five, thirteen and a half stone, Carmody assessed him; he was smart, had a lot of lip.

"Hey!" Carmody shouted his name.

He was sucking the unlit butt of a cigarette, keeping the flavour of tobacco in his mouth. With his cap pushed back, a paler rim of dust about his eyes could be seen. He turned in the direction of Carmody's shout.

"Yeah, you!" Carmody shouted. "Come here."

He was a fair distance away; he stood and measured Carmody for a few moments, and then walked slowly towards him.

He said to Carmody, "Are you having trouble with something?"

"With you," Carmody said.

"That's a shame."

Carmody turned the consignment sheet towards him. "You can read as well as talk?"

"I can read."

"Twenty loads ordered. You collected twenty loads."

"Nineteen."

"Twenty. Move off, don't come back. Fast. If you dropped off a load somewhere, you can pick it up again. Or if you're looking for an extra load, it isn't here. Move!"

"You're calling me a liar, you bastard!"

Coping with trickery was part of Carmody's job, and he was good at it; he knew the ropes. But foul language pierced his soul. Silence settled along the crowded quay, the bag-filling ceased, a loaded skip swung above the hopper, and a donkey engine on the boat was silent.

Carmody was carelessly arranging his feet and shoulders, balancing his weight, storing power.

"You said something?"

"You got your sums wrong. You owe me a load, bastard."

Carmody's weight was on his left foot and his hands were hanging free. He always waited for the attack.

It came.

This young hero of a Free State, untamed, came in, hands flailing, shouting filth at Carmody. Carmody was motionless; then suddenly releasing his power, he struck. A short jab, the weight of his shoulder behind it, his fist tightening at the moment of contact. The attacker was frozen, as if stricken by sudden illness, then his knees and joints loosened and he fell almost soundlessly on the granite setts. Not even taking his count, he pushed himself up to battle again.

Carmody's flinty stare swept along the watchers; he held out two pointing fingers and spread his hands apart to draw a line. This was Carmody's business, he was saying: keep out.

The contender was on his feet again. Carmody had caught him on the point of the jaw, and he was unmarked but unfocused. Carmody moved in to punish him: he hammered on his ribs and, as he felt him folding, with a single blow he left him gasping, struggling for air. He hoisted him on to his cart, tied the reins to his wrist, and prodded the horse on the quarters. The cart and strange cargo plodded away along the quayside.

It had been a two minute break. The donkey engine lowered the skip; the hopper was working again, the bag men shouldered their loads, trotted on their journeys. The rain began to fall, a slow drizzle: it caught and grounded the flying dust, formed a black scum along the paved granite. A crewman came down the gangway with a long oilskin and sou'wester for Carmody. There was another two hours' work, and men would suffer wind and wet and slime. It was eating away their days and years, but work was survival. Some of them made pointed cowls of the heavy coal sacks and moved about like comic monks behind a wall of rain.

The work day dwindled away, the last loads were filled, driven off into the obscurity of mist. The donkey engine was silenced. Carmody climbed up the gangway on to the metal plates of the boat. He washed and tidied in the captain's washroom, took his tweed cap and gabardine raincoat from a hook.

From the gangway he watched the captain behind the glass of the bridge, saw his hand raised.

Carmody nodded, didn't look back again, went on his way. The whole world was wrapped in silky mist.

The captain called him "Pat".

"The name," Carmody whispered aloud as he walked up the steep hill from the river, "is Joseph Carmody."

Guttersnipe English seamen and their captains and mates stuck "Pat" like a cattle tag on a whole race. Their filthy breed of soldiery was gone now, their native police disbanded, gone into hiding some of them, but the carriages and motor-cars of their lords and masters were still on the streets, and their great provision stores shone with fresh paint. Their houses, in town or sitting on vast acres of estate, were still there. Yes, there was a lot of clearance still to be done.

He walked unhurriedly in the mist to a fine imposing church, entered it to pray for a while in its twilight. God was in his tabernacle behind curtained gilded doors, and the light of his perpetual presence flickered from an ornate suspended dish. Carmody looked with reverence at the enclosed bowl of colza oil and the floating wick. He bowed his head and asked God to forgive him his human iniquities.

Scattered about in the half light were more than a dozen supplicants, lost in the hushed crepuscular sanctity of this spacious place. Light from a grey, darkening sky came only from the clerestory surround, high up, close to the great wooden beams and trusses. The far-spaced lower windows were stained and leaded, the names of their donors engraved on brass plaques beneath them, a little sweetener for the keeper of celestial ledgers.

Carmody whispered his Ave Marias to himself ten times, a decade of the rosary, repeated, pondered like a Sanskrit mantra. He stood and genuflected in humility to God in the tabernacle. In the church porch he dipped his fingers in the stoup of holy water and made the sign of the cross. He looked out at the churchyard, the cut-stone walls, the ornate iron railings, the gateways, the good streets and quality Catholic housing that had grown around it. He would have a house here one day.

He glanced up at the heavens, laden, incontinent.

He walked across the churchyard to the presbytery, the residence of the anointed, the ordained, as well as lesser orders who praised God through menial work, servility. It was a stone building, three storeys high with tall chimney stacks, cusped windows and a studded door.

He rang.

A lay brother opened the door and stood before him; a faint smile, patient.

Lay brothers gave their lives to serving others, carrying out day-to-day work that must be part of all places of residence. The priests were devoted to serving God and their parishioners; lay brothers found solace in toiling with their hands.

Carmody said, "Good evening, Brother."

"Good evening, Mr Carmody." He held the door open for Carmody to step inside. "You'd like to see Dr Cafferey?"

"Yes." Carmody took off his cap.

The residences of anointed clergy, of whatever rank, have a beautiful stillness of death about them; like a corpse cleansed and groomed, they have a waxed gloss painted on the outer skin. Carmody admired the polished woodblock floor, the wainscotting, the walls distempered with the faintest green, pictures of venerable men in ceremonial robes. Not a sound. Men in holy orders, like spectres, must drift soundlessly from place to place, passing through walls and doors. He was escorted to a reception room that had a polished table and stolid upholstered chairs. Only a single item broke the bareness of virgin blue walls: a black crucifix with a suspired Christ hanging from his hooks, with bloodied ring of thorns pressed into his scalp, the red wound of the centurion's lance in his side. A beautiful white figure sacrificed for mankind. The curtainless windows were of opaque glass; there was no fireplace. The chill was penitential. Carmody stood and waited.

Behind him a door opened and a voice seemed thunderous, exploding in this lifeless place.

"Good evening, Joseph."

Dr Paul Cafferey – a doctor of divinity – was a young man in his middle thirties, of medium height but tending towards fleshiness; his hair was receding and his face a pink smiling orb.

"Sit down. Sit down, Joseph." He went through the act of blessing: a tiny weave of hand and fingers before his breast. "Thank you for coming, Joseph."

Before he sat, Joseph bowed his head at this act of benediction; he made the sign of the cross.

Dr Cafferey nodded, spoke quickly. "The soup kitchen is no more, Joseph. I've had a full account from a dozen sources. Thank you for delaying your visit to me until the dust had settled. Or should I say, until the smoke had cleared!" He sat and joined his hands. "An unfortunate accident, they say. I have prayed for that woman who was struck down in her act of sinfulness. But we know that our God is an all-merciful God. May she rest in peace."

"Yes, Doctor."

"Sergeant Cosgrave at the Garda station is a reliable man. He'll go far. Very valuable." Dr Cafferey paused and gazed at Carmody. "He ensured that there was no Garda activity that might have obstructed proceedings that evening. He was quite impressed at the speed of your moving in and moving out. Military precision, he called it. Excellent."

"Thank you, Doctor."

Information came from the sergeant's telephone to Dr Cafferey; Dr Cafferey had a messenger to rouse Carmody and his men. It was a simple arrangement and distanced the man of prayer and the man of law enforcement from whispers of complicity. And Carmody? Carmody had a healthy fear of God.

"I called you out twice that evening," Dr Cafferey said, "and you didn't renege, Joseph. The destruction of the soup kitchen has removed a running sore from our society, but dealing with Mr Burke was vital, too."

Carmody felt a trace of pride at his importance in the scheme of things. "We followed instructions, Doctor. We laid Burke up for days. He was absent from his school. Not a mark showing on the street, but he was black and blue underneath."

"Yes, I received the information. A fine job." Cafferey smiled the faintest of smiles. After a long silence, he said, "Did you know why we punished Mr Burke?"

"He's an apostate, married to a woman in sin, who teaches children of a renegade religion."

"Well spoken, Joseph. You're skilled in words. There was another reason."

Dr Cafferey stood and paced about for a long time, his plump lips pursed in thought. He let the silence and waiting prepare Carmody.

He said suddenly, "A half an hour before you and your comrades waylaid and punished Burke, he had called at the Garda station to report the soup kitchen incident."

"To the sergeant?"

"To the district inspector. He refused to talk to Sergeant Cosgrave. Mr Burke feels that he has social rank, you see. He was advised to drop the matter." The doctor paused. "There was no possibility of recognition?"

Carmody shook his head. "I was wearing glasses, just peering over the rims of them. A cap, a scarf. It was dark, midway between gaslights. A big crowd. No one recognises Joseph Carmody. I can deal with people."

"Good, Joseph."

"Did he think the district inspector could help him?"

"He thought that the death of this Protestant woman added weight to the removal of the soup kitchen. Manslaughter, even murder perhaps, was attributable. That's what took him to the district inspector's office. He must learn times have changed."

"The sergeant heard him?"

"Overheard him. He hears every word that's spoken in the inspector's office. Cosgrave is a clever young man, ambitious and hard. He is a man of the future."

"What about the district inspector?"

"Dangerous, Joseph. Irish, of course, but tainted. He served in Palestine in the armed police. He was commissioned there, which gave him importance. He would have been tolerated at early evening drinks gatherings. I know about colonial life, Joseph. My uncle was principal of a very select school in northern India. He retired with a good pension and a disdain for Irish country people. Peasants, he called them. Tainted, you see?

"But I'm rambling. The inspector thought it would be wiser for Edward Burke to forget the whole incident. Kindly advice, friend to friend. We are living in bad times, you can't trust your neighbour. That kind of thing."

"He's not afraid, is he?"

"The district inspector? Only of backing the wrong horse."

Carmody paused and asked, "Was my name mentioned at the Garda station?"

"The sergeant assured me that no names were mentioned."

There was a soft rapping on the door and a lay brother entered carrying a tray. A single cup of tea, sugar and milk, and a thick slice of dark fruit cake were placed before Carmody.

"You carry on. I like to pace about when I am thinking. Body in motion, mind in motion."

Carmody had been in this room a dozen times in two years; he always felt that the sanctity of the church gave it a special importance and that he was privileged to sit here as a guest. But to be offered refreshment! He was overcome, filled with humility. The food, the drink had no taste in the dryness of his mouth as, almost in dread of offence, he picked and sipped at it with hands that were clean but had an ingrained shadow of two decades of coal dirt.

"Now," said Dr Cafferey, "I have given it some thought. It isn't possible that Burke recognised you during the street altercation, is it?"

"No, hardly likely, Doctor. It was black as pitch and a quick job. Half a minute, hardly more."

"But you gave him a little warning?"

"Yes."

"He might remember a voice, that's all. Nothing to worry about there." The priest sat facing Carmody. "I like to go back, to experience the episode again, step by step. It's perfect. I'm very happy about it, Joseph."

Carmody nodded, as assured now as if he were on his dockside pitch, a man in charge, papers in hand, hiring and firing. Dr Cafferey was the ringmaster. The sergeant reported to him. The district inspector was a man of rank and little authority.

"There's no danger, Joseph, but there is an aspect of this affair which we must examine. The pollution of Catholic blood. You understand? This Bennett woman is in congress with Edward Burke. She is carrying about his Catholic seed in her body. We know that God will punish them for ever, but they must be seen to be punished here, in this city. Would you think so, Joseph?"

"Yes, yes!"

"The Burke family is old and Catholic and has been wealthy for a long time in our history, but they are a dying breed. A father and two sons already buried. One son in a foreign uniform of a foreign king. The other, a reject, diseased from women and alcohol and laudanum. But they had more honour than their sibling, Edward, who goes to lie down each night with this filthy Bennett woman. Roderick Burke, the parent, was a spiritless man, cowed, lucky to have died and avoided shame. He is buried beneath a great family monument in our cemetery."

Dr Cafferey resumed his pacing, hardly aware of Carmody.

Carmody waited, as still as the figure on the crucifix.

"Yes," Dr Cafferey said, swinging about with a forensic histrionic sweep. "There is the relict, the widow, Catherine Burke. A woman of strange habits. She had two sons, and then twelve barren years before the birth of Edward. And, it is said, she didn't share a bed with her husband for many many years. Strange, isn't it?"

Carmody was silent.

"But she is a Catholic, Joseph, and we musn't make judgments. A sudden reconciliation perhaps, a bed shared for a single night. There is an old wasted priest at one of our city churches who visits her. I must ask him to come and see me. He would keep me informed."

Carmody said, "She is very wealthy, Doctor," and was immediately sorry.

"The Church is concerned only with her salvation, Joseph."

"Yes, yes, of course."

"This old doddering priest brings her the sacred Host for holy communion once a month. She doesn't attend church services. Something about a lot of people in a confined space. She is an eccentric person."

"I see her walking miles along the river bank every day."

"Yes, solitary in a great wilderness. She has lost her husband and all her sons, we must remember that. All of her sons. This last one, too. He has deserted her, crossed over into the awful state of heresy. Heresy, Joseph."

"Yes, Doctor."

"We must show our displeasure to him and the blood he has chosen to mingle with. Could you suggest something? A group of three or four people, perhaps. Not a physical attack on this occasion, Joseph."

"I see."

The doctor helped him. "They live in the city, don't they?"

"The Bennetts? Yes."

"And Burke and his wife?"

After a few moments silence he said very softly. "They have houses in the city."

"We could deal with Burke and his wife first."

"Windows," Carmody said. "Three men, two paving stones apiece. It can be over and done with in ten seconds."

Dr Cafferey showed his satisfaction. "A good idea," he said. "Windows. Yes, that would be fine."

"Soon?" Carmody asked.

"Sunday is a good day," the Doctor said. "A holy day. A day to take up arms for God." Carmody tightened his gabardine about him and pulled down his cap against the drizzle, but he felt impervious to wet or wind, insulated by his achievements that had drawn admiration from Dr Cafferey.

He walked down George's Street, past the Town Hall, and

crossed the Abbey River at the Customs House on his way to the club. There were plans to be laid.

It was late, past midnight, when he journeyed back through Irishtown to his dwelling.

On the instant the key touched the lock, his wife pulled open the door. He could see her anxiety.

"You've sat up late," he said.

"I'm worried."

"For Michael? He has a chest cold, that's all."

"Seven days in his bed . . . ."

"It takes nine days for things to pass."

"His breathing is hard."

"He has a chest cold. I'll look in on him in the morning."

About half past ten in the morning, in the turmoil of dock-side unloading, Carmody's wife sent a horse cab for him. He was burning with anger and resentment when she met him on the doorstep.

"Diphtheria," she said.

"Diphtheria?"

"Michael. They've taken him to the City Home."

"Where?"

"The City Home."

"The City Home is for paupers!"

"There's an isolation ward. He's at death's door. The district nurse arranged it."

"My son in the City Home!" He made the sign of the cross. "My dear Jesus, Mary and Joseph . . . ."

He was gone. In the stabling area of his coal yard he tackled up his pony and trap and drove in the busy morning traffic across the river to the workhouse.

CHAPTER EIGHT

THADDEUS BENNETT HAD thrown off his surgeon's gown and footwear and was scrubbing in the washroom adjoining the theatre. Some of the wearying heat of radiators and the accumulation of hospital-generated wattage suspended above the surgical table lodged out here to spend itself. He sponged and dried his body and, cooler, began to dress.

Illnesses came in waves, he thought; they lay, almost dormant, for periods and then were suddenly in vogue. This was the decade of appendicitis. It struck from royalty to road sweeper. He had just removed two of these little tubes of human detritus and poison. The leakage and inflammation from one would require care for days.

From the door of the theatre he nodded his thanks to the nursing staff clearing the mess. It was a well-equipped theatre, with its swivel and tilting table, the high wattage lamp above it, three-tiered frames holding enamel basins, and enamel pails for refuse. There was a trolley with an upright cylinder, a mixture of alcohol, chloroform and ether, fed by a tube to the anaesthetist's location, where he had a tiny panel of two gauges to measure pulse and dosage. At times he used pure ether dropped on cotton wool and held at the nostrils.

The floor and walls of the theatre, and sometimes perhaps the ceiling, could be wiped down with disinfectant, but invisible strings of streptococci would always be waiting to invade. A trolley of glittering instruments was pushed away for sterilisation.

Taddy climbed to the next floor, to the matron's office.

"Two calls for you, Taddy," she said. "Brigid telephoned them through. You have a good housekeeper there."

"Yes. I'm lucky to have her."

"How is Matilda?"

"There isn't any change."

She handed him a sheet from her notepad; he read it.

"Diphtheria from the sound of it."

"Yes, sixteen cases reported in less than a week. Compare one or two for September-October. It's peaking now. It could be a bad year. Isolation units in the city are full, so it's home treatment until there are discharges or deaths."

"The City Home?" he read aloud.

"One of your cases is there. A district nurse rang your housekeeper, didn't leave a name. Everyone is so rushed."

"Yes."

"Be careful. When you finish your calls each day come and sit for half an hour in our little scouring unit. It's only formaldehyde but it helps. Leave a change of clothes here."

Taddy moved down the stairway quickly and along the corridor to the porched doorways looking out across the river. Traffic and people moved about, seemingly unaware of illness, smoking, saluting, laughing in the same infected world. He drove through them, turned to cross the Wellesley Bridge and pushed on past the secluded residences of the wealthy, hidden behind a screen of tall trees in large grounds. Newer houses of brick, for merchants and professionals, were visible from the road but set well back. He reached the Union Cross and halted at the City Home gates.

The City Home was a gloomy complex of stone. A hospice for the dying, he thought, rows of beds and withered faces on pillows. The days broken by intervals for cleansing of bodies, defecation and changeless, tasteless meals. And loneliness at the end.

It was an institutional place of rest and care, where the staff did their best. It had been a workhouse in famine days, and frugality seemed to have lodged there. Although Miss Henrietta Holmes was the archetypal matron – strong, square, squat, formidable – she was also a gentle person, with good features and expression.

She met him in the entrance lobby, smiling. "Dr Bennett. Thank you for coming. It's a neglected case. Come this way," she guided him. "We'll avoid relatives in the waiting-room and corridors." They moved along.

It was just midday. The church bell at St Munchin's, sounding out over the white tumbling flow of water that ended the navigable estuary of the river, came faintly to them from the distance.

In an annexe to the ward Taddy donned a long white robe and rubber gloves. He took a flask from his pocket and drank a little whiskey. "Tired," he said. "A long day yesterday. Morning surgery and a lot of house calls. There's influenza about, too. Sore throats and diphtheria on everyone's mind. But it keeps them alert, I suppose."

The matron asked, "How is your wife, Dr Bennett?"

"Not very well at the moment."

"I'm sorry to call you out."

"No, you must call me. I'll come if possible. This is a bad case, you say?"

"Yes, downhill. Very late coming in."

Taddy followed the matron into the ward; the bed of his patient was nearest to the door and had a portable screen about it. He read the chart: "Michael Carmody. Age 14 years". His temperature was dropping. A good-looking boy, he was ashen grey in colour now; his glands were enlarged. Taddy took his temperature again. Still dropping. His pulse was rapid, and he was battling for breath.

Taddy gently opened his mouth, held his tongue with a finger of his gloved hand. Diphtheria formed its suffocating membrane at the back of the throat. Taddy looked at the yellowish-white skin virtually covering the vocal chords. He needed air; he was dying.

Taddy said, "It's bad. Is there a relative?"

"His father is in the waiting-room. Not a very easy person to converse with."

"I'll talk to him."

"Here?"

"Somewhere quiet."

"There isn't anywhere, Dr Bennett. Every corner is crammed with patients, geriatrics, terminals of all kinds – a whole general ward of isolations. We've closed the gates on visitors, relatives."

Taddy paused. "The mortuary? There are bodies there?"

"Of course."

"Are they covered?"

"I'll see that they are."

"Bring him there. I'll come." As she turned away he said, "Matron?"

"Yes."

"Have a surgical trolley and a tube ready."

Taddy went out to the deserted private corridor, where there was a door to paths and flower beds. He took another drink from his flask, smoked a cigarette, and then walked across the open space to the single-storey row of buildings at the rear. A quiet place, deserted. Inside, he counted three bodies beneath their sheets. He heard footsteps approaching.

The matron arrived and ushered in Joseph Carmody. Taddy saw a strong body and face, a barely controlled aggression and angry eyes viewing him from head to toe. Taddy knew that a hand held out in commiseration would be ignored.

He said, "Mr Carmody?"

"Yes, I'm Mr Carmody." As he gazed about the cloaked trolleys of death, realisation was slowly coming to him. He stared at Taddy, the matron. Belligerence, anger, fear.

"Mr Carmody . . .," Taddy began.

Carmody said, "This is the deadhouse, isn't it?"

Matron said, "This is the mortuary. These are dead people beneath these sheets. We treat the dead and the living with respect, Mr Carmody."

"My son is alive!"

Taddy said, "We needed a quiet place. We have to talk about your son's treatment. He is seriously ill, and we are wasting time."

"So we talk in a deadhouse?"

The matron paused and broke the rhythm of his anger. "Privacy, Mr Carmody," she said. "This is a crowded hospital."

"A crowded workhouse!"

"A crowded hospital where this is the only place to discuss your son's illness."

"I can pay for a bed for my son at Barrington's."

"They would have to refuse. It isn't an isolation hospital."

"It is a hospital."

"Where patients need care, not infection."

Taddy held up his hands for silence. "Mr Carmody," he said very quietly, "I need you to sign a form giving your permission to carry out surgery on your son's throat."

Carmody was thunderstruck.

Taddy said, "Otherwise he will be dead in three, four hours."

"The boy has a sore throat for a few days . . . ."

"A boy who has diphtheria, Mr Carmody. A few days is the difference between life and death. At first signs we might have been in a better position to help."

"You *might* have helped, Doctor?"

The matron shot her anger at him. "Time!" she said. "The choice was yours. With surgery, your son has a chance, only a chance, of living. Without it he is dead. He will be here beneath a sheet, Mr Carmody." She spread out a printed form on a table behind her and held up a fountain pen. "Sign it or leave it! All of us here are rushed off our feet."

Carmody read the form of consent. "It means you can pass your incompetence on to me, doesn't it?"

The matron chastised him. "This is Dr Bennett, a most competent surgeon. He is a voluntary worker in this epidemic. You should offer your thanks."

Carmody signed the paper and studied Taddy. He said to the matron, "Dr Bennett. He's not a Catholic, is he?"

"He is a doctor."

Taddy said, "There's no guarantee that your son will live; you understand that, don't you? Diphtheria causes a membrane, a skin that is, to grow across the breathing passage. Your son is choking and poison is already moving about his body. He arrived here too late. Who first diagnosed his illness and sent him here?"

Matron said, "Mr Carmody's wife called in a district nurse. She sent the boy here."

"When?"

"Two hours ago."

Taddy paused. "The operation entails making an incision in the windpipe, cutting an opening and inserting a breathing tube to keep him alive while we treat him. He has less than a one in five chance. I must get to work now, Mr Carmody."

"I hope you have a steady hand, Dr Bennett. You smell of whiskey."

Taddy moved away, back along the corridor to the ward annexe. Sterilisation was a lost battle in these confines, but he changed his rubber gloves that had been polluted not only by air but by nicotine and his whiskey flask. Carmody had seemed less perturbed by his son's illness than his removal to the City Home, the workhouse, and the stain that non-Catholic hands might leave on him. He was upset, of course, but he was offensive.

The matron said, "I'm sorry, Dr Bennett. He's a bullying fool. I'll find some place for him. There will hardly be good news. This is a daily chore for me."

"He's distressed," Taddy said.

She pushed a covered surgical trolley into the ward and drew the screen about the patient's bed. The grey face and mouth made the noise of a failing pump. She pulled a sheet of oilskin beneath him from head to shoulders, loosened the clothing and exposed his throat.

She said, "He's too weak for anaesthetic."

Taddy put his finger on the throat. "Rest a pad of ether there for a minute or two. Numbness will have to suffice. Thank you for handling Mr Carmody. Illness of nearest and dearest takes people in different ways, from anger to tears. Religion complicates it."

"He is a very zealous defender of the faith, I'm sure," the matron said.

"A confident man."

"Too confident. A bullyboy." She laid bare the trolley of instruments and dishes, towels.

Taddy took a scalpel; the matron stood opposite him holding a dish of swabs. Taddy felt about with his fingers for the projection of cartilage and took his bearing from it. He pinched the flesh and skin, pierced it with the scalpel and made a clean inch and a half wound, then cut gently again to expose the trachea. The matron, with swabs in each hand, soaked at blood, back and forth. Taddy cut through the rings of trachea cartilage and forced open the incision. The chest heaved with the intake of air. Taddy slid in the tube and let the incision close on it.

The matron said, "I'll deal with the bleeding and closing."

Taddy nodded. With a still rapid pulse and falling temperature, Taddy knew he had only the remotest chance.

"Do what you can, Matron," he said.

When he entered the annexe again a nurse was waiting to take his gown and gloves. He scrubbed his hands and rubbed them with formaldehyde compound. The nurse, a pretty girl who reminded him of Abigail, sprayed his clothing and handed him a rinse for his mouth and throat. Taddy smiled his thanks.

He went out into the open air, put a cigarette in his holder and felt the comfort of nicotine. The gates were held open for him and he drove into the city again, turning into George's Street. The pavements were peopled, shops and licensed premises open. Another day. He thought of the white stillness of the mortuary at the Union Cross.

His two sons had been at boarding school in Dublin and had taken the expected arts degrees at Trinity. Then he had put them into trade to learn buying and selling, shipping and transport. They would have comfortable lives. Medicine was a hard, dedicated grind. Abigail, of course, was determined. This would be her battleground against the poverty of the city.

He drove beyond the railway station, parked and walked down a laneway, ten feet wide, smelling of rot and ordure. He looked at the address Maggie Norris had given him at Barrington's and stepped carefully along the littered cobbles. Doors everywhere were shut. News of disease spread quickly and people shut their doors against it; or perhaps locked it in.

He knocked and saw half a pale face peering through a crack in the small curtained window. Why had they built these single-storey hovels without purpose except to hide away poverty? Agents called for rents to satisfy their own margins and pass, without detail, a residue to landlords across the water who had never set foot on Irish ground, or in this city climbing up out of its darkness. The final rebellion had come and had been punished. They had risen again, but the shackles had only been loosened in this Free State.

Freedom had a long road to travel yet.

The door was opened into the twilight that was the daylight of these dwellings. Awful poverty came as no shock; he had been face to face with it through almost two and a half decades.

A child had opened the door and a woman, poorly dressed with a black heavy shawl on her shoulders, now peered from behind it.

Taddy said, "I'm Dr Bennett."

She nodded, or bowed, and held open the door. There was no fire, but children sat close to the empty hearth. The father stood there in shirt, braces and trousers. He had laced working boots, tied with leather thongs. He took off his cap and offered his thanks.

Taddy followed his wife into the small adjoining room. Other than four makeshift beds, hammered together from oddments of dry perished timber and boxwood, the room was bare. A girl of perhaps eight years looked up at him, wondering at the richness of shirt and suiting, the cuff-links, the tie-pin. He smiled and put his hand on her forehead.

The mother said, "I was afraid it might be diphtheria. It's raging, isn't it? A bit feverish and chilly and pains in her back and legs. The throat is sore, too, and swollen."

"Since when?"

"Yesterday. I hope I didn't bring you on a wild goose chase."

Taddy said, "I wish everyone had your wisdom." He said to the small girl. "Open your mouth. That's good. I only want to look inside." He took a flashlight from his pocket and shone it on her throat; the yellow-white membrane had only begun to form on the tonsils.

"Yes," he said, "it's diphtheria, but we've caught it early. There are no beds in isolation hospitals. You must treat her at home. I'll call and bring you a paraffin heater. Can you open the windows a little?"

"My husband will do it."

"And he must take all these beds out. This is the patient's room, and you are the only person who comes and goes here.

Her delph and everything she uses must be kept apart. We can probably kill the illness at this stage, and there will be some treatment for you and your family." Taddy smiled. "You've done a good job. I'll be back within an hour. I have some things to collect and I'll bring instructions."

She held out her hand, holding a half crown. "Whatever it is, I'll pay it. The rest as it comes, I promise you."

Taddy put a pound note in her hand. "There isn't any payment. Use this for heating and food. Milk, soups, I'll make a list for you."

She saw him to the door, her cheeks wet. Oh God, he thought. He stepped between rubbish and waste. The low narrow houses enclosed him like a canyon, doors closed but eyes following him through the windows. He reached the main street and its traffic. Horse cabs and motors collected arrivals from the station. A newsboy ran past with his armful of broadsheets to meet them. Two warm, well-shod policemen walked past in the slow pace they had learned in training.

Taddy got inside his car and sprayed it with disinfectant. Diphtheria was carried from one person to another, so infectious that germs lived in discarded clothing for months. Many normal persons carried it for varying periods in their systems and transmitted it. The first president of America was reputed to have died of it. It was as old as Babylon. It was on record that a doctor had died within twenty-four hours of a child coughing into his face. An old wives' tale? Who could tell?

Taddy grimaced at the puny efforts of mankind against disease. There was something out there to kill each one of us. He drove back down through the near elegance of George's Street and crossed the river again. The City Home would have antitoxin.

The matron met him in the hallway and guided him to her office where she pointed to a chair.

"I have a case," Taddy said, "perhaps a family, I can save. I shouldn't waste time. You can give me antitoxin?"

The matron said, "Michael Carmody is dead."

Taddy stood in silence for moments. "Tracheotomy was a despairing effort. He died without a murmur, I would think."

"Yes, heart failure."

The membrane manufactures poison, the bloodstream delivers it.

Thaddeus remembered the smart, snappy phrases, the mnemonics of college lecture rooms. He remembered the grey ashen face, thought of the great effort of breathing.

"When did he die?"

"An hour ago. He's prepared now, in the mortuary."

"And his father?"

"He's waiting out there. He has to be informed."

Thaddeus said, "I'll be in the mortuary. Bring him there."

The matron paused. "I didn't expect you," she said. "I do this kind of thing every day. You have patients waiting. You should go."

Taddy nodded his appreciation. "Bring him," he said.

Taddy walked the journey to the mortuary. He found the stretcher trolley and folded back the sheet. The young boy's face, released from death agony, had a peacefulness. He was a handsome boy with fair hair brushed across his forehead. In death his ashen colour had paled.

Quick hurried footsteps sounded. The matron was trying to restrain Carmody, who was babbling with anger, pale, almost frantic. He ran to the stretcher and made an awful hopeless moan of despair. He never touched the body, as if he might be afraid of it. He swung a blow that glanced along Taddy's forehead and stumbled back, ready to charge again.

The matron gripped him, struggled, waited until he had sobered.

He pointed at Taddy and said, quietly now, "You'll pay for it."

Matron said, "I can have the Gardaí here to remove you. You have enough trouble and grief, Mr Carmody. Come again, bring your wife to see her son. He arrived here a week too late."

He told her, "My son is a Catholic, christened, confirmed. You allowed dirty, drunken, hands to touch him. Guards!" he said. "Gardaí! Bring them. I'll have a story to tell."

The matron said, "It's time you were going now, Mr Carmody. I want you to wait outside. I have other patients and illnesses to cope with. Your son was neglected, dying when he arrived here. Surgery to give him air was a last chance, but diphtheria can make a lot of poison in a week."

Carmody stood and looked at the calm still face of his son. The matron took his arm and he shook her off; she gripped him again, surprising him with her strength, and pushed him out into the gardens.

In her office she completed the death certificate: diphtheria, toxaemia, cardiac failure. Taddy, looking through the window, saw Carmody crouched on a garden seat. A threatening man.

So much to be done, he thought suddenly: a return trip to the laneway with antitoxin, disinfectants and instructions. A good, intelligent woman there. Then to Barrington's to cleanse himself.

As he took the matron's fountain pen and signed the certificate, he said, "Thank you for your help, Matron. It's unfair to judge people at a time of bereavement. It's a time of confusion."

"I don't have your patience," she said. "I dislike the man. I dislike religious flag-waving. I enquired about him. This is a city of religious confraternities. He is in a large one, a head-prefect of sections: a little position of power. A stevedore on the docks. Another little position of power. In these days he could be a dangerous enemy. There's distrust and plotting everywhere. In trouble-times he was a ruthless man, they say, burning, pillaging, leaving shells of fine manors along the river banks."

Taddy nodded; he said, "Yes, I understand, but it's over now."

The matron studied him. "This man is a Jacobin," she said. "Six years ago they fought an open, bloody, civil war.

Murders were committed in this very hospital. Now it's a secret war. No, it isn't over, Dr Bennett. Be careful. Republicanism is out there everywhere."

"Yes, thank you," Taddy said.

"In epidemics like this when patients are foisted on you, show them your Protestant hands. Let *them* make the choice."

Taddy nodded. "I understand," he said, "and thank you, Matron."

He used her telephone to instruct Brigid to send a change of clothes to Barrington's.

CHAPTER NINE

EDWARD BURKE HAD finished his day's work at the Latimer School and walked along the quays towards the Wellesley Bridge. The tide was full. Seagulls in little groups swooped and perched, gliding with the wind or banking suddenly against its flow. Seagulls sixty miles inland from the coast? Wiseacres would look at the sky and the water, working on some abstruse problem, and finally reach a conclusion. 'A bad sign, storm weather on the move.' Storm weather was high wind and rain and the rattle of windows; perhaps a flood tide that crept over the quaysides and paused midway along the adjoining streets.

Edward hadn't walked these quays for many days. There was this plague of diphtheria and threats of school closure. With Taddy's help he had arranged heat and ventilation, the spraying of classrooms and walls, and they were still free of the single case that would shut them down. Taddy was worn but indefatigable. Virulence waxed and waned. It might pass. It might return. It might stay with them until April banished it.

Coal boats were unloading, horses and iron-shod wheels making a thunderous noise, the whine of the crane and the donkey engine screeching a treble. Scavengers followed loaded carts, hoping for falling slivers and slack.

Edward watched the crowding gangs for the figure of Carmody. He should be an easy man to recognise. He wasn't there.

Edward felt what was almost a sense of relief.

He said to a waiting car-man, "Where's Carmody?"

The man looked at Edward's respectable dress. "A funeral. He lost his son. Diphtheria."

"Bad luck," Edward said.

"Not bad enough." The car-man spat and walked away into the dust and clouds of grit.

Edward returned to the pathway by the wall and walked its paved surface. He let his resolve weaken, ebb. He would have liked to confront Carmody, tell him in simple words that he was a shallow hero, marching with his militia to smash and destroy; coming out of the darkness with rags and blackened faces to kick and preach the gospel. And Lucy Langford was dead.

He walked along the pavement, turning Carmody's absence over in his mind. Death was a hard blow to everyone; death pierced the skin. He felt a trace of sorrow for him. The Garda inspector had given good advice, he knew: steer clear, let sleeping dogs lie.

But deep anger was hard to banish.

He walked on. Schoolchildren were crowded around a drinking fount with water gushing from the lion's head, swapping the chained cast-iron cup from one to another. He saw them run ahead like greyhounds, bare-footed, shrieking, laughing. There was a public lavatory at a corner, an open-ended, white-washed rectangle. They ran through it, whooping like Indians. Then, in a crocodile line, they vanished into the alleyways.

Edward stopped at the lavatory. Skins of limewash had

formed into a kind of brittle armour. The awful smell, even in the tidal breeze, crept about him. He walked into the Hades underworld light. Oh God, he thought. This was a midden of solid human faeces. Infection was thriving there every day, every year. He had passed it in ignorance so many times. A fifteen-inch pipe had been cut in half, lengthwise, and raised on two piers to form a trough. Its entire stretch was piled high with coiled and liquid excrement. Big and small flies settled on it. Who came to clean it, to scoop and shovel out the filth? Now it had been dusted, like a grand confection, with chloride of lime.

Edward hurried out, stood on the pavement and faced the wind, tried to cleanse himself. He felt illness in his throat.

He hurried away. On two little protruding lay-bys on the dockside there was patchy grass, spotted with litter, and always empty wooden seats. He climbed the steps up to the level of the Wellesley Bridge and the fine edifice of the rowing club. He seemed to have emerged from some awful underworld. The old Thomond Bridge and the castle browsed with dignity over the great spreading river. Soldiers of old battles and sieges had milled about these riverbanks. There had been hunger and blood, fear, lust, all the ancillaries of warfare. And raging plagues: Cromwell's men had found walking dead behind the breached walls. Only four score years had passed before the Williamites from the Boyne had set up their guns again. Edward watched the river flow out of sight where defeated troops had sailed away to join foreign armies. The world was a continuum of blood-letting.

He was en route to visit Arnie's son, Harry, in his secure nursing home, not more than a couple of miles beyond the Union Cross, between the river and the neglected roadway into Clare. Arnold, Taddy and Edward took turns to visit him at regular intervals.

The nursing home had been a manor house purchased by the Protestant businessmen of the city to care for their less fortunate members: the manageable insane, the witless, the addicts to alcohol and laudanum, those who had contracted illnesses of rot and decay. It was a fine building of more than thirty rooms, hidden in beeches and towering pines, reached by a long secluded avenue from the roadway. There were locked gates and a porter's lodge.

Edward could hear Thaddeus' thoughtful, unhurried monologue. "Whiskey is good medicine. Whiskey, with faces around the table, excites confession, brings a sense of relief and close friendship. I need it more these days. Matilda is fifty-four. I don't think she'll see another birthday. She was a sparkling girl, you know."

He could see Arnie laughing, silent, raising his glass to drink a little, saying he sometimes wondered what Harry might have amounted to. A clever enough boy, athletic, good looking, moving into years of rugby, rowing, hockey, cricket. He might have been good.

Edward remembered him growing up; you saw him once, you didn't forget him.

Arnie's rambling monologue had continued: "At sixteen he was so big, confident. Maybe that was the trouble. Young things of twenty-one were looking at him, too. I watched them at fêtes and garden parties. How could I tie him down, keep a rein on him? The young things at parties would draw the line at the rim of a stocking or a button or two loosened on a blouse, but Harry went for young kitchen maids and dockland brass-nails when they arrived fresh on the street. He was stealing money from Ethel. Young whores don't look after themselves. The old ones do. Harry got poisoned with syphilis. I didn't notice a change, but he was troublesome at school. I caught him one night in a little kitchen lassie's bedroom. I knew he wasn't a beginner. There was a bed, but he was having her naked on the floor. I took him out of school and brought him into the business, paid him well, but I knew he was dipping in the cash-box. He was missing for days at a time. He lived in brothels. I couldn't tell Ethel. He'll settle down, Arnie, she'd say, he's full of life, look at him."

The shattering blow had been delivered by his wife, Ethel. She was a person of private means, of course, and she had deserted him. The murder and bloodshed of the country's road to freedom had scarred her with fear; and Harry's disgrace had tipped the scales. She lived somewhere in Norfolk, near her family home. She had been gone three years. She was beautiful then as she had always been and he hadn't expected her hardness. She had told him she didn't want letters or visits. Arnold still loved her.

Taddy pouring drinks again, saying, "With syphilis it's always too late. Harry got into dangerous water, that's all."

Arnie nodding. "Ethel felt guilty, Dorcas felt guilty. Don't ask me why. They felt helpless. All of us were helpless."

Edward remembered those conversations, infrequent little evenings of friendship, sentiment, as he turned down the sloping roadway that was beginning its fall to the distant riverbank. Trees and wild shrubs were everywhere, growing spiky with the ageing year. It was an unmade rutted road with grass margins that were soakaways for rainwater. He reached the gate of the nursing home and used the loose ring that was a knocker. Here, isolated from traffic and people, it made a loud, clanging noise. The gatekeeper came from his lodge.

"Ah, Mr Burke," he said, opening the gate.

"Thank you," Edward said. "I came to see Mr Bennett."

The gatekeeper locked the gate and walked up the long avenue with Edward, escorting him to the entrance doors and ringing the bell. The door was opened and he returned to his post.

From this entrance lobby two corridors led right and left, and a fine broad staircase rose to the upper floor. There was an aura of peace and restraint. A smiling attendant, ununiformed except for the muted austerity of her gown, ushered him to the superintendent's office. There were no titles or descriptions of rank that might be associated with hospital life or the medical world. It was a kind of Victorian concept of disguise: in the same way as the realm of business and mechanisation had to be dissembled behind country-cottage railway stations or turreted redbrick façades hiding columbariums of pen and ink clerks, illness of the mind had to be hidden from the world of sanity.

"Good day, Mr Burke," the superintendent said. "Please sit down. How is your wife and the other members of the Bennett family?"

"Taking each day, ma'am," Edward said.

"Mr Harry's condition is distressing for his family, and for the staff here who know the long history of the Bennetts in the city, and their worth. Watching his deterioration is not pleasant."

Edward listened patiently. It had been the wish of Taddy and Arnie that he should be privy to the details of Harry's illness and its progress.

"We have had to put a heavy wire screen across his room. Sit well back from it. There must be no contact."

"Then he is very ill?"

"He is mad, Mr Burke."

Edward was silent.

"It's the progress of the illness. Madness, paralysis. But he is calm now. You can see him, but don't touch him. When you are ready to leave, there is an attendant sitting outside the door. Do give my respectful wishes to the Bennett family."

"Thank you, ma'am."

An elderly man dressed in dark serge escorted Edward across a broad courtyard to a separate dwelling that had once been a run of coach houses and stabling. It was silent now.

He talked without stop, glad of an ear to listen. "I've worked here all my life. I'm seventy-five, started work when I was twelve. His Lordship was here then. I started mucking out stables, wound up driving his coach and four. He went back to Berkshire when the shooting started. That's twelve years gone under the bridge. Then this nursing home bought it and he recommended me. It's a nice quiet job when years are creeping on. This place had been my home."

Edward said, "It saw some fine days."

"Oh, I've seen ten coaches resting here, and horses stabled, when they were banqueting in there. Big names that are gone. Or dead and gone."

These coach houses and stabling area had been converted into four units with separate doors and brightly coloured windows. It might have been part of an improving working-class street but for little circles of glass, Judas spy-holes, in place of knockers.

The attendant rang and said, "It's ringing, but you don't hear it from here. Lovely little houses, I always think. Of course, I remember it when there was a hayloft. Housing for six coaches, and stabling for eight horses. His Lordship used to ride out on horseback, just cantering across the fields, stopping and watching and listening. He never liked hunting. There used to be shooting parties, but he never joined in them either. He used to write poetry, they said, and send it to London. He was a good man but a bit strange."

There was a period of silence and the door was opened by a man hardly more than thirty. He was more like a soldier than a ward attendant, Edward thought, and although strong and agile, he was also mannerly and gracious. This was a tiny reception area, almost surgically clean and bare of any adornment.

"Good day to you," he said.

Edward nodded.

"We've had to move him to total isolation. The superintendent would have explained to you, I think."

"Yes."

A door opened on to a corridor. An attendant sitting outside the room of confinement allowed Edward to enter and then closed the door behind him. Harry and his bed were caged off behind two walls of half-inch mesh. The air was warm, comfortable. Harry, wearing loose-buttoned night clothes and woollen slippers, sat on the bedside and stared at Edward.

Edward sat on the only chair beside a small table where there was a hand-bell. Harry's face was disfigured with ulceration, a corrosion of decay, his lips and nose oozing sores. One side of his face was a huge bulge of tumefaction, and beneath his night clothes, his body, his orifices, would be in suppuration. His hair was lank and grizzled. He was an old man.

"I just dropped in to see you for half an hour," Edward said.

The movement of Harry's muscles, the stir of his hands and feet, seemed slow. His blank expression changed to puzzlement as his gaze fixed on Edward's face. His voice was distorted with the growth of illness, almost unintelligible.

"Who are you?" Harry asked.

"I'm married to your Aunt Lillian. I'm Edward."

"I don't know you."

Edward asked, "Do you feel a little better?"

Harry's gaze seemed to turn inwards on himself; the ulcers at his eyes might be great monstrous tears. Five minutes had passed when suddenly he made a sound that was laughter, a great choking gurgling sound as if he might be remembering an outrageous moment from the past.

"I was thirteen," he said suddenly. "The old people had a big place in Castleconnell by the river. Down the slope to the falls, the river always a raging torrent. I used to sit and watch it. The old people loved me, thought I came specially to see them. I came to peek through the kitchen window, to watch the young skivvies at work. I didn't know why! Swear to God I didn't know why!" The choking smothering laughter again, fading to hoarseness. "I used to watch them. There was bare skin beneath their skirts. When they bent over I could see lovely thighs and great moons of bottom. I was excited, stiff as a poker. And I didn't know why!" Every word was laboriously shaped and floated with his memories; laughter was a gigantic effort of breathing; then the pause and storytelling again. "They might rest a while, sit and swing their legs on the table, and their skirts would fall back and the movement of their legs was unbearable."

There was a long silence. He was the sole occupant of this little terraced house, always under surveillance. His attendants slept here, of course; they cooked his meals, fed him, washed his clothing, his body. They had protective clothing, restraints. They followed their routine with robotic monotony, without emotions, without feelings. People for every job.

Harry was laughing again, wheezing his way into words. "A beautiful woman taught me all the mysteries. She was thirty-seven, older than my mother. She was a beautiful bitch, a relative visiting our house by the river. I was left in her care all day. She could talk and laugh, fill the house with music. She called out to me from her bedroom. She liked me, she said. She was at her dressing table, combing her long fair hair. Suddenly she dropped off her shoes, rolled off her stockings. She undressed, every wisp of clothing, and I thought she was shining with beauty. She came and undressed me and brought me to lie on her bed. I was trembling. But she did everything for me. Oh, the softness, the beauty of it. I never forgot her. Every whore and skivvy I screwed, in my mind it was her body, her hands, her breathing."

He was silent again for long minutes, letting the room, his prison, take shape around him again. He stared at Edward.

"Who are you?"

"Just a visitor," Edward said.

"I don't know you."

"No."

His body was tightening in rigor, his teeth clenched. Edward rang the small hand-bell on the table. In ten minutes he was walking down the country road homewards.

In George's Street he called at the hotel and drank a measure of whiskey, alone.

CHAPTER TEN

TWO WEEKS HAD passed since the burial of Carmody's son. In secrecy, in a time of raging illness and confusion, except for a circle of close friends it had passed without notice. A son of Carmody would never be seen to be taken from a workhouse ward, through the streets of the city, to his grave. There would be no record of his admission inside that place of pauperism and hopelessness.

Carmody walked alone now through the business streets of closed shops and shuttered windows, and remembered his anger. He had won a battle that day in the workhouse and walked away unscathed. The city newspaper had given it only a few lines: a fire, a tragic accident. The fire had been a time of panic, a time to take a small body from the dead-house and drive past the gatekeeper and the open gates; and while it still burned, with a few friends to form a tiny cortège, he had driven into the countryside. The fire, the matron's death, were forgotten now. And his son, hidden away, was at rest.

He walked the streets with a faint warmth of satisfaction. Gaslights were closer; the carriage lamps of jarveys were specks of light; motor traffic was scarce. He counted the Catholic shops and considered the proprietors and their loyalties. How many of them had taken up arms in rebellion or in its aftermath of civil strife? None would be Carmody's summation. But they had made their secret donations to conservatism, to the shadow-patriots who were in government now. Times would change; Carmody was sure of that.

He walked to Thomond Bridge and past the castle, into a poor area of neglected housing, of penny-halfpenny shops, of people not far from raggedness. Respectful salutations were made and, silently, he nodded.

He reached his destination: what had been an empty shop and back room. The shop window was curtained with heavy cloth and gaslight barely glimmered through its weave. On the doorway, a neat plaque had been fixed: 'GAA. St Paul's Social and Athletic Club.'

St Paul's was an athletic club devoted to the furtherance of native games. It had a young membership of boys under the age of eighteen and a training field, not far distant, where playing and coaching took place. But full membership, and the use of these rooms, was by proposal and seconding of mature clubmen and the ultimate agreement of the committee.

Carmody was chairman of the committee.

He raised a hand to salutations in the outer room where a card-drive was in progress. Six tables with four to a table at a shilling per player, that amounted to twenty-four shillings, with ten shillings to the winning pair and fourteen shillings to club funds. The air was heavy with tobacco smoke; a good turf fire burned in the grate. Carmody passed through to the inner room.

A fire burned here, too, and its window was curtained; the gaslighting was bright. This was the committee room. The meeting was at eight o'clock. Carmody looked at his pocket watch. It was on the stroke of the hour. He closed the door.

Six members sat in conversation about a trestle table. Carmody smiled, hung his coat and cap on a wall rack, took his place as chairman and faced them.

"Thank you, gentlemen, for your punctuality. I declare the meeting open. The secretary will read the minutes of the last meeting."

The secretary, who had opened his school notebook, said, "Mr Chairman, before reading the minutes, I would like to speak on behalf of the members. We offer you our condolences on the death of your only son, Joseph, a boy of brilliant promise, whose demise, almost inexplicable demise, cast a shadow on so many lives. We will pray for him. Black armbands will be worn by St Paul's team on its next outing."

The meeting proceeded: minutes, a treasurer's report, a routine agenda. No further business.

Formality was abandoned now. The meeting might have been a hurried prelude to the real business of the evening. Tobacco smoke floated about, chairs were moved and tilted. It was a quiet discussion among equals, but always the last word seemed to be Carmody's. Sometimes he stood and held the floor.

"The death of your son is a tragedy, Joseph. The loss of a son is a blow, the loss of an only son is a great cross." A pause. "Word is whispered here and there that his treatment was neglected."

Words suddenly everywhere now.

". . . that they experimented with him . . . less than a day in the hospital and he's dead . . . diphtheria is a killer we know, but taken in time . . . knowing you, Joseph, you couldn't have wasted time . . . you'd have had him in a hospital bed if you had to carry him . . . who was the doctor? . . . there should be an enquiry . . ."

Carmody held up his hands for silence; it came slowly, words fading away unevenly until there was stillness.

Carmody spoke.

"My friends," he said, "the hospital was the City Home,

not long since the workhouse. You know I would have given my son better than that, but they had carted him away without my knowledge." A pause to study them. "I humbly accept the will of God. He took away my only son. He took away my name and my blood. My wife can bear no more children. The name Carmody dies with me. But God, too, gave the life of his only son for mankind. Christ came on earth to show us how to live our lives without fear, with courage and honesty. That is our mission."

Someone said, "May we be worthy of that."

"Amen."

Carmody nodded. "Without fear, with courage and honesty," he said. "I hope I speak with those convictions. I know illness when I see it. I talked with my son." A long pause. "He was a healthy boy. A mild cold, perhaps flu. A few days and he would have been running to school with the best of them." Carmody had their silence; he stood and watched them again for moments. "I took his hand before I left for work that morning, felt his forehead. Not even a temperature. But I returned to find that he had been taken from his own house."

"You weren't consulted, Joseph?"

"My wife," Carmody said, "is a person of great faith and virtue. She tends to my home and my needs. But she is not equipped to question the decisions of doctors or their ilk. She is a humble person. She was waiting on my doorstep for me, a broken woman. Diphtheria, I was told. My son had been taken to the workhouse. Yes, gentlemen, my son had been taken to the workhouse. An awful name, an awful place. People mumble 'Union' and 'City Home', but it's a workhouse, gentlemen. It was built as a workhouse and will always be a workhouse! If my son needed hospital treatment, I could pay for the best bed in Barrington's." Carmody's voice was rising, sharpening his anger. "I said, if he *needed* hospital treatment, but he was a healthy, thriving boy."

"Who sent him?"

Carmody could omit what he considered unimportant in

the pursuit of justice. District nurses and matrons were bit-players.

He said, "The doctor concerned was Bennett, a Protestant." He paused; his words were slow and seemingly discreet. "My son was a Catholic. He sent my son to isolation in the workhouse. Gentlemen, I don't have to tell you that a child with a cold or a mild flu is defenceless in a diphtheria ward. My son, unimportant, was pushed away out of sight. Would Dr Bennett have sent a Protestant child to the workhouse?"

"A bloody outrage."

"He should be brought to book."

"Wasn't there botched surgery, too?"

Carmody was careful not to affirm anything. "I signed a form for him to be treated with everything that medical science could supply for his survival. You, too, gentlemen, would have signed that form. Your son. Your only son."

In the silence there were wide eyes, mouths agape. They saw this awful moment of terrible decision.

"Even it was a black doctor, you would have signed! I couldn't see my son; he was locked away from me, a danger to everyone, I was told. But I wanted him to live. I took the pen in hand and signed."

"Of course, of course!"

"But the surgery, Joseph?"

"I was told," Carmody said, "that a hole had been made in his windpipe and a tube inserted to allow him to breathe."

The secretary laid down his pen and joined his hands.

Silence and shock sat on the faces of the committee.

"Bennett did this?"

"Bennett was the surgeon. The matron assisted him. My son died within a couple of hours."

"Will you take action?"

"No," Carmody said. "If doctors aren't Protestant, they're from the moneyed Catholic breed. The same thing. You buy your way into medicine. Most of ours are brainless, too.

Some of them take ten years to scrape through examinations."

"What can we do?"

Carmody waited for silence. "We can punish Bennett. The Bennetts. We want him and his seed out of our country."

The committee stood and applauded. Carmody motioned them to sit, surveyed them with the ghost of a smile that was his approval. He settled himself in his chair, looking beyond them in thought for a little while.

Carmody liked to talk, liked others to listen, and always gilded the conclusions of meetings with some prepared dissertation to enlighten his membership.

"Twelve years ago, 1916, we struck the blow for freedom. Every man at this table was out there with a gun in his hand. This island was an occupied colony. Remember? 'George V, by the grace of God, of Great Britain, Ireland, and of the British Dominions beyond the seas, King, Defender of the Faith, Emperor of India.' Remember? But we fought him for five years, every regiment of scum that he sent against us. And we won."

Carmody put his palms flat on the table and stared down at them. These were all studied moves. When he was impressed by speakers, he remembered the tricks of their trade – the trade unionists of 1913 and later, the strike leaders here in the city – and applied them himself. Carmody was a good speaker, careful about the simplicity of words, the necessity of reaching every illiterate in his audience. That was the trick.

With this committee, of course, he could be more expansive; these were working men of some schooling and intelligence.

"We won, gentlemen. We won the war and lost the peace," Carmody said. "We sent weak negotiators to London who brought us back nothing. Oh, we'd have a government in Dublin, of our own people, of men who'd say 'God Save the King' before they crossed the threshold. And we wouldn't be Ireland any more, we'd be the Irish Free State of the British

Commonwealth. And two-thirds of Ulster would be a bolt-hole for Protestant and Presbyterian. Ulster, a new country where the Catholic Irish would be the whipping-boys. That was the peace they brought back to us!"

Carmody suddenly threw up his hands with a great disparaging outburst of sound, a manufactured sound of flatulence. The committee was applauding, red with enthusiasm.

"Gentlemen, gentlemen!" Carmody stilled them. "That peace was accepted! There were flunkies where we never expected them, cap-in-hand grovellers." He paused and waited. "But our leader called on us and we followed him. We walked away from that signed document of dishonour. We parted company with the flunkies and they outlawed us. Shot us with British guns. Executed us like animals. For a year they shot us with their Irish Free State army." Carmody brought his fist down like a hammer on the table. "But we never surrendered! We're still fighting."

The committee was fired now.

"We left gaps in their Free State army."

"We shot them in their Sam Brownes and polished buttons."

Carmody let them threaten and disparage. He took his breather. There was fertile ground in abundance to be seeded. He let the babble of voices lessen, begin to fade.

He said, "No, gentlemen, the shooting days are almost over. Politics is a more deadly weapon. Politics and the *threat* of force. An election will come one day, and we'll be ready to fight it. We must creep into committees and corporations, become the people's friends. Every man and woman has a vote, the wealthiest and the poorest. Who needs help most? So we talk to the working man, give him importance. But we reassure the wealthy."

"The wealthy?"

"That we will protect them."

"The wealthy Irish?"

"Yes, a growing force."

Carmody stood and took his coat and cap from the rack, wrapped himself in warmth. "I must leave now. Thank you for your attendance gentlemen," he said. "I always leave these meetings with great hope and optimism. In the near future we must discuss political committees and representation in our city's government." He smiled. "This is *our* city. This is *our* country."

Carmody took his leave. He walked past the church of St Munchin and the Treaty Stone. That was another treaty, he thought, that had been dishonoured without great lamentation. There should be no lamentation about breaking treaties.

Carmody had been born thirty-nine years before, ten miles from the city centre, on the skirts of a small village in another county. He never mentioned it, but he was a blow-in to this city he had adopted. The Carmodys, a father and three sons, were a family of blacksmiths and farriers. Farriers shod work-horses and hunters, but blacksmiths worked with iron to shape it for gates and railings, to make the iron bands for cart wheels. They were the complete tradesmen. His father boasted that he could make racing plates more precise than the experts of County Kildare.

But Carmody had grown up in the image of his mother, a quiet woman of silent resolve. In her bedroom, a box on a small table, draped in white cotton, was her "altar". Statues of Christ and His Mother gazed down on smaller figurines of lesser saints, a vase of flowers. A wax candle in a holder and bottled holy water were there in the event of the arrival of death, a lighted candle to be held in the hand of the dying and holy water to be aspersed for the awful passage to eternity. She knelt there every night for half an hour in prayer. Carmody tried to shape himself, but he knew he could never reach her immense resolution.

Blacksmiths worked up a thirst in heat and sweat; and when he was still a young boy he went to the village pub with the rest. He learnt his politics there, and was drawn into the anonymity of the city.

The muscle of his trade made work in the holds of coal boats easy for Carmody. He saw a stevedore standing with his book and pencil, the smartness of him, and suddenly he had ambition. He had a goal to reach. He had become abstemious, was devoted to, afraid of, God and the Church. But he waged his political war without mercy. Daytime, a black figure on the quays; night-time, a blacker shadow laying his charges of explosive at police barracks, or burning the great houses of implanted Protestants. Yes, Carmody had taken life in a just cause. He had no need for a confession or an absolution.

He crossed Sarsfield Bridge, the Wellesley Bridge, as so many people still called it. The Sarsfield Bridge, Carmody always reminded them. It commemorated the hero of the city's final siege. Sarsfield held the passes of the Shannon, and highwaymen rode with him. They knew the tracks of the county and the scenes of battle. Sarsfield had ridden furtively out of the city with five hundred dragoons and, with one great explosion, had destroyed the armoury, ammunition and baggage of the enemy. *Sarsfield* Bridge!

Carmody spat. Wellesley, twice Lord Lieutenant of Ireland, was a plundering governor of India, too; Wellington, his brother, fighting pitched battles with toy soldiers, thought his men were dirt. A pity Waterloo had been saved in the nick of time. The Wellesleys of County Meath honoured with a bridge across this city's great river. And Lord Fitzgibbon on a pedestal surveying it: a hare-brained horseman racing at point-to-point speed toward Russian guns. A twenty minute gallop and four hundred dead men. Carmody spat again.

He turned into George's Street and walked at a slow easy pace to the east. He missed nothing: the cars and carriages, the tweedy strutting group on the grand pedimented porch of the County Club, the lighted windows of the hotel and the hall porter costumed like a music-hall comic.

He was thirty-nine, he thought; forty coming up. He was pleased to be reaching forty. You only came of age at forty;

with maturity came judgment, care, a little restraint. He would make his name in this city of well-heeled aldermen and councillors.

He thought of the family forge, the black walls, the pull of the bellows and the shades of heat changing on the metal, the rhythm of the hammer and the ring of anvil noise, the rolled up sleeves, the sweat. It was gone now, the work that burned life and life-blood.

His father had died at fifty-five, raising up the heavy hammer for the last time and dropping on the earthen floor. His brothers had gone to Boston and vanished into silence. His mother had died of loneliness. The care of them all had been her life, but suddenly there was no one left. She was kneeling at her altar when she passed away on her last journey. The dwelling-house and forge stood empty now.

Carmody walked on past the Crescent, past the lights burning in a Bennett house, and moved towards the church that was his destination.

Dr Cafferey had told him, "I look forward to your visits, Joseph."

CHAPTER ELEVEN

THE BISHOP'S PALACE was outside the city, approached by a gateway and a long avenue and surrounded by extensive grounds. The house had more than ample comfort: carpeting and furnishing, polished floors and windows. The bishop's private quarters, a complete household, had, in addition to comfort, the feeling of his presence and his sanctity. There was a private chapel or oratory.

The remainder of the dwelling was for the reception of lesser or greater rank: bedrooms, a communal dining-room, a study, access to the library. Nuns from a local convent carried out staff duties with the expertise of professionals. Two were resident, only a bell call away, day or night; for a large function there could be a dozen in attendance at short notice.

Dr Paul Cafferey came by horse-drawn cab. The smooth surface of the avenue wound between trimmed foliage and the fine beeches and oaks and elms with a beauty in their haphazard planting in the rich and undulating ground. Around an easy bend the palace came into view, a fine stone building with a marquise and steps to its doors.

He directed the cab driver to the rear, where the nuns would give him suitable food, and climbed the steps to ring the doorbell. He could hear its gentle sounds in the distance. He stood like a proprietor viewing the property. It brought a feeling of richness. He might one day, he thought, be the incumbent here. It was possible.The bishop wasn't growing younger. Other, more senior men than Paul Cafferey called here, he knew, but he brought with him the gossip of the parish, the diocese. And the prelate, His Lordship, Bishop John McEnteggart, was intrigued, sometimes holding up his hands in wonderment. He could drink a glass of sherry with Paul Cafferey, and they could laugh.

There were breaks in the clouds, and sunshine, pale gold, flowed across the parkland, fresh-tinted the thinning autumn leaves, showing the naked limbs beneath. It was a beautiful day suddenly appearing in the approach to winter. Winter light, shorn of brightness, light that brought a greyness, a despondency to the world, would settle to permanency soon. The middle-aged felt older; the aged wondered if they might see another spring.

Dr Cafferey, when he had left his presbytery house, had walked to the city centre before taking a horse cab. Wearing a light, double-breasted overcoat, a velour hat and carrying a rolled umbrella, he was a very recognisable figure in his smart clerical attire. He nodded to salutations, occasionally smiling.

He walked unhurriedly in the minor poorer streets. It was the morning-break time at schools, and clusters of children scrambled about. He patted some on their spiky heads, knowing that adults were watching and would nod at his gentleness. He took the back entrance to the People's Park and walked across the patch where football games were played between goalposts of piled clothes, eventually reaching the higher ground of pathways, flower beds, shrubs and trees. Philanthropist Monteagle's column threw its shadow along the sloping grass. Spring Rice had been his name, but he was revered by people who confused him with Edmund Rice and thought of him in black soutane, a pioneer of schooling and instruction for the poor. Dr Cafferey, with his non-committal smile, didn't disabuse them. You won little battles and big battles and battles you didn't fight. You didn't preach it aloud, for example, that the fine cut-stone library by the exit gates had been donated by a Scottish Presbyterian.

He walked on in the pleasant diluted warmth of the sunshine. Dr Cafferey's journeys might seem haphazard, but they always had purpose. There was a church in the near distance and, in an open space, a clock raised on a plinth surrounded by iron rails, commemorating another dead dissenter. A group of schoolgirls was approaching, heads down, chattering. They were on the brink of their teens, Dr Cafferey thought: impressionable, curious, fond of talking.

They walked erect and silent now, ready to make their obeisance as they passed. Dr Cafferey stood before them and made a little movement of blessing with his hand. They stood and bowed their heads in a show of respect.

He gave his little winning smile. "Just the group of smart young ladies I needed to meet. I had heard some news. Have you heard anything unusual?" he asked, looking towards the church a hundred yards away.

The looked at each other as if there should be some ready answer for this holy man.

Their spokesperson said in a whisper, "No, Doctor."

"Oh, you must call me Father," he said. "I am your priest first. The rest is just a reward for my studies."

"Yes, Father."

"Nothing unusual then?"

"Nothing, Father."

"Is there a side altar to the Blessed Virgin Mary in your church?"

"Our Lady's Altar, Father."

"And her statue is there?"

"Yes, Father."

"There's a story going about this morning that her eyes moved, showing great compassion for the people in prayer."

The young things were motionless, in bewilderment.

"I only overheard it on the streets," he told them. "I don't know anything more about it. I thought I'd ask you. Always pray to the Mother of God, won't you? For truth and purity."

"Yes, Father."

"She may have come to help us through this time of sickness and disease." He gave them his discreet blessing again and was striding off to George's Street and the cab rank.

Dr Cafferey was a pragmatist. Faith could wane; it could wither and die. It needed stimulation. In the confessional the penitent should almost hear you groan, listening to the recitation of his sins; or, from the pulpit you should hold him, frozen, with roaring rage, or a whisper, at his iniquity and the dreadful screaming punishment of hell, and the irrevocable moment of death. And finally, you told him of God's infinite mercy.

Strange inexplicable ghostly shadows, apparitions, statues that wept or bled, or perhaps moved, brought a mixture of dread and wonderment. A Celtic phenomenon. The invigoration of faith was the purpose of the priesthood, Dr Cafferey thought. You spurred it on with even a little gentle hocus-pocus.

The double doors behind him were opened and a nun in her long robe, her face looking through a window of stiff fabric, held a door with each hand.

Generous Dr Cafferey gave her his blessing and she curtsied and crossed herself. "Good day, Sister Agnes."

She smiled and dropped her gaze for a moment, and he passed into the comfort of the carpeted lobby with its hall-stand, chairs, panelled wood and a warm fire. Before a large hardwood cross and a dying Christ, there was a prie-dieu where he knelt for just a few moments in prayer.

When he rose from his instants of devotion, Sister Agnes spoke.

"His Lordship is expecting you."

"Yes, I telephoned him."

She took his coat and hat and umbrella.

He followed her along the corridor, shining and smelling of wax and cleanliness and adorned with heavily framed pictures of popes from Gregory XVI to Pius XI. Dr Cafferey knew this passage well.

Sister Agnes announced him – "Dr Paul Cafferey, Your Lordship" – and left.

It was a fine room with its french windows displaying the gardens and trees and sky. There was no excess of religious decor, ornaments or bric-à-brac, but everything had a place in the comfortable aura. It had been a bare, cold place, almost penitential, in the days of his predecessors, but this incumbent, with Dr Cafferey's assistance, had furnished it. His Lordship sat in a fine square Spanish chair of hardwood and studded leather facing the fire, his slippered feet resting on a footstool.

The bishop turned his head and smiled. "You're welcome, Paul. Sit, take a comfortable chair. It's a wonderful day out there, but I'm not fond of chilly weather."

"It's a pet-day, old people still say. A reminder of good days gone and winter days ahead."

The bishop bore signs neither of asceticism nor indulgence. Tall, not carrying excessive weight, the bishop had a face, when it adopted a more serious mould, that had immediate authority. He was sixty-six, looked younger, and had been in his holy office for more than five years. With others, Paul Cafferey – possibly because of his doctorate – had been chosen to meet and install him. Without exchange of words, there had been immediate rapport.

A week later, when relative calm had returned, Paul Cafferey had telephoned for an appointment. He found the bishop alone. "Being raised to a bishopric is like a bereavement," he had been told. "A great gathering at the burial and then the bereft is left in solitary confinement."

They had been friends since that time.

The bishop now went to his cabinet and brought a decanter of sherry and poured two generous measures. They drank. The coal fire threw out its warmth about the room, enhancing the creeping bareness of the outside world and the pale colour of sunshine.

Paul Cafferey took a sheet of notepaper from his pocket and opened it. "A few items here on my agenda," he said. "I'll take them as they come."

"Good, good," the bishop said.

"In St Brigid's parish there is a curate. Father C, as I note him here."

"Yes?"

"Not a young man. Forty, I suppose. He has what I would call an over-friendly relationship with a female person. She is a confraternity person. She arranges flowers, altars, that kind of thing. About his own age, perhaps a year or two younger."

"Married?"

"No. A plain-faced, well-made woman."

"Has there been misconduct?"

"I don't think so."

"Good. You can leave me his name. A discreet move to a more distant parish should reinstate him, don't you think?"

They sipped their sherry again.

Paul Cafferey continued. "There's a serious diphtheria epidemic raging in the city. A high percentage of deaths. There's a lot of fear about."

The bishop said, "Yes, I had some news of it. I could arrange for an announcement at all Sunday masses till further notice."

"Yes." Paul Cafferey had already written the bishop's distress and benediction on his sheet of paper, but he adopted an attitude of thought, a search for words. "Yes, that would reassure the flock."

"My sympathy and feelings, that kind of thing?" the bishop mooted.

Paul Cafferey looked out across the lawns, thinking, composing aloud, "Your beloved pastor, His Lordship the Bishop . . . offers deep sympathy to his flock at this moment when God tests your courage . . . and would like to assure you that you are daily in his prayers. He sends his blessings to you all."

The bishop smiled. "Excellent, Paul," he said.

"Spirits are flagging," Paul Cafferey said. He spoke carefully, pausing, showing the circumspection, the discretion that he had exercised. "I have seen a shadow of defeatism on a great number of faces. Faith needs to be raised to a higher flame, I think."

"Faith must always be kept alive, Paul."

"God understands that we must be clever as generals on the field of battle to win the war against evil. And, in winning the war, if we can restore confidence and good faith, then it is a memorable victory. Christ turned the water into wine. Or was it an illusion? Perhaps it was the inspired legerdemain of a great general."

The bishop listened with attention.

"Miracles, the supernatural, have always stirred and excited the faithful. The Mother of God, even in recent times, is reputed to have materialised for people of great sanctity or untouched innocence. Of course the Church stands on neutral ground. She is aware of fixations, deliriums, dementias. But she does not proscribe. Even an illusion, an imagined phantasm, can win our battle."

The bishop liked to hear Paul Cafferey's flow of words, so effortless, so convincing. "Ah, you should have been a politician, Paul. This country could use good politicians. Only yokels and gunmen in Dublin run our affairs. Now, tell me, what have you set in motion?"

"There is an area of great poverty skirting the church of one of our mendicant orders," Paul Cafferey said. "At mass time the entire aisle facing the altar of the Mother of God is crammed with the heads of shawlies."

"Shawlies?"

"Poor people without hats, or even coats, wear coarse shawls. Shawlies is synonymous with poverty."

"Poor people."

"Yes, and they occupy fertile ground. Passing close by today I met some schoolchildren. I mentioned that I had heard a story of the altar of the Virgin Mary. Had they heard anything unusual? No, they hadn't heard anything. Something about the eyes of the statue moving? I dismissed it, gave them my blessing and moved on."

The bishop considered it carefully. Finally he smiled. "Yes, yes, it may help them through this crisis of disease. Astonishing how people, even educated ones, will grasp at shadows."

"Panic and fright are difficult to cope with. Perhaps they even open doors to disease." Cafferey paused, lowered his voice. "I have a good friend in a local newspaper. He could be of use."

The bishop poured them a little more sherry. "Yes, you are right, of course," he said. "We cannot entirely depend on prayer." He raised his glass. "Lunch will be ready very soon. I told Sister Agnes to include you. Pork steaks sewn around bread stuffing and herbs, roasted, basted with hot juice, roasted potatoes and beautiful marrowfats. You like that, I'm sure?"

"Very much."

"Was there other news?"

Paul Cafferey pondered a while. "We all know that the major businesses of the city are in the hands of Protestants. There is a rising tide of Catholics, of course, but Protestants are in the preponderance."

The bishop said, "It might be better if it stayed like that for a decade or more, I think. They are a dependable community. They are accustomed to having money and not squandering it."

"Precisely. Our entrepreneurs have a lot to learn. I only draw the line," Paul Cafferey said, "where our brothers are being absorbed into marriage with them. Or won over by some specious charities. Where events are in the public domain, we must be seen to take action. That is, seen by a careful few who will keep the city informed."

The bishop smiled. "There is a specific family, is there? Someone you have in mind?" He had gone to his desk and taken a hardback quarto notebook from it. He sat again and flicked through it. It was indexed.

"Bennett is the name," Paul Cafferey told him.

The bishop was reading. "An impressive little dynasty. Merchants, professions." He looked at Paul Cafferey. "Reaching back to Napoleon and his wars. Some of them fought at Waterloo."

"A very good family," Paul Cafferey said.

"Exemplary help in famine times. Considered by some of the landlord class to be over-liberal in political views," the bishop read.

"The Bennetts were, of course, in trade and professions. Landlords didn't work. There are always social divides. Trade wasn't a polite word in landlord dialogues."

The bishop finished reading and closed his book. He nodded his agreement with Paul Cafferey. "Yes, I see," he said. "They crossed the line, didn't they? A pity. An only daughter, Lillian, married to Edward Burke. She wasn't young either, was she?"

"Thirty-eight when she married Burke. He was ten years her junior."

"She had money."

"Of course, but strangely attractive, too. You can be sure she is among the anonymous charitable donors to *our* diocesan funds. Has been for years. Substantial amounts."

"Her charity didn't begin with mixed marriage?"

"No. She had a soup kitchen for the poor until very recently. It had to be closed, of course, but the violence was unacceptable. Rowdyism, even blackguardism, you might call it. A nervous helper of hers suffered a fatal heart attack. She had led a sheltered existence, no experience of street life. Unfortunate."

"And Burke is principal of the Latimer School. A strange marriage, a strange workplace. Burke was a Norman name, of course. Does he attend his Catholic duties?"

"Outwardly he is a practising Catholic."

"Tell me about these Burkes."

"Of very comfortable means. Only the mother and this Edward fellow survive. You could call them a conservative Irish family. Two brothers, much older, twelve or fourteen years older, are dead. One, in action in France. The other drank himself to death in London. Our school principal spent the war years in Trinity. All were clever boys."

"Strange, this extraordinary age gap between births. Perhaps some malfunction and then sudden restoration of fertility. These things happen, I suppose."

"Catherine Burke lives alone. A strange woman, I'm told."

"A recluse?"

Paul Cafferey paused. "It's difficult to describe her condition. She walks a mile and a half of the riverbank every day. Silent, unapproachable."

"Condition? Not mentally ill?"

"There are so many degrees of mental illness. Being charitable, I would say she is eccentric to an extreme. Her surviving son is allowed to visit her for a half an hour each month. But, once in a week, a group of three or four people visit her. They spend whole evenings together."

"Who are they? Friends?"

"I don't think she would accommodate friends. They are mostly spinster women, perhaps a little younger than she is, but as withdrawn, forbidding."

"Do they sit and talk, or play card games? Listen to music, perhaps?"

"Music hasn't been heard in that house since the death of her eldest son in France. His bloodied uniform, hat, Sam Browne belt, hang at the end of her bed. The blinds are always drawn and the house is almost in darkness."

The bishop sipped his sherry, gazing out at the pale sunshine and the mark of winter on the trees. Paul Cafferey told a tale well. He was a good man to put at the helm of affairs: curious, observant, and without too much religion.

He said, "But you have never been in the house?"

"No."

"How have you gathered your information?"

"There is a city church not a great distance from Catherine Burke's house. There is a spiritually failed old priest there who wanders about. He is given odd jobs to do. A dissolute old man. Catherine Burke does not attend church services. Due to a nervous disorder, she claims . . . ."

"This old priest?"

"He is known as Fr Tom Tom. He brings the Sacred Host at intervals, and she allows him to pray aloud for fifteen minutes. She pays him generously. I pay him a little."

"And he talks to you?"

"Guardedly."

"Is there a story?"

Paul Cafferey considered it for a moment. "Yes," he said, "you could say there is a story. Hearsay all of it, of course. You put pieces together and guess at the missing ones. Old Tom Tom is hardly a reliable witness. Purely circumstantial, My Lord."

The bishop laughed.

"I'll tell you what I've heard and what I think," Paul Cafferey said. "Catherine Burke didn't share a bed with her husband for many years. She had a fine bedroom on the ground floor. He was a quiet, ineffectual person, I'm told." Paul Cafferey paused and looked at the bishop for moments. "From birth she had an obsessive love for her eldest son. From the time of birth, all his life, he slept in her bed. She cared for the needs of the other boy, and her husband, but had no love for them. She probably disliked them. When her eldest son was fourteen, a son, Edward, was born."

They sat in silence for moments. Outside a little breeze was rising, shivering along the grass, brushing the sunshine to a paler gold. It would be a cold evening, with a sprinkling of hoar frost. The bishop's gardener moved about near the flower beds, and disturbed birds in the shrubs fled like arrows. Paul Cafferey sat motionless, in silence, waiting.

Eventually the bishop said, "An incestuous relationship?"

"Possibly."

"Not possible that it was her husband?"

"Fr Tom Tom says no."

"Edward Burke is the son of his eldest brother?"

"He might well be."

"Did he know it?"

"He was just a child when his brothers were grown men. Children aren't aware of these things."

"Does he know it now?"

"Difficult to say. He grew up too close to it. We possibly have a clearer vision from a distance. But we can only surmise."

"Catherine Burke receives the Host?"

"Yes."

"Perhaps she has confessed and been absolved."

"Perhaps."

A bell tinkled distantly in the silent house. His Lordship and Dr Cafferey would be expected in the dining-room in ten minutes. The bishop took a pocket watch from his waistcoat pocket and studied it.

"You don't think she had confessed?"

Paul Cafferey shrugged. "She is not a repentant woman. A purely personal opinion, of course."

"We speak in absolute confidence, Paul. Incest doesn't shock us. In remote communities, on sparsely peopled offshore islands, we know that abuses exist. Fathers and daughters is the usual pattern. But union of mother and son is rare."

"And pregnancy and birth."

"Yes," the bishop agreed.

"We must, of course, encapsulate it in secrecy," Paul Cafferey said. "The sanctity of the Church and its members must be preserved. The greater good, the common weal. I think you can leave it safely in my hands. I will keep him under surveillance. He is an apostate."

"I leave it in your hands, Paul. The Bennetts bring trade, revenue, give employment. We need their ilk for some time yet. The Burke widow, too. She is a person of substance, a degenerate Catholic we agree, but she has property and wealth. We will send her the Sacred Host and pray with her. This Fr Tom Tom, does he know these people who visit her? Who are they? What is the purpose of their meeting?"

"I'll pursue it," Paul Cafferey said, "with the care and discretion you would wish."

They spread lunch over an hour and a half, enjoying the well-prepared meal and drinking good wine imported by the Bennett family, which was generous with its gifts to the bishop's commissary. The wines were delivered; bills were never presented. Eating was an almost silent time of satisfaction. They rested and smoked . . . .

A little later, Paul Cafferey was back in his horse cab, trotting away from the quietude of the bishop's palace towards the clamour of the city.

Paul Cafferey came from one of those genetically untraceable sources. His parents' union was one of lacklustres, where sexual connection even in marriage was close to sinfulness, and the purpose of sex was the birth of Christian souls. The Cafferevs lived in the ample space above a thriving small town business: grocery and provisions, a vast range of farm ironmongery and hardware, and a licensed section for the sale of beer, wines and spirits. His father had worn an apron from breakfast to bedtime; his mother had cooked and baked and washed and scrubbed, and was available for the almost nightly ritual of blessed union.

She had been a dominant figure in her family's lives. Even in times of few and distant hospitals and doctors, with only the homespun skill of midwives, ten of her twelve children had survived childhood, and she had driven them on to excellence. There were degrees of excellence, and the service of God was the highest.

Only one of seven sisters survived in the task of bringing Christ to the Chinese; she wrote to Paul piously at Easter and Christmastide. His two brothers still practised medicine in Irish Boston and sent Christmas cards as a reassurance of survival. The parents, too, were dead, he in apron, she in rolled sleeves, no doubt looking down from their heavenly seats in approval.

Paul Cafferey had attended boarding school for four years, observing and avoiding the dormitory abuses and the gentle smiling approaches of clerics. It was a preparation for a further four years of novitiate training before ordination to the priesthood. Strangely he had found no attraction in women or men; his youthful occasional emissions in sleep he had taken as a passing phase to the adult state that would be gone like childhood illnesses. The celibate life was a natural state for Paul Cafferey, and he enjoyed the power of his priesthood.

While still at boarding school he had seen the weaknesses of the ordained and with an innate confidence had challenged it. A dean of discipline had preached to them of "touching forbidden parts of the body", he had mentioned pleasure and damnation; but he had avoided the sinful word: masturbation. During ensuing weeks boys were summoned to his private rooms, remained silent about their experiences there, mentioned only that it had been a spiritual assessment of their progress.

"What happened, boyo?"

"What do you mean?"

"Up in Spider's room, that's what I mean."

"He talked, that was all."

"Talked about what?"

"Spiritual assessment."

From the beautiful sunshine of a spring day in the compound, Paul Cafferey had been summoned. The dean's quarters were on the highest level of a four-storey building. He climbed the cold terrazzo staircase, knocked on the dean's door and entered. There was great comfort: a carpeted floor, pleasant furniture and heat. The warmth had the gentleness of an embrace. A single window looked out at only sky and cloud. Only God was privy to the dean of discipline.

In an armchair facing the doorway the dean was reclining on his lower spine, buttocks and legs outstretched, hands behind his neck. He was a big man of early middle years, with a bulging stomach, and his total baldness shone in the bright air. He motioned Cafferey to a similar chair, facing him.

"And who are you?"

"You sent for me, Father."

"I asked who you are."

"Cafferey, Father."

They sat in silence for a full minute. Cafferey studied the carpet pattern; he knew that the interrogator's eyes were measuring him. A sad, fat, bulging man. Seconds ticked on slowly.

"What is the sixth commandment, Cafferey?"

"Thou shalt not commit adultery."

"And what is adultery?"

"Unlawful intercourse by a married person with any other except a lawful partner."

"You're very articulate."

"Thank you, Father."

"There can be adultery with one self."

"Masturbation, Father?"

The dean remained perfectly motionless, but his eyes had a fresh interest in Cafferey. "Do you masturbate?"

"No, Father."

"Have you seen it done?"

"No, Father."

"But it has been described to you?"

"Yes."

"Here in this seminary?"

"It was discussed in the course of weekly confession," he said.

"You had confessed it?"

"No. My confessor spoke to me about the dangers of impurity."

"About touching yourself, exciting yourself?"

"Something like that."

The dean pulled his cassock about him, sat more upright. "Your conduct has been under scrutiny for some time, Cafferey. I think of you sometimes and am often in doubt. That is why I have requested that you come and see me. The purity and virginity of pupils is my responsibility. I must ask you to remove your clothing and stand before me."

"You want to examine my genitals?"

"Precisely."

Cafferey stood and looked across the room at the comfortable piety of it and at the sky and cloud beyond the windows. This pitiable man of authority was restless with excitement: the unbuttoning, the dropping away of clothing, would bring a tightening of passion.

Cafferey said, "Where is the doctor?"

"Doctor?"

"A doctor to examine my body. You will be present, Father, as my spiritual advisor."

The dean was suddenly enraged. "Your parents have placed you in the jurisdiction of this seminary. Obey me, or I'll be forced to recommend your expulsion to the rector."

Without warning Cafferey crumpled in his chair, head bowed, sobbing, his hands and legs trembling.

"Quiet!" was hissed at him. "What are you whimpering about! Quiet, quiet!"

Cafferey didn't raise his head. "My expulsion, Father," he said. "It will kill my parents."

"Expulsion for what?"

"Disobedience, Father."

Paul Cafferey had learnt early how to win battles.

The cabby slowed his horse to walking pace and leant down his long behatted head to ask, "To the presbytery, Doctor?"

Paul Cafferey handed him money. "Put me down here," he said. "I enjoy walking on a late sunny day."

George's Street's broad thoroughfare honoured Hanoverian royalty who spoke broken English, or perhaps none at all, but its four-storey brick houses, without embellishment, had elegance and grace. Its new name would honour Catholic Emancipation now.

The rattle of combustion engines and iron-shod wheels of horse traffic made it a noisy place. Pedestrians filled the pathways and jay-walked across the wide stretch. Corporation men with push carts, shovels and brooms lifted up the horse droppings and carried them away. It was good ground manure and worth a fair few pence a day.

The new police, the Gardaí, saluted him respectfully as they passed. Men raised a cap or a hat, or touched a forelock, and women averted their gaze in respect.

Paul Cafferey passed the great Protestant stores and the smaller ones of emerging Catholics. A music shop had pianos for sale and a plethora of sheet-music in its window. Woolworths had arrived from America.

Paul Cafferey walked on to a newspaper office. The local newspapers were weeklies, self-important, inky, ponderously written broadsheets. They concerned themselves with sales and settlements, weddings and new arrivals on the planet, the movements of gentry, their sports and entertainments. Great care was taken with news, a carefully balanced comment without sting of criticism or any hint of approbation. They were widely read for the announcement of deaths and funerals.

This newspaper was in a terraced house with steps rising up to what had been the entrance to a substantial dwelling. A polished brass plate fixed in the brickwork announced its title. The front door was open into a polished hallway where there was a small enquiry office. A middle-aged man sat there, aware of his importance. At first he ignored the shadow of some new arrival at his window, seemingly absorbed in the perusal of slips of paper that were probably destined for memorial columns, or sales and wants.

He looked up alarmed. "Dr Cafferey, my apologies!" He pushed away the papers. "I was absorbed with these pieces of illiteracy. My daily penance. Our new men in power in Dublin have a steep educational hill ahead."

Paul Cafferey said, "No, no, you do important work. Editors make the excellence of our newspapers. You'll forgive my intrusion. I wondered if . . . ."

"Of course, he's available."

Ceasing his editorial chores and coming out to the hallway, he led Paul Cafferey to a spacious room where a heavily suited man, sitting at his desk, looked up from his work. An upright telephone, with earpiece resting on a loop, was a symbol of his omnipotence.

He stood up at once. "Dr Cafferey, what a pleasure to see you."

The escort drifted away unnoticed.

Paul Cafferey smiled, raised a hand to shoulder level: his blessing. "Good of you to see me, Bernard."

"My door is always open for you." He motioned Paul Cafferey to a chair and they sat facing each other across a desk. "A small glass of sherry?"

"Thank you, but no. I had a spoonful of sherry at lunchtime. I was visiting His Lordship."

"A fine man."

"Yes. We discussed pertinent matters and I told him I would call on you. He respects your judgment."

"I'm flattered."

"This plague of diphtheria is taking a few lives and breeding fear among the poor, the very poor, the overcrowded. The poor lose faith very easily."

"I have always been aware of that. They forget the power of God."

"His Lordship has decreed that special prayers be recited at Sunday masses until this cross is lifted from us."

"Amen."

"And his own masses will be offered for the flock of his beloved city. He is deeply distressed. He hoped you would make the facts known."

"I will try to do him justice."

"Thank you, thank you," Paul Cafferey said; he joined his hands and held the finger tips to his lips, deep in a kind of troubled thought. "There is another matter."

"Yes?"

"There has been a story about for a day or two concerning the church not far from here. The statue of the Mother of God."

"Yes?"

"It has been said that tears flowed from her eyes."

A stare froze on the face of this man of power.

"It seems well authenticated. Perhaps a sign of her compassion and that she will pray for us. Her prayers are always heard by her beloved son. I haven't seen it myself, of course, but good people came to me. I always think it is best to avoid names. You could mention the occurrence. It would restore the courage and perseverance of our people. And God will remember you."

Paul Cafferey was personally escorted to the hallway, almost to the street door. He said, "You will be in my humble prayers, Bernard."

"I am greatly honoured, Dr Cafferey, greatly honoured."

The sun, weakening now, made a little aura about the smart figure of Dr Paul Cafferey as he moved out of sight.

CHAPTER TWELVE

GOOD WORKING-CLASS houses – aspirants to lower middle class – were monuments to respectability: clean windows, net hangings, solid aged brickwork, filled and painted woodwork and embrasures. Hallways opened at street level on to pavements, and door furniture was well polished. A ground floor window, too, was a place of display for some piece of almost valueless pottery: a memento perhaps of a single day spent at the seaside.

Carmody's ground floor window housed a bamboo table, dressed with an embroidered runner, on which sat a pair of glaring spaniels. Carmody had won them with a ticket at a church bazaar. Their association with religion earned them a special place.

Out of earshot, Carmody would have been called labouring class, but he had pushed fearlessly across his Rubicon to get a foot on the ladder. As a freelance stevedore, he considered himself a contractor, a sub-contractor, who tendered for work and controlled his men, and now he had crept into the fringes of the business world. Carmody: Coal Merchant. From his coal yard adjoining his dwelling-house, he sold now by the bag or the bucket, but he would sell by the cartload soon. To small houses and big houses, too. He would lift the coal-hole covers of the high and mighty and, bag by bag, empty a cartload into their cellars, leave them short a bag or two if they weren't as alert as stevedores.

The ground-floor window stirred and Carmody's wife, Veronica, carefully dusted her display and moved out of sight. The floor was covered in good lino polished to a glistening sheen; a square heavy table and four chairs were its centre-piece. There was a what-not, corner fitted, of three shelves, which should be cluttered with gewgaws, cheap glass and snapshots, but which held only three objects in descending order: a crucifix, a gaudily framed photograph of their buried son and a figurine of Christ with a hand raised in blessing.

The fireplace had a screen and a fender that enclosed fire-irons. There were framed photo-prints of patriots on the wall: a schoolboy martyr, a city mayor shot on his doorstep, and a hunger striker who had died in south London.

The room and the fireplace were never used. It was a show place, and now a mausoleum display for a dead offspring.

Veronica Carmody, her skirt to her ankles and a head scarf fixed like holy veil, carried a piece of torn flannelette for a duster. Chairs, table, the what-not and its items were carefully polished. When she had finished, she stood for moments to survey it. Then she knelt before the what-not and prayed.

She walked now through all the rooms of her house in their bare pristine cleanliness. Each day she cleaned them, and the stairs and the hallway. She was meticulous. She was accustomed to being alone: her son had been at school, now he was dead; her husband was out early till late, always in search of something, pursuing something. Following the funeral and burial, he had taken her aside and told her that he would be sleeping in his son's bedroom for a year in a gesture of mourning.

She had been filled with loneliness, even terror. She was a

meek person who dreaded coffins and graves. Now, not only days, but nights, too, were spent alone, cold in her bed, in awful darkness.

Weeping, she had talked to him. "I'm alone all day, from early hours to late hours. At night-time I need your strength, the warmth of your body . . . ."

"Don't mention bodies or flesh!"

"I'm cold, forgotten."

"Your son is cold, and except for us, he is forgotten."

"I get no rest, waking, sleeping, tossing all night."

"Do you think I sleep?" he said.

She paused.

"Do you?"

"No."

"That's God's test of our faith."

"It seems like punishment," she said.

"Punishment cleanses us. It will give us strength. Count what you have, not what you haven't."

"Why, why did it happen?"

"The will of God. Perhaps God's will is to point us at the source of evil. There is a purpose in everything."

"Evil?"

"Yes, somewhere there was evil."

She had loved her son and wept for him every day, but illness had taken him, she knew, not evil. What was *evil*? Some stain of original sin that we carried about? Or some impalpable force sent from hellfire? Why was God so cruel to take young lives?

She sat in her kitchen, the one place of comfort in the house. The range shone and sent out heat. There was nothing left to do except remember, ponder. She nodded into moments of sleep and jerked out of them in panic. The hours crawled past. She drank tea and ate baked wheaten bread at the time of midday dinner. The hours after midday were easier. She sold little quantities of coal and took money. Her meekness vanished.

"Just a half bucket of slack, Mrs Carmody, and I'll pay you without fail tomorrow evening."

"You'll bring me the money tomorrow evening and I'll give you a half bucket of slack tomorrow evening."

"Just for a day, Mrs Carmody. The children aren't well and with all these deaths . . . ."

"I'll solve my problems, you'll solve yours."

"Mrs Carmody . . . ."

"Tomorrow with money."

She ran his huckster coal yard with cold efficiency; she was a good partner for crashing into a new society. While she was at business, she became alive, hard, confident, and she could momentarily forget the loss of her son, the coldness that religion had bestowed on her husband. Alone in her house, in the dark bedroom of night-time, she diminished. She had married a domineering man who had become cold, remote, unreachable, living a life apart from her that he never discussed. His son had been taken, and more would die until this cloud of disease had passed. He was bitter, with anger that needed to be spent.

She might see him tonight, or in the early morning when she served him breakfast. She gave him a packed lunch that rarely varied: thick slices of fat bacon between bread and butter, hard-boiled eggs, a paper of salt. Evening times, in the warm oven of the range, she left a great quantity of meat, cabbage and potatoes, against his erratic time of arrival. For Carmody, a good meal was a big meal, an overflowing plate.

Darkness crept in until it had settled by seven o'clock. Inside her ground-floor window she perched a notice: Coal Yard Closed. As she arranged it she was aware of kindly eyes watching her. At a glance she saw the respectable clothes, the half-veiled hat, the gloves, a rolled slender umbrella. The face smiled and looked towards Veronica's doorway.

Veronica Carmody considered it, then moved slowly out to the hallway and gave this person admittance. Beautiful, long, flowing clothes, a hat of style and quality. Yes, a lady of reasonable importance.

"Good evening," she said. "I realise I am intruding."

"No, of course not, ma'am. Can I help you?" Veronica Carmody closed the door, its noise melting into the silence of the empty house.

The visitor said, "I am Miss Bellingham. I know who you are."

Confidence was slipping away from Veronica Carmody. This was a woman of breeding. Her clothes and style were excellent, her speech faultless. Veronica Carmody was confused.

"I don't understand."

"Of course not. But now you must hurry. We have an appointment to keep and there is a horse cab waiting outside. Wear a coat or a cloak. Dress isn't important. We are going to meet friends."

"My husband may be back . . . ."

"He will be very late."

Veronica Carmody was silent for moments. "You know?"

"Yes."

She felt suddenly unburdened, secure in the confidence of this smiling person. She had no fear. She hurried up the stairs to her bedroom and put on her best coat and hat, took her soft kid-gloves. She hadn't dressed like this since the death and burial; she was confined to plain black serge for a year of mourning.

She hurried again downstairs. Miss Bellingham opened the door.

In the seclusion of the upholstered cab they drove through the gaslit streets, past shops still open and a movement of working people on the pavements. The new Gardaí walked in pairs. Soldiers were there too, Irish soldiers. Free State soldiers, they called them. The enemies of the Irish republicans, Veronica Carmody knew.

Miss Bellingham said, "You had a little education, child?"

"I was a school monitor," Veronica Carmody said. "A

pupil-teacher. I liked teaching. But Mr Carmody came to my parents and asked for me in marriage. They liked him. He had discipline and ambition. I obeyed, of course."

"Of course."

They drove down into the older part of the city, the fringe of the more ancient part, where indigenous enterprise had taken root a century before, when the blight of total bondage had begun to lift. Craftsmen, skilled artisans had built fine dwellings here, stone and brick buildings, in the style of rich rural holdings.

The horse cab made its way from a busy street, down a steep cutting, to a corner house close to a parish church. The façade of the house, the gates of a work yard with its storerooms and benches shut off, redundant, had an aspect of neglect. At the windows, blinds and dark heavy drapes kept the world at bay. The cabby halted and Miss Bellingham and her visitor alighted.

This was their destination, the residence of Catherine Burke, sole occupant, relict of Roderick Burke, a businessman who had been held in high esteem in his native city.

Miss Bellingham rapped gently with the great lion's head knocker and the door was opened to the sparse light of the hallway. Catherine Burke led the way through the drawing-room with its fine glowing fire to a room empty of everything except a circular table and five chairs. Two women sat there in silent welcome.

Catherine Burke addressed Veronica Carmody. "I am Catherine Burke," she said. "You have met Miss Bellingham. Those seated are also my friends."

They took places and settled. Veronica Carmody saw a great length of window curtain, and walls covered in pale green unpatterned paper. The floor was polished wood. It was bare except for their table and chairs. There was one door and one window and a wall-fitted gaslight that was turned down to a weak glimmer.

Catherine Burke asked, "Are you feeling at ease?"

"Yes."

"There is nothing to fear here. We know you are troubled and that your child is in the cemetery. Your home is disturbed and you are almost alone. We felt we could offer you comfort."

Veronica Carmody felt a warmth of happiness. The faces around her were those of kind women of reasonable years wearing clothes of good fabric and reserved in style.

"Yes, I am troubled," she said.

"You must have no fear in this house. We are friends not only in a time of misfortune. We are always here and we share a single faith. Once a month the Host is brought to me from the church, and I talk with the Divine Spirit and feel his strength entering my body. These are pure souls sitting here with you. Feel protected now, and in happiness. Let us pray."

Miss Bellingham stood, a strangely illuminated figure in the glimmering room. She removed an outer gown and stood in a long blue robe. Her hair was beautiful in this strange light, and as she stood with her hands joined at her breast, her purity reached out and embraced.

Veronica Carmody bowed her head.

Miss Bellingham prayed aloud:

Come Holy Ghost, Creator, come from thy bright heavenly throne,
Come take possession of our souls, and make them thy own.
Thou who are called the Paraclete, best gift of God above,
The living spirit, the living fire, sweet unction and true love.
Thou who are sevenfold in thy grace, finger of God's right hand;
His promise, teaching little ones to speak and understand.
O guide our minds with thy blessed light, with love our hearts inflame;
And with thy strength, which ne'er decays, confirm our mortal frame.

Far from us drive our deadly foe; true spirit to us bring;
And through all perils lead us safe beneath thy sacred wing.
Through thee may we the Father know, through thee the Eternal Son,
And thee, the Spirit of them both, thrice blessed Three In One.
All glory to the Father be, with his co-equal Son;
The same to thee, Great Paraclete, while endless ages run.

There was silence for moments, the outside world had dissolved and time had ceased. Veronica Carmody felt what might be the beauty of death.

Miss Bellingham spoke again: "Send forth thy Spirit and they shall be created."

Catherine Burke responded, "And thou shalt renew the face of the earth."

Then she rose, kissed the hands of this beautiful entity, and seated her. She stood hands outstretched, cruciform, a body without a cross. She moved and took her place at the table.

She said, "Amen."

From the stillness that had pervaded, there was movement now: the raising of heads, the clasping of hands. Only the lady in blue existed for Veronica Carmody; the rest dissolved into a white circle that might be shadow or substance.

Catherine Burke's voice was saying, "Can you hear me?"

"Yes," Veronica Carmody said.

"Let me talk to you about death. And after death."

"Yes."

"There is no place of reward. Or place of punishment. The spirit leaves the body to decay and goes on to greater good; or returns to evil.

"The spirits of the wholesome remain for a long time, here about us, perhaps until our grief is healed.

"Evil will wander the earth until it is destroyed; destroyed, made nothing, by the power that controls it."

It was almost a prayerful chant now.

"Evil assails country after country; makes the slave set himself above his place; makes the son of the house leave his father; makes the old into foolish men; makes a road of virtue to damnation. Demons lay snares for us and they are attended by innumerable armies, legions of darkness, who seek to undo all good and spread foulness and sin in their wake. A battle of good and evil. Demons have taken possession of the bodies of the impure. You sit with them in church or pass them in the street each day, or they share your workplace. When they are spent they are insane. That is their death.

"At the sight of the madman protect yourself with spittle from your mouth."

Catherine Burke bowed her head. "Divine Spirit, I pray thee watch over us unceasingly; protect us; visit us; defend us against every attack of evil, waking and sleeping, day and night; every hour and moment be our helper, everywhere be our companion."

"Amen," Veronica Carmody said.

"Your son is a child of purity. When his time on this earth is spent he will go out to limitless worlds. He will find peace. Look and see him now. Be still, watch."

Veronica Carmody looked and saw her son standing by the window. His face had such peace and happiness. He smiled at her. She felt no urge to move, only a great surging peace inside her. She was weeping.

The twilight of the room became a wash of colour, the silence was intense; not even a footfall from the winding street outside. Catherine Burke was speaking from a distance now, clear, distant words.

"Your child in its illness was touched by impure hands. But he is at rest now."

The colour was fading into darkness again, consuming the room and its supplicants. Veronica Carmody felt herself waking from sleep. She heard muted sounds of traffic from the street, the shifting coals and little pulses of heat. She opened her eyes on the familiar furnishings of her own kitchen: its table, its chairs, the dresser of delph, the chintz curtains that masked the ugliness of the coal yard.

She found herself on a plain board chair before the glowing bars of the range; iron wheels made sound on the roadway, passing voices drifted in, the noises of early evening. She was instantly wide awake, confused. She looked at an alarm-clock on the overmantel. It had scarcely turned seven o'clock. Immediate memory seemed to have deserted her. At seven o'clock she had been in the front-room parlour, putting up the notice that the coal yard was closed. And now, almost instantly, she had awakened in her chair by the stove. Had she walked from her front parlour to her kitchen and sat here and drifted into sleep? She looked at the clock again. Only moments, instants ago? If she had, then the memory of it was lost.

She sat back and closed her eyes, strangely at peace in the midst of such turmoil. She seemed surrounded by sleep again. She saw a beautiful young woman in blue, holding out her hands to her in reassurance. Then the picture faded and she was alone again. Now she remembered words, as if she had learned them like schooltime verse. "Your child in its illness was touched by impure hands." She searched but there was nothing more. She stood and looked at the clock again.

It was half past ten!

The evening was gone, the night eroding away! There was food to be prepared for his arrival! The time! She felt her cheeks and found they were damp. She had been in tears? There was no recollection of it.

Then the pleasant smell of food came to her. She walked slowly to the oven door of the range and opened it. There was a plate and a cover. She took a cloth and lifted them out. The food was what she would have chosen, and it was cooked and arranged in her own precise style. It was warm and ready. A piece of time was missing, she knew.

She went to her bedroom and, in its bareness, dried and powdered her face, arranged her hair. She went back to sit in the kitchen and waited.

Carmody arrived when it was past eleven thirty. He cleaned his feet on the hallway mat, hung his coat and cap on the upright free-standing hanger with its sprouting wooden pegs. Like everything, it was polished and shone. He smelt the food; there was light in the kitchen.

As he entered, he saw Veronica setting his place at the table: she put down a colourful piece of American oilcloth, two knives, a fork, a side plate, pepper and salt. Carmody might be man of the house, in command, but for the etiquette of the future life they were planning she was his mentor. Her father had had a sand-cot on the river, a couple of miles above the city; he worked hard days and earned small money, and had died on the threshold of sixty years. He had been unloading sand on to the hard stone bank of the canal when he toppled. He was dead on arrival at the County Infirmary. His wife had been in service before she married him and brought skills to her daughters. Veronica had three sisters who were in Pennsylvania – Allentown, Harrisburg, Lancaster – and had married well. Veronica was glad that her parents had both been in the church on her wedding day. They were lying side by side in the cemetery now, close to the tall boundary wall with the lunatic asylum: the dead and the living dead.

Carmody's salutation was a single word of Gaelic: "Beannacht." It meant a blessing. He passed through the kitchen to the scullery, which was also neat and shining. It had a square glazed sink, a draining board and a single tap for cold water. Carmody never used hot water; even down at the Island Baths, once a week, he soaped down and punished himself in the icy river. He hung his jacket on the door now and washed and sluiced his face. A fresh towel was always ready for him.

When he reached the kitchen again his food was on the table. Carmody was a big eater. With a fork he split a potato, speared it with vegetables, and filled his mouth.

He said, "There wasn't need for you to wait up. I can take food from the oven and pick myself a knife and fork."

This was a frequent litany.

"You didn't leave an untidy job after you in the docks today, did you?" she asked.

"I start a job, I finish it."

"This is my job. I'm you wife."

He nodded his head towards his plate; that was his apology.

"And you don't have food in your mouth when you speak. You use a knife and fork and lay them on your plate while you are chewing. You use the large knife. You wanted to know all these things, remember?"

"Dammit, woman, I'm at home. Not in the Royal George."

"Home is where you learn."

He picked up the knife. "Yes."

"You want to make a place for yourself in politics, you say. You must know how to dress, to behave, to eat." She turned her chair away from him. "I have time on my hands these empty days. I'll cook you a four course meal soon, and you can see all the cutlery that goes with it. Politicians need competent wives."

He looked at her back, the erect head, the fine hair. She was clean and neat as a pin. He was eating again, but remembering her instruction. All Carmody's meetings and involvements, charities, sporting clubs, religion even, had a deep underlay of politics.

"How were things in the coal yard?" he asked.

"It can take four pounds a week without too much trouble."

"Yes."

"And a lot more as I work at it."

"Yes."

"You'll be a businessman. That's the road to politics."

"Yes."

She allowed him to eat in silence now as she looked at the lessening glow of the fire. The prepared food that she could never remember cooking brought her no unease, but she was searching in her mind for some glimmer of light. Suddenly she climbed the stairs to her bedroom. Hat, coat, gloves were undisturbed. She looked at them only to put her mind at rest; she had no recollection of ever leaving the house. She came back to the kitchen and took her seat. Time had sped, the evening had vanished. Seven o'clock she had been in the parlour; then time had been stolen. The young woman in blue, her calm, her comfort? And the words she had spoken?

She heard the movement of his chair.

She said, "Do you think I'm a person whose judgment can be trusted?"

"Yes."

"Not given to flurry or excitedness?"

"No."

She told him of her missing hours, of awakening suddenly to find time had flown.

She said, "I didn't seem to wake from *sleep*. I was in the parlour and then suddenly here. I don't remember cooking your food. In an instant three and a half hours had gone. Can you explain it?"

"No," he said.

"There was . . .," she paused, "what you might call a 'vision', too."

Carmody was sitting upright in his chair. "A vision?"

"An apparition, something like that. It might even have been a dream. But dreams fade in our minds in seconds. This one remained."

Carmody came round to face her. "What was it?"

"A beautiful young woman in a long, pale blue robe, holding out her hands to me. She brought comfort with her. There was no fear."

"Where?"

"Here. By the table where you have been eating."

Carmody looked at the table and the curtained windows behind it. "Here in this kitchen?"

"Yes."

"Did she speak?"

"Yes."

Carmody took a chair and sat facing her. "Don't rush," he said. "Take time to remember. Are you afraid now?"

"I said she brought comfort, peace."

"Yes?"

"She spoke. She said, 'Your child in its illness was touched by impure hands. He is at rest.'"

Carmody stood still for moments, breathless with astonishment. "You're sure? Those were the words?"

"'Your child in its illness was touched by impure hands. He is at rest.' Those were her words."

Carmody was on his knees. "It is time for us to pray," he said. The sharpness, for an instant, was gone from his voice; he was talking softly to her.

She knelt.

Carmody took his rosary beads from his pocket, crystal glass that had been brought to him from Rome by Dr Paul Cafferey. They had been blessed by the Holy Father, the Pontiff Pius XI, and its pendant crucifix held a relic, threads from a garment of Peter, first Vicar of Christ on earth.

The small pouch that held it was of pale kid-skin leather.

He recited the Five Joyful Mysteries and she responded. It took twenty minutes at his slow devotional pace. Then there was silent meditation. Late night street noises came from the emptying pubs. The wind from the chimney pots struggled in the flue and stirred the remnant coals in the range.

She waited until he was standing before she got from her knees. He was restless in excitement, pacing about, turning erratically, on the point of saying something and then lapsing into silence again.

"Sit for a little while," he said with the same absence of sharpness.

"I can make a pot of tea," she said.

"No, no."

She sat and waited and finally interrupted his agitated pacing. "Do you think it was real?"

"Real?"

"Yes, or just a piece of a dream."

Stillness settled on him as he stared at her and dropped his voice to a whisper. "The Virgin Mother of God came to you in this kitchen tonight. She bestowed Heaven's honour on you. On us." For moments he looked up at the ceiling in prayer. "Came to tell us that our son is in her loving care. And to warn us against evil, poisoned hands."

"Poisoned hands?"

"That renegade butcher who put a knife into my child's throat. I'll see the end of him, drive him out. Bennett. The whole clutch of them and their spawn. I'll drive them out, burn them out."

"You did your burning," she said. "Those days are over. This is a time of politics. There are quiet ways to rid the town of Protestants. Half of them have fled already."

She paused. "The Mother of God who was in this kitchen tonight might have been the work of my imagination. We must be careful, no word of it spoken outside this house."

"She honoured you, and we must show gratitude until death."

"And remain silent. Who would believe us? What is there to show?"

He thought about it. "Yes," he agreed.

"We can pray to her."

"I pray to her every day," Carmody said. "The Mother of God in our city! You heard that a statue is weeping? Yes, a dozen people have seen it. A dozen imaginations? The Mother of God. She will drive out this plague of sickness. I will drive out the Bennetts, the poisoned hands."

Veronica Carmody gathered up the soiled dishes and cutlery and took them out to the scullery.

CHAPTER THIRTEEN

ARNOLD'S HOUSE, LIKE those of his siblings, was in the fashionable nucleus of the city centre. His four-storey and basemented dwelling in a brown-brick Georgian terrace fronted on to the main street of the city at a point where it had left behind the business houses, the hotels, the traffic, and broadened for a short stretch into what was called the Crescent. It was a fine area of substance; an elite Catholic church and a day school had only added to its excellence. Beyond it, and hidden away, had been the garrison barracks, which now housed the Free State army. The area of poverty that existed always somewhere close to soldiery was distant and unseen.

This was hilly ground before the city gave way to the race-course and the open countryside. Another great Catholic church sat on the peak and beyond it a private school of distinction.

As he sat in the study of his private home now, sounds from the basement kitchen reached him occasionally, moments of laughter. Then silence again. He employed a staff of four: a cook-housekeeper, a housemaid, a young starter for the scullery and a handyman.

The Bennetts had lived in this city for more than a hundred years. These shallow opposing parabolas of elegant buildings looked out on a bronze commemorative statue of a great man of conviction, of peace, who had tried to heal wounds and build bridges; and had failed. Where his railed effigy stood now had been a bandstand once and, on sunny days, the garrison band would march down the hill to play for young ladies and their gallants, costumed and coiffed in their balcony windows. Men of rank, of title, hidalgos perhaps, had lived here, but the raising of a monument to a patriotic man of great intellect, a Catholic, had sent some flying in horror to the salubrious countryside.

The Bennetts had remained; they had seen small famines and the Great Famine, little rebellions and lesser ones, and they had never been plundered. The rebels had often been of rank and of their own persuasion, sometimes armed with just cause, sometimes mistaken. An ancestor's word had been passed down to them, and remembered even today: "Be Good Citizens." The freedom that had been won was the Bennetts' freedom too.

Arnold remembered the rebellion of '16 and the awful revenge of a government and its military buffoon; and the unleashing of post-war delinquents to terrorise and brutalise a nation.

He remembered the strike and the City Soviet; he remembered the awful arrival of death that had come with the Spanish flu, ten years ago.

Then peace and freedom and war again, civil war, savagery, brutality, hatred. Where did hatred come from?

It was over now, they said. A new government was in place, with an army and a police force to ensure peace in a free country.

But it wasn't over, Arnold knew. There were still guns and

gunmen out there; every day blood was spilt, and property looted and razed.

His telephone rang. "Yes," he said.

"This is Mulvey. I've been at the storehouse."

"Bad?"

"Burnt out."

"Can you come and see me?"

"Yes."

Dockside storage had been set ablaze; there had been looting and pillage. Arnold had telephoned his insurers for an assessment. He had telephoned a contractor, too, a city man born and bred, a friend, a Catholic who did maintenance on all the Bennett property, private or commercial. He had told him to start his work and they could talk prices another day.

News of the burning and looting had shocked and angered Arnold. The Bennetts had never been victimised. He gave employment from year to year, he thought angrily, he paid a fair wage, he gave anonymously to charities and hospitals. This city was his home.

The family had had good fortune; and bad fortune, too. Thaddeus was dedicated to his medicine and didn't particularly need the income he made from the family business. But Matilda would die soon, of course, and Abigail might have plans for her life; she might want to escape. Thaddeus would be left alone in his beautiful house.

Loneliness was part of living. Arnold was a businessman, clever, a shrewd merchant. He had taken the reins from his father, travelled and swelled the trade. All the Bennetts were partners; they shared prosperity. But Arnold was alone in his house with only the servants. His family life had disintegrated. His son, Harry, had been the grain of sand around which a great ulcerous mass had accumulated; his drinking and whoring, from schooldays, had been unmanageable, and now he was locked away, a wasted syphilitic frame with madness creeping into his mind. His sister, Dorcas, had fled. She was somewhere abroad with an army nursing corps; she was happy and progressing.

Lillian and Edward had married too late for children, but they had a great happiness and, Arnold knew, it would last. Lillian and Edward were made to last.

The business, he thought again? When the time came perhaps Thaddeus' boys would take the family helm from his hands.

Lucy, Arnie's housekeeper, knocked on the door and entered. "There's a man here to see you, Mr Arnold. He's in the hallway." Lucy was careful with her use of the word "gentleman". "He calls himself Mulvey, Mr Arnold."

"Thank you, Lucy. Take his coat and things. You can bring him here."

In a few moments Mulvey was sitting facing Arnold across his desk.

"Thank you for coming," Arnold said. "You can talk. I'll listen for a while." He offered cigarettes and they both smoked.

Mulvey was strong; tall but not too tall. He had dark hair without a rib of grey and his face was unremarkable.

"It's a total loss. The building and the contents. There is evidence of looting before they set it off. They used petrol, thirty, forty gallons, I'd reckon, and opened the windows to make a draught. They know their business. A lot of petrol cans. The firemen contained the blaze, and it didn't spread to other units. The Gardaí were there this morning. Just a quick look about and move on."

"And not a can in sight?"

"No. I walked the ground."

"What can I do?"

"Against terrorists, very little. They move like shadows."

Arnie nodded. "We were a target?"

"Yes."

"First time in a hundred years."

"Someone has put a marker on you."

"Any suspicions?"

Mulvey paused. "Not long ago, your sister's soup kitchen was burned? And there was a death. Heart failure. Your brother-in-law, Edward Burke, was waylaid."

"He reported the fire."

"Yes." He paused.

Arnie said, "Can we trust the police, the Gardaí?"

"Yes, I would say. But it takes only one listening post to pass on news. You reported your dockland fire to the Gardaí, of course?"

"Yes."

John Mulvey had spent twenty years in colonial law enforcement. The son of an old constabulary sergeant, he had emigrated at the age of eighteen. He was forty-eight now. Now, ostensibly, he was a senior official in the city's George's Street Bank. He had a private office there, with living accommodation and transport close at hand. And he had a title – Regional Security Officer – but no dealings with routine day-to-day banking. His brief was the care of certain preferential customers of the bank. These were times of subterfuge and criminality.

Arnold said, "You've been six years in the city?"

"Six years almost."

"You like it?"

"My parents had retired here. I came to see their grave."

Arnie sat and smoked. Revolution made the sticks and stones. The winners sat in government; the losers were pausing for breath. Governments need to survive. Losers have nothing to lose.

"A Free State," Arnie thought aloud.

"That pays allegiance to an old monarchy, and pierces republican souls."

Arnie nodded. "They still burn and pillage. Some day they'll inherit the chaos they are creating. It's an old political story."

There was a knock on the door and Lucy reappeared.

"Everything's ready now, sir. And the family is here."

When she had gone, Arnold said, "No sleep last night. I need a drink. Will you join me?"

"Yes."

"Whiskey?"

"Yes."

He took a decanter from a cabinet and two glasses, and poured drinks. He liked Mulvey. They drank.

Mulvey said, "Your family is here?"

"The Bennett family. All of them are shareholders. We meet here from time to time. I'd like you to be present. The old people live in the country. They're getting on a bit. No point in shattering their peace."

"No." Mulvey was thoughtful.

"Are they in danger?"

"They live alone?"

"Servants, of course. And a driver. I'll put him on the alert."

Arnie walked to the window and looked out at the statue of the man of peace, where once a gilded army band had been seated, sounding muted brass melodies for lovers, triflers, coquettes, during a time of uneasy occupation.

They raised their glasses and drank.

"Come," Arnie said. "It's time."

At the end of the hallway Lucy announced them and left them in privacy. It was a fine room of good drapery and polished wood. Food had been laid out: plates of small sandwiches, biscuits, fruit. Waiting there were Thaddeus and Lillian and Edward Burke.

Arnie announced names and said, "This is John Mulvey." He motioned them to their seats and sat at the head of the table himself. Mulvey sat beside him.

"Take some food," Arnie addressed them all. "I don't want to lose my housekeeper, too."

People smiled again for a moment.

"I telephoned you because there was a fire at one of our

storehouses last night. A serious fire. The building was destroyed, the stock lost. Insurance will cover our losses, but there may be a period of some erratic service to our customers. I telephoned the Gardaí and had a response. They will be investigating the occurrence if malicious intent is suspected."

Arnie paused and waited; he felt he was orating, not speaking.

He said, "This is John Mulvey, who is Regional Security Officer contracted by the bank. He will talk to you in a few moments. I told him that we have never suffered harassment. We have made money when others haven't, but we have given money, too. There is danger now, I think. A time of decision. Many have taken leave of the country. Landowners have left agents to salvage something. They won't be missed. We are part of this city and its trade. We give employment. At the top, we ourselves are workers. . . ." Arnold paused. "Do we stand our ground or go like so many others?"

He looked from face to face.

"Taddy?"

"Stay."

"Edward, Lillian?"

"We stay."

Arnie said, "And I am staying. We, all of us, are staying." He took his seat and nodded to Mulvey.

Mulvey, suited in dark serge, and with a white stiff collar and open-knitted tie, had a military sharpness about him. He was an impressive figure. He stood and paced about slowly on a chosen track, then stopped and faced them. He said, "I've been moving about this city, and the county, since the cessation of warfare. I work at the bank in George's Street, but I am not a bank official. You could call me a watch-dog. The bank contracts me. My name isn't on a door or a window. Few people know me. The security of the bank and some of its listed customers is my warrant. Locks on vaults or doors or windows is bank staff responsibility. Robbery, larceny, violence, pillage: I listen for whispers of them and try to forestall them. I've had good results, but some failures, too." Mulvey paused a while; eventually he said, "There are republican cells in the city. Some of them are clever people, as watchful perhaps as I am. We watch each other. Some of them tire, vanish, emigrate. Fresh ones spring up. There is always danger."

Mulvey paced about again, longer this time, then took his seat at the table. He was relaxed, at ease.

He was very brief. He turned to Lillian Burke. "You had a soup kitchen?" he asked.

"Yes."

"No threats?"

"None."

"You weren't proselytising?"

"No."

"A march of protest was made to your door and someone addressed them. A rousing speech?"

Lillian Burke said, "Yes."

"I was there," Mulvey said. "It was well planned."

Edward Burke thought that Mulvey would be a hard man in a brawl. He looked up and found that Mulvey was staring at him.

Mulvey smiled. "You were standing at the head of the alleyway," he said.

"Yes," Edward nodded.

"And on your way from the police station you were ambushed. How many?"

"Three, I think."

"It was dark?"

"Between lamp-lights."

"No one was recognisable?"

Edward paused. "Perhaps a voice," he said.

Mulvey waited.

"It sounded like the voice of the speech-maker."

"The religious one?"

"Yes."

Mulvey was thoughtful. In every pack, from struggle and confusion, the strong man appears, not necessarily the most balanced, the most gifted, but the most ruthless, the most intransigent. When he speaks the soldiers listen. In a schoolyard he might be the bull-headed one. If he knows God is on his side, he is dangerous. The crucible pushes a lot of waste to its surface and the pure metal beneath is unseen.

Mulvey had seen the speech-maker, but the face had been muffled. He was a new entity in this troubled sea of hatred. A cap, a scarf and glasses gave him anonymity to a stranger. The crowd would recognise him; this was a small city. But, whether he was held in esteem or disapprobation, lips would be held tight. In these days anyone might be an enemy. Mulvey rarely talked to people on the streets. He watched and knew that, with patience, the information would come to him. Sometimes the bank's brougham and driver took him from place to place. At other times he would walk, observe, listen.

He explained to the Bennett family and Edward Burke, "I don't accost or arrest people, I am just another citizen. You'll understand, I don't ever expose my hand, but danger can be curbed or removed."

He turned to Thaddeus. "Dr Bennett."

Thaddeus's placid worn face looked at him.

"The other members of your family have suffered wilful destruction, arson of property, a serious assault inflicting injury. Have you personally been attacked? Or your property damaged?"

Thaddeus thought for moments. "No. These are busy times with a lot of sickness, especially among the poor. I get home to spend an hour with my wife and daughter. And then sleep."

Mulvey said, "Doctors heal the wounds of patients. Patients are not in the habit of wounding doctors. At this moment you are unscathed?"

Thaddeus liked the calm, almost too quiet, approach of

Mulvey. He was strong, healthy. He said, "Sick people want to escape pain, weakness. They need to talk to someone, but they don't need wrangling, contention. Later, in a hospital bed if health returns, they can vent their unkindness on young student nurses. But nurses are a hardy breed, I know from experience."

Thaddeus brought a breath of humour to the company; people were animated, seeing each other again.

Thaddeus waited for a moment or two and said to Mulvey, "Illness we always have in plenty. There is bother from time to time with parents. Understandable."

"Bother?" Mulvey repeated.

"Diphtheria should be treated in isolation, but we haven't units or beds to cope. Some of them survive, some of them die in their own hovels, spreading death as they go. We fight a losing battle. Diphtheria plans its own departure. It attacks the poor, of course, because whole families live in one or two rooms. But no one is safe. The rich, the wealthy, the comfortable, shopkeepers, clerks, artisans. Doctors, too."

Thaddeus smiled. "I'm rambling on," he said.

Mulvey said, "No damage then?"

"I'm showing signs of wear, that's all." Thaddeus smiled. Then he remembered. "There was an awkward incident at the City Home recently. I had almost forgotten it. So many cases."

"Violent?"

"I was threatened," Taddy said. "It can happen from time to time. Parents are naturally overwrought when death occurs. The matron saw him off the premises. A strong woman. Almost manhandled him."

"The patient died?"

"A young boy, hardly in his mid-teens, a comfortable enough home, I'm told. An only son, an only child. He was overprotected by neglect. A chill, a fever, a slight soreness of throat. People don't suspect diphtheria. Just a cold; it'll pass."

"Just a cold, someone thought? A home-doctor?"

"Yes, a domestic diagnosis. There isn't a high temperature. But a swollen throat and difficulty in swallowing should have set the bell ringing."

"Who was the home-doctor? The father?"

"Yes. I can't remember his name," Taddy said. "Different faces every day. A district nurse left word for me. It was somewhere in the old city."

"The district nurse?"

"A blank, I'm afraid."

"The father?"

"He was at work. Where I don't know. His son got the last isolation bed in the City Home. This man called it the workhouse. It used to be a workhouse, of course, but it has an isolation wing. I met him there, a great raging bull of a man. But he had wasted seven days of a dying child."

"You didn't tell him that?"

"The matron talked to him. Didn't leave him in any doubt. I told him surgery was necessary." Thaddeus looked at Mulvey. "A tracheotomy, you know, to allow the child to breathe. But he was beyond saving. He died."

"This man who threatened you, the matron manhandled him?"

Thaddeus paused for a moment. "The matron," he said, "is dead. There was a fire in her office."

Mulvey went to the window and stood there for moments; he turned. "But the man knew your face?"

"Yes, and my religion. My religion didn't seem to please him."

"What was his address?"

Taddy said, "I don't know. Somewhere in Irishtown. A lot of narrow streets and laneways there, but it is a fair house, in good condition, I was told. But there are hospital records at the City Home. Tell them my story. They'll find them. The last I saw of the unfortunate man he was sitting in the hospital grounds."

CHAPTER FOURTEEN

CIGARETTE SMOKE HUNG in the air, weaving patterns for moments before it was drawn towards the fire and the drag of air in the chimney flue. Lillian broke the silence Mulvey had left behind him when he departed.

She looked at Thaddeus. "You didn't tell us," she said.

Arnie had rung the table bell, and when the housekeeper arrived, he said, "Bring some tea, Lucy."

She hurried away.

Thaddeus said, "The matron? I haven't seen you since then. Confronted with death, not everyone is silent, resigned. If tears come, it's a good thing. But to lose a child, an only child. Sometimes, rage. He was an awkward man. Doctors meet them very occasionally."

Lillian said, "He threatened you?"

"He was angry and nearly incoherent. I hardly remember his face, and I don't know his name or his dwelling. He had a distinctive voice."

Edward Burke stood and walked to the window. The patriot, in toga-long cloak, stood on his pedestal, a Caesar looking over a victorious, bloodless battlefield. A drizzle of rain, came upriver from the south-west and settled on the rooftops, seemed to distance the world from them.

Across the way, the Catholic Church of the Company of Don Inigo de Recalde, men of hyperacuity, of prayer and politics, whose part in establishing the God-like infallibility of Rome less than sixty years past had set them apart from their fellow workers in the vineyard. They had been banished from whole tracts of Europe. Don Inigo, once the ardent soldier of fire and sword, for centuries beatified and sainted, had become the champion of Irish Catholic wealth, moulded their children, created a freemasonry of the privileged. Don Inigo de Recalde. Even their church had taken root here in an enclave of Georgian grandeur. Edward looked at its unassuming facade. Working-class feet didn't cross their threshold to kneel and pray and look for weeping statues. They were a breed apart. Horses for courses.

Edward thought now of the rabble-rouser on the night of the soup kitchen disaster, and the death of Lucy Langford. He called to Thaddeus, "I'd remember that man's voice. And his shape."

"His face?" Thaddeus asked.

Edward was silent.

"A figure can fit a gallery of faces."

"The voice had a piercing ring," Edward said.

Thaddeus considered it. "That piece could fit," he said. "Shouldn't we let the whole thing pass without comment?"

"Do we have a choice?" Edward asked. "Lillian and Lucy Langford. Arnold's storehouse razed. He's bringing the war to us."

Lucy knocked and brought the tea. She poured it carefully and left sugar and milk within everyone's reach.

Arnie said, "Taddy is a man of peace. I admire him. He works a hard day. All of us work a hard day. But business and property is our livelihood. We must defend it."

Arnie thought of his son, and heir, Harry, rotting with corrosive illness in the remote parts of a nursing home. He had loved him. In his early wildness he had seen only the emergence of strength and confidence. He had heard of his drinking. But news of his whoring came like a bombshell. Now madness and rigor were seizing him. An awful passage of death. His beautiful sister, Dorcas, had fled from it.

And, Arnie thought, his own wife, Ethel, had deserted the ship. She had been shocked at the whispered scandal; deeply wounded and in fear. With her daughter, she had left him in an empty beautiful house with only servants for company. He was glad she was independent, a person of means; she had repudiated benefits from the Bennett Estate. She had been so beautiful, he remembered.

Once they had been a family of four in a house of noise and laughter, of comings and goings, of love. Arnie had been so confident. Once this house had been alert, looking into the future, holding a steady course. Now he wondered if he had ever been loved in this place of comfort and emptiness.

But he had the ship of Bennett and Company to steer; that was his responsibility, his inheritance. No one would burn him out or dent his courage. Generations of Bennetts had been born in this city; they cherished it, it was their home. They had worked at being patriotic and just. The family vault at the old cathedral held their coffins, told their stories. Arnie knew he was angry, and anger was dangerous.

There were only murmurs of talk at the table, the tiny ring of china.

He held out cigarettes.

Taddy held his polished holder. "I'm smoking," he said.

Edward took a cigarette. Lillian sat close to him. He looked at the kindness of her eyes. He could remember the softness of her body when they were close at night-time, the moments of love-making, the words spoken before they drifted into sleep. He remembered the flames and the smashing of furniture at her kitchen, the awful overpowering lash of religiosity. He remembered the voice, the hammering of fists, the thud of boots. He remembered Lucy Langford's funeral and tears wept by Lillian in the privacy of her own house. Edward Burke, too, was angry.

Edward's father had known the Protestant and Catholic patriots of the century that had passed, had met and spoken with them, supported their causes, stuck with them through scandal and the scurrilous abuse of the Hierarchy. He had worn a black tie when their champion had died.

Edward had loved his father. The dwelling-house was a place of great comfort on the very fringes of the old city. That, Edward thought, had given him comfort and pride. He was city-stock. But it had displeased Catherine, his wife. She would have preferred the new city of brown brick and the importance it had, to drive in her finery through it. A cold, proud person.

Edward remembered that she had never talked to her servants; in her unemotional flat tones she had driven them. He thought of his own breathless passion with Lillian. Had she ever softened into moments of love? Her locked bedroom with access only to Francis, his brother, fourteen years his senior. To a child of five it was just a pattern of living, a room shared, one bed or two beds. He had never known. Had she been promiscuous, was he a bastard? She was too cold for promiscuity, and the penetration of sex would always have been a debasement. A cold, corpse-like woman, she had never wept for his father's death.

He looked about the silent table now, at the comfort of the room and its glowing fire. There was warmth and love here. There had been comfort and warmth in his own house, too, but only his father's love. His spent cigarette had been wasting on an ashtray; he crushed and discarded it.

Lillian spoke into the stillness, saying to Thaddeus, "You look tired, Taddy."

Taddy said, "This diphtheria is taking lives. A lot of lives."

"You must take care of yourself."

"Brigid is a good housekeeper. She cares for us all. Warmth, food. The house is shining."

A few moments' silence passed before Lillian asked, "Matilda?"

"She's failing, Lillian, confined to bed. Almost three months now. She used to like sitting in her basket chair for an hour or two, looking across the park, the flowers and shrubs and Monteagle's monument. She's weaker now, drowses a lot. Only a matter of time, a short time."

"How is Abigail?"

"Abigail is well." Taddy paused. "When everything is over, she'll go to nurse at Barrington's, she tells me."

"Barrington's! At home. Marvellous."

"She could be a fine nurse. A fine doctor. But I won't interfere."

Taddy thought of his two sons at business in Dublin; they were experienced young men now. They would come to Arnie's aid in illness or retirement. He looked about at family members, and at Lillian and her husband, Edward Burke. He thought of family parents in their house by the tumbling river water. They had been respected in a lifetime of city business; and had had their years of grief, too. Two sons killed for Empire by Dutch South Africans. A prissy little overbearing queen had sent off her armies to silence these tribesmen, and politicians had applauded. Bennett bodies were buried there, somewhere. A friend from the War Office had mentioned once the battlefield burials, the horrible mutilations. The Irish had been in so many wars.

Arnie was speaking; he said, "Good. We've eaten half the food, at least. Lucy will be pleased."

Lillian said, "I'll have a special word with her before I leave."

Arnie hardly paused. "When the first Bennett set foot here," he said, "there had been an Irish parliament that might have survived. But members were bought and sold, and it was abolished. London would rule from Westminster. It was fear of the French, of course . . .."

The company began to disperse.

"I must go," said Taddy. "The theatre at Barrington's and then house calls."

Edward halted him. "Be careful, Taddy," he said. "There's a whisper abroad that incompetence at the City Home killed a young schoolboy. You smelt of alcohol. That's how the story goes."

Thaddeus stood in shock.

"He came to the hospital too late. He was dying. He was home-doctored. The parent was the culprit."

"His father?"

"Yes."

Edward nodded.

Thaddeus looked at them all; he said, "I drink just a very little in times like these." He took a four-ounce flask from his pocket. "Perhaps a couple of ounces a day. Three, four sips. The smells, the disease, the dirt. It's difficult," he said. "Sometimes I'd like to be a drunkard, but surgery calls for a steady hand." He nodded his thanks to Edward. "I'll be careful."

Thaddeus walked away; they listened to his footsteps on the stairs as Lucy escorted him to the hall door.

Arnie said, "He works, works, works. That's his therapy. It keeps that sickroom and Matilda and Abigail at a distance. It seems such a short time since she was well and her boys and Abigail were full of noise."

Lillian went to Arnie and embraced him; he carried his troubles well. They went downstairs.

In the hallway Arnie stopped and faced them. "I'm going to Castleconnell," he said. "I telephone them, of course, but I like to call from time to time. Why don't you come with me?"

"Oh yes, Edward," Lillian said. "It'll be a pleasant few hours. It's peaceful there."

And isolated, Arnie was thinking.

Arnie was wearing tweeds and he took a cap from the hall-stand and a three-quarter length driving coat. His car was big and comfortable. They drove down George's Street to the river that had split to embrace the historic island. The tall imposing hospital looked across the water at them. They turned right at the canal gates, where barges were loading and sand-cots had left their yellow pyramids along the banks.

Arnie sped along at road-hogging speed on an almost empty road. The Georgian houses were here, too, their high steps and hall doors mouldering. They passed the convent for fallen women, moved into the country, climbed the steep hill of hedgerows and small trees and the ruin of a little fortress. Rich meadowland surrounded them. It was a main road from the city with a surface that was fair for miles and then suddenly became a bumpier ride when they swung away to the left towards the river.

The house, the Hermitage, didn't cover a large space. It was a two-storey building, ivy laden, surrounded on three sides by a tall stockade of beeches; across a terraced garden it faced the rush of water. A gardener raised his hat and a housekeeper came down steps to meet them.

Arnie said, "I can see you're worried about food, Jessie."

"You weren't expected, Mr Arnold."

"We didn't come to eat."

She led them through a semi-circular reception space to the drawing-room. Its french windows looked out at the riverbanks.

John and Alexandra Bennett, smart and well-kept, were ageing with dignity. Alexandra, a small, neat, confident person, wore a dress of Liberty fabric and a scarf on her shoulders. John Bennett, who had weathered a life of political strife and survived all the storms of trade, of embargoes and depressions, was tall, spare, straight as a ramrod with short grizzled hair. His house had all the comforts he had earned about him.

Both of them came to Edward, took his hands. "You don't come often enough, Edward. It's always good to see you. Does Lillian take good care of you? She used to be a wild young thing."

Lillian laughed. "Thirty years ago."

John Bennett brought whiskey and sherry and poured drinks; a coal fire gave warmth and brightness to the room; they sat facing the gardens and the river.

John Bennett said, "There's peace and quiet here. We get reports of little fracas from the city. They'll pass. How's trade?"

Arnie said, "Fine. Not a ripple. No trouble in the countryside, you say? A quiet life."

John Bennett said, "Yes, a quiet life."

Edward, as on his previous visits, found Lillian's parents' home a place of comfort, warmth and hospitality. This had been a house of movement and noise, laughter and tears, too, he didn't doubt. People talked here. His own house had been almost silent. Once Lillian had shown him the room close to the library that had been a classroom for three hours a day. John Bennett had engaged a live-in tutor to prepare them all for boarding school at twelve. He thought you should be careful not to tire children, not to cram them.

Home-school had its share of talking and laughing, too. The tutor was suitably grey-haired and bespectacled who had seen better days in government service; and had a private pension. He looked as if he might never grow old. He was always gathering knowledge and waiting to spread it.

He had his bedroom and private study, but spent hours here in this room with the family, sat with them at table, walked and fished with John Bennett. He was an Anglican from County Antrim who had fled from the awful fundamentalism of political religion and found happiness here with the Bennetts during his last fifteen years of life. He was buried in the church cemetery, but, if spirits left their graves, perhaps he still walked the paths and fished the pools or spent hours in his beloved library.

He used to quote:

And the night shall be filled with music,
And the cares that infest the day

Shall fold their tents like the Arabs
And silently steal away.

The room was alive with talk now, desultory, but always animated and mixed with laughter. The days were shortening, Lillian was saying, they shouldn't stay late into the afternoon. She didn't enjoy speeding along dark bumpy roads with Arnie, who should have been a racing driver.

Edward had wandered to one of the great casement windows, looking across the flower beds to the river paths and clusters of ancient trees. Only a light breeze stirred the brittle leaves, sending one floating down on the green margin by the flower stalks. Edward would talk to Lillian, he decided, agree with her: they should have a car. They could visit more often. It would please Lillian.

Behind the shrubberies there was movement. A gardener, Edward thought. He waited for him to emerge. An animal, a fox, a rabbit? Arnie had come on this visit today, Edward was sure, to see that the house and its occupants were in safety.

He stood back from the window, out of sight. Suddenly he saw a stooped figure move from one place of seclusion to another. A moment only. Had he been carrying something? At the end of the garden, across the pathway, the grass sloped gently away on to flat exposed rock where the hidden slab of the river bed, resisting the great flow, churned the water into the white torrent.

There was movement there, too, at the riverbank extremity. A head and shoulders for an instant, then only the stir of breeze on foliage. Edward moved to the next window, one which looked downstream to where the fall of water had reached a temporary rest and spread into a great pool of stillness ruffled only by the central current.

He turned back to look across the room. John Bennett was reading a newspaper that Arnie had brought, Lillian was sitting close to her mother and Arnie was seated alone beneath an almost biblical cloud of cigarette smoke. Edward very carefully, with a slight motion of his head, signalled to him. Arnie, casually and without hurry, strolled over to Edward.

"How many gardeners have you?" Edward asked.

"One. Tall, thin as a rake and grey."

"No one else out of doors?"

"A driver-handyman. We passed him at the gate lodge."

"Then," Edward said, "we have visitors."

"You saw someone?"

"I saw two heads and shoulders down there. Skipping into cover. There could be more. They seemed to be carrying something."

Arnie said, "We'll walk to the front of the house." They crossed the room and moved out into the semi-circle of foyer. Arnie took walking sticks from the hallstand and handed one to Edward.

Edward said, "They'll be armed."

"If we see guns, we run, take cover. They'll be running, too."

Suddenly the front door from the steps and portico was thrown open from the outside by Jessie, the housekeeper, who was wide-eyed in terror and bracing herself to scream. Arnie got to her, clamped a hand on her mouth and eased her into a chair. He put a finger to his lips for silence.

She nodded.

"What's wrong?"

"Hartigan the gardener is covered in blood."

"Where?"

"In the shrubbery."

"Go to the kitchen. Don't answer bells. Talk to no one. Understood?"

"Yes."

He nodded to Edward. Travelling fast and taking what cover they could, they went out to the front drive and moved towards the pathway, paved with dressed flagstones and limestone-kerbed, that led down to the river's edge and a dense wind-break of shrubbery. The broad river stretched out of sight towards the village.

"Petrol," Edward pointed.

Beneath the sill of the gable-end window of the house were four metal containers.

"Twenty gallons," Arnie said.

"They've gone for more."

Arnie looked upriver. "The breeze is blowing at us. A forced window, a flood of spirit, a match, the breeze to catch the flame. The end of the Hermitage."

"And now?" Edward asked.

Arnie was in doubt.

"Do we wait for them?"

"No," Edward said. "We don't want a pitched battle. We can spike their guns."

"Guns?"

"The spirit."

Arnie was already in motion. They brought out the cans and unscrewed them, tipped them on their sides and sent a little minor cascade of petrol rolling past the garden to the riverbank. The petroleum smell rose up about them.

Edward said, "Listen!"

There was the sound of heavy metal cans being dropped. Arnie said, "They're moving out!"

Arnie started running, but Edward caught him up and halted him. "Easy," he whispered.

Arnie said, "There's a pool below the fall. They crossed from the other side. That's six hundred feet."

They came to the escarpment rising up from the pool. A flat-bottomed fishing punt was almost midway across; two men used paddles to skim it against the current before it drifted into the calm shallows of the opposite bank. A voice was shouting on the other side, a hard metallic voice.

There was a rifle shot, and the shoreline sandstone at their feet crumbled. As they crawled away into a screen of hollow ground, they heard the sound of a motor-car being driven away.

"The bastards have skipped," Arnie said. "I'll telephone the superintendent over there. Who is he."

Edward said, "Telephone the local Garda station. The old days have gone. The gardener. He's somewhere in the bushes."

Arnie hurried away towards the house. The pathway was still damp, but the petrol was evaporating. When he reached the drawing-room, it was peaceful as a church.

"There was a shot, I thought," John Bennett said. "A bit early for duck-flighting. It sounded like a three-o-three."

"There were intruders in the garden," Arnie replied. "Probably up to no good. They've gone. They had a car on the other side." He said to Lillian, "Edward's out there, all in one piece."

John and Alexandra Bennett were on their feet.

"Edward's all right?" Lillian asked, anxiously.

"Yes."

John Bennett said, "We haven't enemies here. Your mother and I walk down by the riverbank most days. We scratch around in the garden. We sit in the sunshine when it's there. . . ."

"Enemies," Alexandra said in astonishment. "Neighbours. We know them all. We have parties for the children at Christmas. And fêtes at summertime. Our neighbours. . . ."

Arnie was holding up his hand for silence as he cranked the telephone. He waited, then rang again, listened. "There isn't a sound in this damn thing!"

Alexandra said, "Well, there aren't a dozen telephones in the area. The postmistress might be busy at her counter."

"You hear noise in a telephone. I pick mine up sometimes and the whole world seems to be whispering across space. The line is probably cut." He was hurrying away through the lobby to the entrance drive. A distance from the house, he found the line hanging down on the grassland and fallen leaves. When he returned he said, "Yes, it's broken."

John Bennett said calmly, "I have a shotgun and a gross of cartridges."

"Oh wait, wait," Alexandra told him. "They had a car across the river. They've gone. We won't see them again."

Arnie was silent.

John Bennett sat down in his chair again. "Landowners brought destruction on themselves. Evictions, dealing with land grabbers, a free hand to rent-agents."

Alexandra said, "We are merchants."

Arnie nodded.

John Bennett said, "There's a government, isn't there? We have a Free State."

"They want a Republic," Arnie answered.

Lillian interrupted. "Is Edward out there?"

Arnie said, "He's taking old Hartigan to the kitchen. Hartigan took a few clouts."

"Is he all right?"

"A bit bloodied."

Edward arrived. He had washed and dried in the kitchen. "Hartigan has a few marks on his face, a small head wound. He's all right."

Arnie asked, "No sign of stragglers out there?"

"No, they've gone."

Arnie said, "I'll take the car to the police station to report it."

Lillian said, "The *Garda* station, remember. And mention that the telephone wires are damaged. And knock up Dr Morris. Ask him to examine Hartigan."

When he had gone, Lillian stoked the fire, set the flames dancing again. She smiled at her parents. "Quite enough entertainment for one day," she said. "I'm going to the kitchen to see how Hartigan is. I'll arrange for tea with Jessie. Arnie will be back in half an hour." She smiled to Edward. "Father will tell you the history of this old house, its saints and sinners and ghosts," she said.

CHAPTER FIFTEEN

AS HE LEFT the Bennett house behind, Mulvey sat back in the good upholstery of the brougham, comfortable, relaxed, casually watching the pavements, missing little.

He had been living more than five years in the city but was known only to a few. He had stabling for a horse and brougham, and accommodation for his driver, Barrett, within two minutes from the bank premises. He had his offices in the bank, not visible to the customers, accessible only to the manager, who would knock for admittance.

"A change of staff, I see," the occasional client of importance might say in passing as Mulvey could be glimpsed from the manager's office at moments of arrival and departure.

"Well, an addition to our team. Mulvey. Internal Audit Department. Branch discipline, security, that kind of thing. 'Bigger fleas have lesser fleas.'"

That brought laughter as a rule, and an end to curiosity.

He rarely walked alone on the streets. Sometimes he drove

down at night-time into Irishtown and Englishtown. There were pockets of small solvency – shopkeepers or clerks or tradesmen – but great crowded areas of tenements or hovels.

Mulvey had spent more than twenty years as an officer in the Shanghai Police. Shanghai, even in its matchwood acres of destitution, could somehow survive on rice bowls, alcohol, and dope, naked rent-girls too old at fifteen, villainy and murder: there were always ways of extracting taxation from the rich. Sitting in his brougham Mulvey could smell the perfume of brothels and dives. An industrial city.

Mulvey's grandfather had been a tenant farmer in the rocks and stones and fissures of soil of the Atlantic west. Mulvey's father, who had won a place in the old police force and knew the limitations to his progress, had had to stand often in expressionless shame at the evictions and injustices against his own people. He had sent his children abroad: America, Canada, Australia.

Mulvey, just eighteen, had been sent to Shanghai where a relative in holy orders had met him. Irish were strong in colonial police forces, and when the door was opened for Mulvey he didn't hesitate. He was hard, unbending and he climbed the ladder. He liked the life, the generous benefits of law enforcement.

But he had returned from Shanghai to this city with a purpose that was, as yet, unfulfilled. Masonic and Protestant influence had recommended Mulvey, once a Catholic, a colonial policeman, for his almost invisible role in the banking world. He watched for all who had something to lose. He watched Gardaí and men of politics, too.

The country now had its native government, its own army and Garda force, but was still a lawless wasteland. Money, property and lives were always in danger. The banks didn't trust a new police force with a stock of rustic gunmen converted to peace-keeping. They worried for the preservation of capital and the safety of their clients and shareholders. The Bennett family had been high on the list of "special clients".

Strangely, in an almost friendless world, making his initial perfunctory calls on the bank's chosen clients, he had delayed with Arnold Bennett, spent an hour with him. They had something in common: it might be a stubborn sense of duty, ruthlessness perhaps. They met fortuitously at times in the George Hotel and spent a little time over drinks.

The Bennetts were good people, Mulvey thought. He tapped on the small trap on the roof of the brougham, and Barrett raised it to listen.

"Drive to the workhouse, the City Home," Mulvey said. "We're not in a hurry. The matron is dead, I'm told."

"An accident."

"Her replacement?"

"I don't know."

The small square of sky vanished as the trap was dropped into place. Barrett sat high up outside, well-wrapped and hatted. A bachelor turned forty, he was pleasant and a good listener. He had been in the 1914 trenches and returned unscathed. This was his native city; he knew a lot of people, heard a lot of stories. When his evenings were free, he moved about, enjoyed a drink.

The brougham was trotted down George's Street, busy with traffic now, and turned left to pass between the boat clubs and past the statue of Fitzgibbon of Balaclava, to cross the fine elegant bridge.

At the Union Cross they turned right and were at the gates of the workhouse. A metal slab, like a headstone, was set in the wall to mark the city boundary. Barrett tapped on the ironwork gate with his whip.

A porter appeared from the lodge.

"Bank business," Barrett told him.

They drove across the gravel path to the entrance. It was a two-storey building that had been stone-faced in famine and pestilence. It was a geriatric place of death now, with a single isolation wing for the sudden plagues and fevers that came and went from decade to decade.

Mulvey stepped out and entered the reception area. It shone with cleanliness. Passing nursing staff viewed him without curiosity. A tall, willowy, middle-aged person in dark blue uniform approached him.

Mulvey had removed his hat; he smiled.

"Yes?" she asked. She had a patient, unemotional face and tired eyes behind her rimless spectacles.

There had been a fire, Mulvey thought; fire leaves a charred smell that lingers for days, sometimes weeks. He thought of the skeleton of Arnie's storehouse and the damp odour that hung over it.

"I am enquiring about recent deaths," Mulvey said.

"Are you a doctor?"

"No. The bank are interested. They asked me to call. I was told to ask for the matron."

She said quietly, "The matron, Miss Holmes, is dead. I am just a temporary replacement."

There was no flicker of emotion.

"Could we talk somewhere?" Mulvey asked.

"You didn't come to discuss matron's death, then?"

"Not specifically."

"Hospital information is very confidential."

"Yes, the bank is always aware of confidentiality." Producing a wallet that held a framed identity card, Mulvey said, "There's a telephone number. If you're unsure, you could ring them."

She glanced at the card for a few moments. "Follow me," she said. She led the way to a makeshift office and offered him a chair.

He said, "Miss Holmes died unexpectedly?"

"An accident. A little time ago. She came from the midland counties. Her remains were taken there for burial."

"There was an autopsy?"

"There had been a fire in her office. Some second degree burns and smoke inhalation. She had just assisted in emergency surgery and returned to her office, it appears."

Mulvey was remembering Thaddeus Bennett's description of Matron Holmes' manhandling of the "awkward" father. Thaddeus, before he had left, had seen him waiting in the hospital grounds. Mulvey wondered.

"I'm sorry about the matron's death," he said. He looked about this small storeroom for medications and dressings where a table and a couple of chairs had been installed. Despite the cleanliness, the faint smell of the fire was everywhere.

"Matron . . .," Mulvey began.

"I am Sister Callan," she said. "You came at the behest of the bank with an enquiry. Hospital business?"

"In a way," Mulvey said. "It was about the death of a young boy from diphtheria. Quite recently."

"Almost all diphtheria deaths are young. They die every day in the city. They are still dying. What was his name? I might remember."

"I don't know his name."

Sister Callan showed her helplessness. "There are a lot of funerals here, Mr Mulvey. Old people are left here to die. You could say death is our business. Epidemics just swell the ranks. There are three funerals from here today. One was a diphtheria."

Mulvey nodded. "I understand," he said. "I thought there would be a register. Some record files."

"The matron's office was the records office. It was burnt out. Nothing left to us only perished walls and shelves and a floor of ashes. She was pulled out, of course, but too late."

"The fire?" Mulvey mentioned again.

Sister Callan paused. "A paraffin heater like this." She pointed to a portable heater. It was a light metal cylinder, about two feet in height, standing on four legs. "She must have stumbled, toppled it. Paper and paraffin and flame make a quick blaze."

"She wasn't marked?"

"Just a facial bruise from the fall."

"Wasn't there a screw cap on the paraffin tank?"

"Strangely, no. In hospitals good care is taken of portable heaters, but the paraffin tank didn't have a cap."

She walked the gravel pathway with Mulvey. He said, "The young boy I mentioned, he was a neglected case. He lasted only a few hours. He had surgery. Dr Bennett."

"A fine surgeon, they say."

Mulvey saw Barrett bringing the brougham towards the doorway. "All your burials are in the city cemetery, of course?" he asked.

"Yes, you could say that. Old cemeteries might have the odd funeral. Established families, that kind of thing." Sister Callan smiled.

Mulvey nodded his thanks. "I know where the cemetery is," he said. He watched her stepping out of sight; an attractive, graceful lady.

He said to Barrett, "Not even a name. The matron is dead, the records office is gutted. Nothing."

Barrett waited.

Mulvey said, "The city cemetery."

Mulvey sat in the brougham by the cemetery wall and sent Barrett to talk and search. Barrett knew his men from clerks to grave-diggers.

But there was nothing, no burial that might be a sign-post to a name or an address. In such a short time there had been an overburden of incident. He was looking for one man, a Catholic and a republican with a dead son.

And the death of the workhouse matron? The father had been in the hospital grounds. Had he punished her? Had he upset the paraffin heater and slipped away in the confusion?

There were known republicans who were prominent in the city, who wore politics like a badge. Barrett knew them; Mulvey knew them. They would be creeping towards city councils and little positions of influence. Not for them this diluted freedom; they must have everything. A Nation Once Again. They declared that they would cleanse the country of its dross, raise the flags of nationhood and religion.

But this hard man who was slowly emerging had the stuff of the true martinet; he destroyed his opponents. His gathering clique was tight-lipped, dedicated to him; they didn't hold forth in pubs or at street corners. They plotted. Barrett had heard not even a whisper.

Mulvey tapped on the roof. "Find a quiet place and we can rest a while."

They crossed the city close to the Christian Brothers' School and the railway station and came to a stop at the park railings. Barrett used a gas standard for a hitching post and hung a forage bag from the horse's neck.

Mulvey alighted and they walked together through the park gates, past the library and tended flower beds and grass. The gravel pathways were concentric, and "spokes" ran across them, converging at the hub. It wasn't a day of brightness, but the late plants were in bloom, somehow brighter beneath a grey blanket of sky.

At the centre, the fine Doric column honoured Monteagle.

Mulvey said, "Carnegie and Monteagle."

"Invasions brought good and evil."

"Yes."

"Away from the old city, these are fine houses and streets."

"People must mix to go forward."

The winter air was creeping in; it was too cold to sit on the carved wooden seats. They walked slowly, Mulvey smoking.

"People come to find work in the city. They come from farmhouses or one-street villages. Ten miles out, maybe. A great journey for them. They hold an image of it in their minds for a lifetime and almost never go back," he said. "But the occasional corpse goes back to a family grave. Family pride."

"Expensive. A day's work for a hearse. A heavy price for family pride."

"Maybe not pride. Maybe obscurity."

Ragged children, down in a hollow by a side gate played rugby with a ball of paper tied with a cord.

"A foreign game now," Barrett said.

Mulvey said, "Children play at what makes them happy."

They paused to watch. There might be six or seven on each side, switching from scrummaging to half-back, to flying three-quarters, their small bodies tackling each other like giants.

A passing figure stopped and harangued them. "Play the games of Ancient Ireland, of Cú Chulainn and the Red Branch Knights! Not the game of the foreigner! Do you hear me, you little scuts!"

Play suddenly swung across the patch to envelope and pass this preacher, leaving him with hat awry, spinning. He climbed to the steps of the exit, shouting, "I'll send the Guards, I'll shift ye, by God, I'll shift ye!" The game went on.

Mulvey turned away. "No man e'er lived who died in jail and he from Garryowen hail," he said.

A silky drizzle began to fall, gathering like pinhead diamonds on the nap of Mulvey's coat. They stood beneath a great umbrella of oak that still clung to its foliage and watched the threads of rain hanging from the sky, hearing its almost noiseless impact with the grassy slopes.

Mulvey spoke suddenly. "How many undertakers in the city?"

Barrett said, "Three."

"Would they have had a funeral of a boy to somewhere beyond the city recently?"

Barrett considered it. "We can ask."

"You know the hearse drivers and coffin makers?"

"Yes, You'd like to move soon?"

"Now. Leave me in the brougham, a little distant, when you make your calls. The usual routine."

Barrett took a circuitous route past the memorial clock honouring the long deceased clothing magnate, and the church of the weeping statue, past the slaughter-house of a bacon factory, to his first destination. He left the brougham and walked uphill to a broad gateway. Stabling and cover for funeral carriages faced each other in an avenue. Ahead was a forage loft and the workshop of the coffin maker. The yard seemed deserted. A funeral, perhaps two funerals, would clear out the work-force. Barrett made his way to the coffin-shop. An old retainer was there, shaping the shoulders of another coffin with saw-cuts, meticulous as a delicate violin carver.

"Good day to you," Barrett said. "You look well, Timothy. But times are busy, aren't they?"

Timothy squinted and focused. "Ah, Mr Barrett," he said. Barrett was a bank employee; you gave him his title. "Very busy," he said.

"This sickness can't pass soon enough," Barrett said.

"Money for the undertakers, mourning for the rest."

Timothy didn't stop in his sawing and shaping. Spare coffins were stacked around the workshop, some varnished and padded, others in raw timber. There were small coffins, too, for the young.

Barrett said, "I'm trying to trace a funeral."

"I just make the boxes."

"You might recall something."

"A lot of graves are filled every week."

"A funeral that might have left the city for a country graveyard. A few miles out. Maybe no village, just a townland. I don't even have a name for the corpse."

"Names mean nothing to me." He seemed to be devoted to the paring and shaping of wood. "I don't remember anything. A lot of deaths."

"Even a passing word in a pub?"

"We don't talk about coffins over a pint."

Barrett thanked him, walked past the coffins awaiting tenants. There was a mingled smell of wood, glue, stain and varnish. The tall gibbous figure of Timothy bent over his work like an ancient grey alchemist.

"Thanks for your trouble," Barrett said.

"Wait a minute."

Barrett turned.

"Funerals from the city to the countryside are expensive," the coffin maker said. "You'd get a village carpenter out there who has a horse and a second-hand hearse. He'd be glad of the business."

"He'd come for the body?"

"You'd bring the body to him. Wrap it up on the floor of a pony and trap. Travel at night-time, a couple of hours. Lift the body from the trap to the coffin. Walk behind the hearse with relatives. The curate says a few prayers at the burial. That's all."

Barrett looked at him. "There was a country funeral?" he asked.

The coffin maker laid down his plane and emery paper; he said in a low voice to Barrett, "Yes, I heard of a funeral. Just a few words, that's all. People have their own reasons. Poverty, pride. City grave-plots and funerals cost money."

"A name?"

"No name."

"Where?"

"We talk in confidence?" the coffin maker said.

"Yes, in confidence."

"There's one crossroads cluster of houses eight miles from the city. It has a small crumbling church with a leaking roof. . . ."

Barrett added, "And a small river flows past it?"

The coffin maker went back to his work. "Yes, that's it. Let the dead rest, Mr Barrett. Don't disturb them."

"I won't disturb the dead."

Barrett descended the stairway to the yard and walked down two hundred yards of street to where he had left Mulvey waiting. He opened the brougham door.

"Anything?"

Barrett said, "No name, but a place. Eight miles. Now?"

"Yes."

They passed from the city through the Cathedral Square, north along the main highway. Barrett let the horse break into a steady even trot. The drizzle had blown past. Countryside had begun almost at once; a last few straggling houses and lush fields and weathering hedges made the landscape. On the hill was the ruined castle and a tended road to the golf course.

Mulvey sat and pondered. Taddy Bennett had forgotten the name of his patient. In a daily mêlée of emergency, unexpected house calls, field-surgery and death, who could blame him? Even names had been pushed from the memory of Sister Callan at the workhouse. With blazing records, names vanished. And in the confusion of fire-fighting, taking a small body from a mortuary might be possible. And how had the matron died?

Mulvey lay back in the brougham and lit his cigarette.

Four miles from the city they turned into a poor rutted roadway; the brougham swayed and bounced, even in the hands of Barrett. The terrain had changed, too. Gone was the richness of pasture, trees and hedges. This was moorland, bogland. It stretched away across flat miles of winter heather and gorse; pools of black water dotted it. The scars of turf-cutting had dried to a hard dark brown. A lonely wasteland, Mulvey thought.

He was closing with this crafty gunman, who would have been pushing his way to the top in the recent years of rebellion and civil strife. Mulvey visualised him: a worker who made cash and drove his men, a fervent soldier in the army of God, too, tight-lipped, thunderous in the condemnation of desire and naked flesh. Bad times of centuries had let religion grow wild, and it would hang about freedom's neck for decades.

They were leaving the bogland, coming into rich land again; the occasional big house of gentry sat in clusters of woodland. They were probably empty or gutted, Mulvey thought. He sat back and smoked. Yes, he thought, the hunt was on; we are closing the gap.

In minutes short of two hours they reached the small river with its narrow hump-backed bridge, with side-refuges, niches for pedestrians who might inexplicably have found themselves in the way of His Lordship's coach and four.

The village of perhaps four dozen houses had grown up in the heart of gentry-land. Its shops were small and unplanned. The draper's large window displayed shapeless dresses on coloured cardboard cut-outs, but he sold men's heavy boots and serviceable shoes for women, too. The hardware shop was a confusion of everything of utility: buckets, shackles, chains: everything from scythes and billhooks to storm lanterns. The grocer was postmaster and publican, too. Great bags of meal with scoops stood in corners, and there was an indestructible weighing scales to measure out into paper bags his quantities of tea and sugar. There were blocks of salt and a tapped metal drum of paraffin. The bar was a small counter, chest-high, that hid thirty-six gallon barrels of stout on a rack and, on the shelves behind, thick, heavy, pint-size tumblers. A lone bottle of whiskey sat beside a half-glass pewter measure.

The aproned publican was observant, wary: there was an air of authority, of officialdom, about Mulvey.

"Travelling far?" the publican asked.

Mulvey answered, "Driving about."

"The roads are confusing here."

Mulvey smiled. "They lead to bogland, a river, a lake, a graveyard. That's the usual pattern." Mulvey ordered whiskey for Barrett and himself.

The publican was pleased that he had excited humour; he brought the whiskey. "Well, it's the best road in these parts, rutted and all as it is. Twenty-four miles across the county."

"Yes," Mulvey said. They drank.

"There's nothing much to be seen here. Go right or left. Downhill to a broken mill, uphill past the graveyard to the mines. I never remember the mines working, and I'm not young. They mined for silver once. Money was made there, they say."

They finished their whiskey slowly. Eventually Mulvey said, "Stick at your counter. There's a better return on whiskey and porter."

They left.

Barrett turned left, up a twisting road out of the village street. It was hilly country, rising in the distance to more than two thousand feet, but in ten minutes they had reached the graveyard.

The sagging rusting gates were tied with a rope bleached by winters and summers. Barrett let the horse stand and graze on the prodigal roadside grass.

They climbed across the stile beside the gates.

Old graveyards become neglected places; heavy grief spreads itself over a couple of generations and dissolves into forgetfulness; a family line is ended, spent, has emigrated. Grass and weeds grow tall, and briars and convoluting wild creepers weave a carpet of obfuscation. Stones and their messages to posterity darken, tilt, seem to struggle for survival. Only a few grave plots, still "alive", had a semblance of care. Pathways had vanished, and they trod carefully, feeling for level ground. They found a few graves with the earth stripped of grass and vegetation, but where the ground had settled.

Barrett called out, "It might be here."

Mulvey made his way to him and nodded. Fresh moist clay, displaced by the coffin, was a proud ridge.

"Yes," he said. "A fresh grave." He looked at the old weathered stone and read from it aloud: "Carmody." There hadn't been a burial recorded for more than fifteen years; it was early days yet for the stonemason to chisel out this new arrival. "The last interment 1913," he said. He looked about. "A good place of concealment." He looked at Barrett. "Carmody?"

Barrett said, "We can find him."

They climbed the stile to the roadway; Barrett held open the door for Mulvey, saw him seated.

Barrett said, "There's a Carmody somewhere? Churches, committees? A secret mover?"

"You know where he can be found?"

"No. Somewhere in the city. I'll find him."

"Good."

CHAPTER SIXTEEN

At the unadorned, important church of the elite, the Catholic middle class and aspirants had dressed for the occasion of Sunday morning mass. Overcoated men with polished shoes and bowler hats climbed the broad steps. Women were in fashion costume, too: expensive three-quarter length buttoned coats, hats, silk stockings, pointed shoes and loose furs arranged with carelessness.

Broughams dropped their pilgrims on the pavement and drove away to obscurity to await the end of this weekly courtesy call on the Creator. A few motor-cars remained parked at the kerbside, humble badges of success left for a short while in thanksgiving, an adornment to His House.

At the end of mass, clerics, perhaps two or three, would stand on the steps with a word for some and a nod for others. All part of the ritual.

Arnie stood at the window and looked down at the street that was quiet, clear of Sunday family walkers, of the little noise and laughter of younger people, groups of boys or girls, courting loving couples. Soldiers, on a day pass, polished even to their shiny faces, should be moving down to find the company of women in the old city.

Arnie said, "It's quiet down there."

Lillian said, "There's a procession."

"Oh yes, I forgot."

Sunday lunch was at Arnie's house. They had sat down to this weekly sharing of company, food, drink and talk at two o'clock. John and Alexandra were rare visitors from the Hermitage. Arnie had collected them and would drive them home before dark.

It was always a special day for Lucy, the housekeeper: an empty house all week and then suddenly people. The kitchen, its staff, the upstairs maids were all of a bustle. Lucy asked for perfection: napery, cutlery, glass, everything pristine. Flower arrangements that had beauty, but were different. A luncheon of melon, consommé, smoked salmon with lemon on wheaten bread, rib of beef, an array of vegetables, sauces. Then it was always a rice pudding – a concession to Arnold – and tea with biscuits and *petits fours*.

They were still gathered about the table in conversation. Alexandra said, "A procession? You didn't mention it, Arnold."

Lillian said, "It's a religious event, Mother. You remember processions? They say the diphtheria sickness is passing. This is a kind of thanksgiving. They call it 'Homage to Our Holy Mother'. It's a good act of faith. It circles the city."

Arnie said, "It'll pass under our window in an hour. Final devotions are at the church up there on the hill."

"You don't approve, Arnold. I can tell from your lips."

Thaddeus said, "Diphtheria isn't passing. It's standing still."

Arnie said, "I feel for the people. It's a shining bait for the poor. They'll snap at it, of course. First we have a weeping statue. . . ."

John Bennett had left the table to read his Sunday

newspaper: it had been ironed in the kitchen and its narrow spine stitched to hold it intact. When he moved it there was a loud crepitant noise like the approach of a fire.

"A weeping what?" he asked.

"Statue. A church near the park."

"Oh, those things keep cropping up now and then. No offence meant, Edward. Weeping faces in the graveyard would be nearer the mark."

Edward nodded.

Arnie said, "The church is crowded every day, with penny candles flaring from dawn till dusk."

Old John went back to his newspaper. "I don't understand these things," he said. "Divine spirits must have seen illness coming. They could have stopped it, saved Thaddeus and an army of people all this hard labour."

"This is an expression of gratitude, isn't it?" Alexandra asked.

"Yes," Edward said, "you could call it that. Gratitude perhaps that we are keeping abreast of the illness. It still rages."

Thaddeus nodded. "Precisely, Edward."

Arnie, smoking his cigarette, returned to the table. "Who spreads these weeping statue stories? Religion should be a sensible thing. All this magic and puffs of smoke make a sideshow of it."

Lillian said, "How people worship is their own affair. Religion should be everyone's personal secret."

Sunday, a momentary pause for rest from the work-a-day world, had become, almost for all, a day of attendance to duty of the Church. Arnie thought of morning communions and evensongs; masses and benedictions.

He said, "God rested on the seventh day. He didn't come on earth to visit us or flap around in processions. Rest, that's the word."

Old John crackled his newspaper again. "Processions? Not good, I think. Whenever I planned a trip to Belfast, I made sure to steer clear of them. Grown men with brollies and hard hats and these orange scarf things about their necks, marching. Put me off flautists for ever."

Lillian said, "That's just politics, Father."

"Yes, yes, I suppose so." He went back to his reading.

Edward said, "It's politics here, too."

Lucy and two maids came to clear the table.

"A wonderful lunch," Arnie told her; everyone agreed.

Lucy clasped her hands and smiled.

Arnie led the way to the drawing-room. Its two embrasured windows looked down on the same street scene. A great coal fire burned, and a sofa, a *chaise-longue* and easy chairs faced it. Lillian sat between John and Alexandra.

"You should come in every Sunday," she said. "Arnie has a motor-car, and Edward and I are going to buy one."

"We have a car and a driver," Old John said as he put away his newspaper. "A fine lunch, Arnold," he called out. He turned to Lillian. "Except for business, I was never a city man," he said.

"Then we'll come and visit you."

"Wonderful!" Alexandra said. Arnie had brought them drinks: pale sherry for the womenfold; a stiff whiskey and soda – Scotch malt – for John. "Wonderful, wonderful!" Alexandra said again. "I love to see your cars coming up the drive. And Jessie and her house staff would surpass themselves."

John Bennett held up his glass and peered through it; he leant over to inhale its bouquet. "Good malt here, Arnold. No soda to spoil it."

Arnie said, "From Skye. Twenty years in the wood."

"Jameson can be a good round whiskey, but I never say no to a drop of good Scotch malt."

Alexandra was saying, "Before we leave now we must arrange a date for your visit. All of you. Thaddeus, you can get a locum once a month or six weeks, can't you? You must come."

"There's Matilda. . . ."

"Poor darling Matilda. I pray for her every day."

"She's very comfortable. There isn't much time left."

"Does Matilda ask for us?"

"She doesn't have a lot of strength. She smiles to me and I know she's without pain. Tuberculosis is the great enemy. These plagues of diphtheria and fever come and go, but tuberculosis is unending."

Silence settled for a few moments; the fluttering of the fire was the only sound. Thaddeus had finished his drink; he stretched as he drowsed in the heat. Since Matilda's illness he carried weariness about with him from day to day. Alexandra looked at his fine gentle hands, then at the black and yellow patterns of the fire. Lillian put her arms about her shoulders to arrange her shawl.

At the window, Arnie and Edward tipped glasses.

"The Hermitage is safe, I suppose?" Edward asked.

"I left three men to look after it. Three shotguns."

"What about Mulvey?"

"He works well. A lot of barriers. The workhouse matron is dead and buried. The records office gutted. No names, no pack drill for a long time."

"And now?"

"An out-of-town burial. Eight miles out?"

"A name?"

Arnie spoke softly. "Carmody. We know he's in Irishtown and we'll trace him. Carmody," he said again. "People are tight-lipped these days, aren't they? Loyalty or fear, but tight-lipped."

Edward didn't change expression; he was looking down on the quiet Sunday street. A few more people about, hurrying uphill towards the church. The forerunners of the procession, hurrying to get good seats for the final performance.

Arnie said, "The name has a familiar ring, but I can't place it. Carmody. Is it a common name?"

"Not very common," Edward said.

Arnie stared in silence for long moments, gazed out at the

streets again, poured fresh whiskey in their glasses.

"You know him? You've talked to him?"

"I know his voice."

"Where from?"

"On the docks. He's a stevedore. He has unloaded your shipments. He'd know who you are. Who we are."

They drank; Arnie said, "But he's clean as a whistle, isn't he?"

"Yes, clean as a whistle. He probably set off the record office blaze, probably left the matron senseless with a single jab, but clean as a whistle. In the confusion the boy's body could be carried off, but the records are in ashes."

"Clever."

"Dangerous."

Arnie looked at him. "You'd kill him, Ed, would you?"

"Probably. Lillian is my wife."

Arnie said, "I'd kill him, too. Not just for the warehouse and previous sins. The Hermitage: people in retirement; the rifle shot, the petrol. But I gave the job to Mulvey. I'll talk to him."

The head of the procession, more than a mile long, pushed into the broad crescent, passing the patriot statue. Acolytes in soutanes and surpluses carried a crucifix mounted on a tall brass tube, and behind it, the little black and white retinue with joined hands and bowed heads seemed to glide. Following them was a cleric in flowing cassock and biretta. They were the outriders.

The pavements, in a few minutes, had become crowded, a waiting congregation whom age or profusion of children had forced to the sidelines. There were the wheelchairs and crutches of the stooped, the lame and the halt. Rosary beads hung from hands everywhere.

The sound of a brass band, playing church music in slow march, reached them: a fine melodious sound from practised bandsmen. It grew louder.

Alexandra Bennett called to them, "What is that?"

"The procession is arriving."

"Isn't standing at the window a bit rude, Arnold?"

The heavy lined curtains had been thrown open since morning, but Arnie had drawn across the lace-panelled drapes against the window.

"We're out of sight," he said.

John Bennett, who had found his newspaper again, looked up. "Who are we hiding from?" he asked.

Lillian said, "Not hiding. Just peeping from their little coign of vantage." She brought him a fresh measure of malt.

Thaddeus slept soundly in his armchair.

The city was a city of churches, each with its platoon of clergy from monsignor or canon to the lowliest curate. Churches had confraternities and sodalities of men and women, and waiting lists of young boys to join the ranks of acolytes. It was a vast network of communication with God.

A serried block of clergy led the way, their vestments moving like an iridescent slab catching the light and shadow of the day, their lips moving silently in prayer. An ageing monsignor carried the monstrance, a sunburst of gold-washed metal, studded with semi-precious stones: and its orb, the Light of the World, was a consecrated wafer of unleavened bread that had become the body of Christ, the Son of God. Four canons walked with him to constantly relieve him of his burden. Nearing the end of this march through the city, he was growing unsteady beneath a great ornate canopy held aloft by pillars of the church, men of substance and property if possible. An endless army of confraternities, men's and women's, carried banners to announce themselves. The faces of the marchers were as solemn as funeral mourners; they wore badges and sashes over their Sunday-best clothing. White and pale gold of papal flags fluttered everywhere, and national tricolours, blessed by anointed hands, mingled with them. Bands, in the distance, played their own music, and visiting clergy led their congregations in prayer or singing.

Finally, the statue of the Mother of God came, held aloft by chosen men of dedication to the faith of their fathers. Her canopy was a rich magnificent baldaquin, portable, carried by clerics in white albs and girdles. Her raiment was gleaming white satin, and a web of diaphanous fabric floated down from her head. A banner, wide as a country roadway, proclaimed: "Hail Queen of Heaven". The mitred bishop, in his open carriage, held up and fluttered his hand in blessing. He was surrounded by men of importance, clergy and laity.

The procession took an hour to pass beneath the Bennett windows. So many bands, so much music, so many hymns, so much booming recitation of prayer: it should have made a great cacophony, but the procession passed by with an almost frightening dignity.

As the blessed statue passed below them, Edward said, "There's a guard of honour for Our Lady of Deliverance from Disease. A line on each side?"

Arnie said, "Yes, I see them."

A leading member on one line, in a sharp penetrating voice, called out the First Joyful Mystery of the Rosary of Our Holy Mother. When the time of response came, he raised up his hands in exhortation, urging them to shout their prayers to heaven. It was a great roar.

John Bennett lowered his newspaper. "Is there trouble out there?"

"Just prayers," Edward said.

"Sounded like a battle-cry." John Bennett was deep in his newspaper again.

Lillian was smiling.

Edward said to Arnie, "The leader of the prayers down there. . . ."

"The loud fellow?"

"Yes, the loud fellow. It could be Carmody. He's a high prefect in his confraternity, too, it seems."

Arnie gazed down on him, the solid build of him, his face twisted in a distortion of sanctity.

"He knows this is my house. The crescendo of prayer was for us, I imagine. For the Bennett family."

"Probably," Edward said.

"Not for our salvation."

"No."

Edward said, "I remember his voice, the trembling praying voice down there. That's all."

"Thaddeus might remember his face."

"Thaddeus is a worn-out man. He needs rest. Let him sleep. We've met Carmody face to face. Mulvey will get to know him better."

At the top of the hill, the procession had been turning, out of vision, to the church and its acres of paved and concreted grounds.

The magnificent statue in regal attire, a great potent fetish of holiness, had passed below them; in minutes it would be gone from sight. The pavement crowd was dispersing. Quiet Sunday was returning.

Arnie said, "Tonight I'll telephone Mulvey."

Mulvey was an early riser, the habit of a lifetime. His apartment, study, bedroom and kitchen were tidy. He didn't need a body-servant. An unfussy eater, he cooked oatmeal porridge on his gas stove and took it with a little glucose powder and milk. The city bakeries made fine bread, oven baked with good texture, and Mulvey had learned his tea-making in China. He took one other meal, in the early evening, when Barrett drove him to a small select hotel. In Shanghai there were beautiful women who would spend evenings or nights entertaining chosen clients; you paid them and you were acquitted, unshackled. He missed them. There were no beautiful concubines in this city; there were only whores and diseases. And even whores prayed and carried rosary beads. But Mulvey could screw down his passion. He made occasional trips to London, sometimes on business, but always for pleasure. He was contented with life.

He hadn't arrived in this city merely to tighten the security of a bank and its priority clients. He hadn't wandered back, still a young man, from the East where he had a good life for this daily scouting of good and bad streets, watching faces and movements, examining plundered shops or gutted storehouses, finding zealots and thieves.

He had reached good rank in the police, completed twenty years service, and was still in his thirty-eighth year when he had become uneasy.

He had parents. His father, a sergeant in the Royal Irish Constabulary, had served his last ten years on these city streets. He had retired before its disestablishment in '22, and moved with his wife to a small farmhouse and a few acres of land three or four miles beyond the city boundary.

Mulvey had read their letters looking out from time to time across the teeming shoreline and the Woosung River crammed with shipping and junks, always relieved that they had reached retirement unscathed and even found happiness with their own hearth and a few acres to till. He wrote to them every month. They were alone, the family scattered.

And then their letters had ceased. His father had been the letter writer. Perhaps he had died. His mother, though ill-educated, could manage a rambling, slipshod few lines, but there had been silence.

There was a routine weekly exchange of meaningless correspondence between Shanghai headquarters and Crown Colonies Office in London. Mulvey had tapped it for information. The reply from Millbank had said, '. . . your father, retired, is listed as dead, for a little more than three months. His pension has been discontinued. He received a certificate for exemplary service. There was an accident, it appears, in which your mother also perished. Our deepest sympathy. Things are still very disturbed in Ireland and lines of communication haphazard. . . ."

No mention of cause of death. Mulvey's service entitled him to retirement and fair pension. He set sail from Shanghai on the trek to Singapore, Madras, Suez, the Mediterranean and the winter Atlantic all the way to the Mersey and Liverpool.

Banks in Ireland were mainly Protestant and Masonic, and Mulvey, a colonial servant with an honourable record, was *persona grata*. These were dangerous times and men of integrity at a premium. He had asked for a contract in what he called "his own city", where his father had served with distinction. Freedom had just been won with high praise to God; the ensuing civil war had been a bloody savage affair. The government of this Free State within the king's Commonwealth sat uneasily in Dublin, and its opposition, staunch republicans, were a secret army.

Day-to-day crime of the city was smalltime thievery and brawling that a new Garda force could keep in control. Prostitution in the docklands hinterland found discretion in the darkness of unlit lanes and alleys and was ignored.

Mulvey was seeking bigger fish. Small diehard partisans, spoilers, meeting in secret to plan campaigns of burning and mayhem, needed money. There were targets in plenty. Although the banks, monuments of lingering foreign power, were tough nuts to crack, there was, even in failure, a trumpet blast of propaganda. Raids sent long ripples of threat to a fawning government and a striving middle class of shopkeepers.

Mulvey watched, too, for isolated groups and sources, and Barrett, his driver, found names and places for them. He sent his information to the bank's special office of security in Dublin. The bank's men of power could meet Garda power to remove dangers and irritations.

Mulvey didn't talk to the Gardaí. In the city he was a senior bank official going about his business.

He had taken a couple of weeks to settle in his bank office and his living quarters. He had recruited Barrett, an ex-soldier of the '14 war, who had carried sergeant's stripes. Barrett knew the city from its broad streets to choking slums and alleyways; he knew a lot of working people in the right places. That was five years past.

Mulvey had said to him, "My father was a police sergeant in this town. He served his last ten years here. He retired three or four miles out beyond the Union Cross. I'd like to find the house."

Barrett paused for moments. "I knew the sergeant," he said.

Mulvey said, "I know he's dead."

"Yes, he's dead."

"And his wife."

"Dead."

"How?"

Barrett said, "A fire."

Barrett had driven him out the three or four miles to where the road branched away into the rising ground of hill country. It had been a small house, but now only the black-streaked shell was standing. If there had been a residue of furniture or delph, it had been pilfered. Mulvey stood and examined it, pacing the ground where they had last walked.

"Fire-raisers?" he asked.

"Yes."

"The civil war was over?"

"Before the civil war. A lot of killing was done."

"Where are they buried?"

Barrett had driven him to the graveyard that seemed distant from a village or a church, and he had stood on a bare plot where grass was springing to life again to remove all trace of it.

"You were at the burial?" Mulvey asked.

"Yes. Only a few people."

"See about a stone and a surround. I'll give you particulars."

Mulvey didn't remove his hat or bow his head in prayer. "No arrests?" he asked.

"They didn't find anyone."

Nearly six years ago, Mulvey thought, and he had discovered nothing. He had kept the bank and its priority customers safe from harm until the Bennett trouble. Mulvey pondered it:

the soup-kitchen fire, the punishment of Edward Burke, the threat to Thaddeus Bennett, the death of a matron, the death of Lucy Langford, the arson attempt at the Hermitage, the rifle shot. A spate of incident to be examined there. But, in the gutting of a small retirement house, the deaths of two ageing people: nothing.

Every day he pondered it.

There was the sound of a door knocker; that would be Barrett, the only person who knocked on Mulvey's door. Nine o'clock sharp. The army had been an exact training school for Barrett. He looked out of his first-floor window. The horse and brougham were at the pavement.

Mulvey lit a cigarette, took his leaded cane and went downstairs.

It was two hours before the procession would congregate, and he had arranged that Barrett would drive him along its as yet uncluttered route.

Barrett stood on the pavement and held open the door for him. "Looks a good day for street walking," he said.

Mulvey laughed. "Leave the roof-flap open. I don't mind fresh air, and we might need to exchange the occasional few words."

The city, on a bright early winter day, exposed all its beauty and its ugliness. The stillness of Sunday morning between church bells and between masses crept along the broad sweep of George's Street. The brickwork was in light and shadow; church steeples were fixed in the frosty blue of the day. It was a fine place.

Barrett drove down to the city's main intersection of business thoroughfares and turned uphill, and at the top went left into Irishtown. This was part of the route. The street was suddenly alive with people and colour: flags flew from rickety windows, and greenery, wild flowers, drapery and ribbons adorned altars of timber oddments and boxwood. Statuettes of the Virgin Mary were everywhere. There was a sad haphazard beauty about it all.

Mulvey, from his brougham, studied it. Drab house fronts had been transformed in a wealth of imagination. Men and women worked to sanctify these common side-streets, knowing that the Mother of God would walk unseen through it in a few hours, and the anointed clergy of the diocese, in humility, would lead her. Bunting was strung from gaslight standards; papal colours were twisted and knotted; framed pictures of Jesus Christ and his saints stood on window sills.

It was a great act of homage to the Unknown God from his lonely people.

The horse and brougham travelled at walking pace. The long street down to the river was busier today than on the market days that gave it sustenance. Outside one door, polished and gleaming, a gramophone was perched on a window table and the Count McCormack sang *Panis Angelicus*. It was almost drowned in the clatter of preparation.

Mulvey spoke to Barrett, sitting above him. "Slow, very slow here now. There's a great display at this coming doorway. Do you see it?"

"Yes."

"And there's a picture. It's a big picture, isn't it?"

"Yes."

"Keep it in your mind," Mulvey said.

A neat altar had been cobbled with care. Against a screened wall stood a wooden niche, a canopied upturned box which sheltered the Virgin Mary's statuette. There were candlesticks, flowers and greenery. In a tabernacle with an open door, a small statuette of Christ stood on the threshold. The window was covered in fabric and the picture symmetrically placed. Women fussed about with final arrangements while a man, no doubt the householder, stood, arms folded, and watched passers-by stop to admire it. He smiled, satisfied, and went indoors to rest.

When the brougham had moved on, Mulvey said, "You can leave me sitting outside the hospital."

They crossed the bridge to the hospital and Barrett stopped and climbed down from his perch.

"Walk back," Mulvey said. "Just stroll along, a spectator. The woman of the house is there. Give the altar your praise and the picture a perusal, but not a lot of praise. Just say that it's nice."

"I know the picture," Barrett said. "They call it 'Our Lady of Perpetual Succour'. You find a few of them around. Not popular. Not in everyone's bedroom. Most people like an innocent smiling Virgin."

"A bit forlorn, even ugly," Mulvey said. "I'm not interested in the picture. Examine the frame. Don't touch it, just look at it. Try to find out where she got it."

Barrett walked back across the bridge where a fine papal flag was fluttering in the breeze; he crossed the Mall and walked into the wonderland of devotion and competition. He stopped to admire here and there en route to his destination. When he arrived he stood nodding, smiling his approbation.

"It must be the best," he said to a stout woman in blouse and long skirt.

Pleasure flowed across her face. "My husband did the woodwork."

"A handy fellow. But it's the dressing, the flowers and the candles, that make it so rich."

She said softly, "I love decorating things."

"It's fine," he told her.

He moved a step or two and stared at the picture, raised his chin, squinted his eyes a little, moved closer.

She said, "I'm not sure about the picture. Should I leave it there, do you think?"

Barrett considered. "It's a foreigner's idea of Our Lady and her Infant Son. He was probably a sincere man, did his best."

"But not a good painter?"

"No."

"Should I leave it?"

"Oh yes. Our Lady will be pleased with your generosity.

Leave it. Everything is beautiful."

She thanked him.

Barrett stood for moments to study it, to examine the frame: heavy plaster covered the wooden shape; one corner was badly chipped, the mitred joint exposed. There was a chain pattern of connected links almost obliterated by layers of paint. The cheap, gaudy oleograph had lost its glitter with time.

She was still beside him. "You don't like it, do you?"

"It's important that it fills the window," he said. "It's a good size."

She nodded. "I'll leave it," she said. "An important friend of my husband brought it to us a few years ago. A very devout man. He saved it from a fire. Risked his life, I suppose. He said he couldn't stand and watch holy objects being swallowed up in flames. He'll be passing in today's procession."

"Yes," Barrett said, "he'll see it. He'll be pleased."

"Do you know what I call it?" she whispered. "I can never remember the big long name it has, so I call it 'Mr Carmody's picture'."

They both laughed.

"A compliment," he said. He tipped his hat, left her happy with her decision and moved away into the crowd.

In ten minutes he was back beside his brougham. When Mulvey lowered the window, cigarette smoke drifted out.

Barrett said, "It's a cheap print gone a bit faded and brown with age."

"The frame?"

"Plaster under skins of paint. Chipped bare to the wood at one corner."

"There's a pattern?"

"Still showing. Chain links. Eternity, I suppose; no end. The picture was a gift to her husband by a man very strong in the faith. He saved it from a fire a few years ago, she said."

Mulvey was leaning forward, "Yes?"

"She calls it Mr Carmody's picture."

"Carmody. From gravestone to picture frame." Mulvey sat back in his seat. "Good, good," he said. "We can move for home now before the streets are crammed."

Barrett trotted the horse from the hospital, by the riverside wall, crossed the bridge by the Customs House and passed the Town Hall on his way to George's Street. The fine imposing clock above the drapery emporium told that the procession would be gathering and on the move now. Mulvey alighted and parted from Barrett at the bank.

In his quarters Mulvey wore a black quilted jacket and house-shoes. There was a broad overmantled gas fire and armchair, and when he brewed tea in the kitchen, he brought it, black and unsweetened, to his fireside table, drank it and smoked.

He had grown up in a half dozen police barracks where his father had served and where accommodation had been sparse and meagre. His mother was a homemaker. With a fire and an oil lamp and a kettle swinging on the open hearth, she shut away the grey days of winter and summer. She cooked, baked, knitted and sewed; she hung curtains on the windows. They had what furniture they needed; no more. Police constables and sergeants, who were transferred at the drop of a hat, travelled light. There were three pictures: a wedding photograph, a chocolate box landscape, and the one of earliest memory with its patterned frame and broken plaster. He remembered God's Mother and her strange Infant Jesus. The picture and trappings of furniture that had travelled with them through life would still have been there when death arrived.

Carmody had rescued the "holy" object from the flames: in dread, no doubt, of the wrath of God and the burning niche in hell that might be held in punishment for an act of cowardice and neglect. He was a God-fearing man.

Mulvey sat in comfort until the procession was below his window; then he watched it for ten minutes. It was dull. The Chinese could teach them a few tricks of display. He took a book and settled into his reading. Mulvey liked Edgar Wallace, kept abreast of the excitement of a mythical crime world. He read the pulp magazines, *Black Mask* and its pale rivals. Spending a lazy day was easy.

In the evening time his telephone rang. It was Arnold Bennett.

"I'll talk to you in the morning," Bennett said, "but Carmody is a stevedore on the docks."

It was dark, time to have a drink. Mulvey poured a measure of whiskey, brought it to the table and lit a cigarette. Strange, he thought, you searched for five years for a pinhead of information, and there was nothing. Then suddenly the floodgates were opened.

CHAPTER SEVENTEEN

CHRISTMAS PASSED SADLY for the Bennett family. Matilda slipped away into deep coma in the first hours of Christmas Eve.

Abigail had watched her wasted face, the great fighting effort to breathe, the hoarse grating sound that the friction of flesh and air could make. The tidy, once humorous mouth gradually fell open as if death needed to imprint vulgarity.

Abigail damped her lips and wiped away gathering mucous. The pale hands clutched life again and her fingers picked at the woven fabric of the counterpane.

Thaddeus was exhausted, she knew. He had arrived home after ten o'clock, Brigid had come to tell her. Brigid had brought him a stiff whiskey and insisted that he should eat something. She had been cross with him. In the eighteen hours since he had left the house, he had made a dogged effort to fit his normal day of surgery and calls into the increased activity of a fresh surge of diphtheria that even weeping statues and processions hadn't halted.

But he would want to be here now at the end. Abigail pulled the floral porcelain bell-handle for the kitchen. When she heard steps on the landing outside, she opened the door to a weeping Brigid.

"Madam is dying tonight, isn't she?"

"How did you know?"

Brigid said, "I saw her in the kitchen. I was sitting by the range, and she came in like in the old days to talk to me, to thank me, to wish me and the staff a Holy Christmas. It was so real. She was wearing her Arnott's dress and her hair was bobbed. Her short hair and her beautiful face. . . ." Tears were gathering again for Brigid.

"She was so fond of you," Abigail said. "Yes, she's slipping away now. You must call Mr Thaddeus."

"God give me strength. Mr Thaddeus has suffered too much, Miss Abigail. I'll dry my face and go to his room. What will I say?"

"Tell him I asked for him. He'll understand."

Abigail turned back to her sanatorium and for a moment looked hopelessly at her mother's grasping fingers, holding on. She cleaned her face and arranged her hair, then walked to the window and looked out at the street lights fencing the park. The monument was a black smudge against the sky. In the past, Christmastime had been jingles of music, coloured paper, little pine trees loaded with gaud and glitter, and wrapped presents on the floor; a half-crown for the postman and the dustman, and presents for Brigid and her staff. The food: turkey-meat and ham, sprouts, marrowfats, potatoes mashed and roasted and in their jackets, the fragrance of wine and brandy, the blue flare of the lighted pudding. Laughter and maybe tears. Songs at the piano.

It seemed only yesterday when there had been children's birthday parties and outings and holidays in Atlantic coast hotels. Yesterday.

She heard Thaddeus arriving and changing into protective clothing. She opened the door for him. He looked a haggard old man. She closed the door and took his hand at the bedside. She stood slightly out of his vision. He stood erect and proud and spoke in a very steady voice.

"Is she long in coma?"

"A couple of hours. The dean came from the cathedral to say prayers."

He took a damp swab and gently brushed Matilda's face as if he might be caressing it and she might be smiling her old love at him. He arranged her hair and held her hands in stillness for moments.

"She's still beautiful," he said. "And she loved us all."

"Yes."

"I don't know any prayers," he said eventually. "Not a single one." After being silent for a while, Taddy quoted:

> To every thing there is a season, and a time to every purpose under the heaven:
> A time to be born, and a time to die; a time to plant, and a time to pluck up that which is planted;
> A time to kill, and a time to heal; a time to break down, and a time to build up;
> A time to weep, and a time to laugh; a time to mourn, and a time to dance;
> A time to cast away stones, and a time to gather stones together; a time to embrace, and a time to refrain from embracing;
> A time to get, and a time to lose; a time to keep, and a time to cast away;
> A time to rend, and a time to sew; a time to keep silence, and a time to speak;
> A time to love, and a time to hate; a time of war, and a time of peace.
> What profit hath he that worketh in that wherein he laboureth?

Abigail crossed to the window and looked out at the nighttime city, leaving him in closeness with Matilda. The orbs of gaslight on the streets seemed to burn in requiem and in the distance lighted windows hung in the darkness here and there: Christmas revels or perhaps other lonely vigils being kept. Matilda's rattle of breath diminished and for moments ceased; then the tearing intake of air would come again, a resumption of dying.

Thaddeus sat by her bedside. "The only prayerlike thing I know," he said. "For everything there is a season. A time to be born and a time to die." Ecclesiastes. My mother copied it into her leather-bound lifetime diary. Once it suddenly came to mind in student days in the anatomy room at Surgeons. You see the crowded organs of the body, so neatly packaged, so still in death. So many pieces that must be in movement to keep the brain alive."

Abigail turned to him. "That's all we are, a brain."

She poured a measure of whiskey for him.

He nodded. "I was never one for churches or prayer-books. The Bennetts were never churchgoers. I can't remember a single prayer." He drank half of the whiskey measure. "We doctors drink a lot. Puzzlement, I suppose."

He stood and pressed his lips against Matilda's forehead, sat again and held one of her restless hands. Abigail sat at the window watching the park gateway, the iron railings and the library catching the soft gaslight.

Brigid left tea and light food on the landing table and called out. Abigail heard Thaddeus' glass fall from his hand on the wooden floor and roll erratically to the skirting. He jerked back from sleep.

"I nodded," he said.

"You're exhausted. Will it be soon?" she asked.

"Yes, soon."

Matilda died twenty minutes after four o'clock.

"You musn't worry, everything will be taken care of," said Abigail.

"Let it be known that her funeral and home are private," he instructed.

"All right. The boys would be coming for Christmas tomorrow, so I'll ring them very early to come today. I'll ring the rest of the family later. Brigid doesn't need instructions."

Thaddeus said, "Ring Maggie Norris at Barrington's. She'll send someone to help. And Lillian will arrange the funeral."

"Arnold has gone to Castleconnell. They'll come in the morning," she said. "Brigid has brought some tea."

"Whiskey," he said.

Abigail made her telephone calls, and the Bennett family and Edward Burke arrived.

Matilda's death brought grief, but happiness, too, that it was over and she was at peace. She would celebrate Christmas with them this last time. She would never be left unattended. People would always be close, talking aloud as if she might be listening.

Beautifully dressed and arranged, she lay on her bed for Christmas Eve and Christmas Day. On St Stephen's Day she would be taken to the mortuary chapel at the cathedral, where she would lie overnight.

Waiting for the remains to be moved, Arnie and Edward had sat in conversation with Thaddeus for more than an hour. They had talked and slowly sipped whiskey. It was a quiet, sober conversation. Something had been discussed. Agreement might have been reached.

The church reception had the chilly warmth of churches. The prayers were quiet, and the tears that were shed were shed in silence.

After the funeral, Edward said to Lillian, "I must make a trip with Arnie in his car. We'll be a couple of hours; not much longer."

"Take care of each other," she said. "We'll look after Thaddeus for his first trip home to a house without his Matilda. He'll be happier when he's back with his surgery and his patients."

"His boys were fine. One each side of him."

"They are young men to be proud of," Lillian said. And

Abigail. Matilda gave him a fine family." Lillian smiled and held Edward's hand for a moment.

Arnie drove through the St Stephen's Day traffic. The pavements, too, were crowded. Christmas Eve had been a day of shops open till late hours, shop windows that at Christmas had some special glow of warmth. Piety was abroad, revelry and drunkenness. On Christmas Day, the Feast of the Nativity, the morning churches were filled, and the crib was unveiled inside the sanctuary rails. Then it was a day of closed doors and deserted streets.

But now it was over. It was the day of St Stephen, the martyr, who had been stoned to death. A forgotten man. It was a day of release, of closed shops and open public house doors, of heavy drinking, even street brawls. The new cinemas and dance halls were bright. For a few it was a time of remembrance, for a visit to the cemetery to stand in a forest of memorials in prayer.

The venerated one on this day was a small bird: the wren. This, colloquially, was "The Wren's Day". Groups dressed in oddments of clothes and comical hats, wore masks – eye-fiddles, they were called – and sang from door to door. There might be a bodhran or a melodeon. They carried a bit of greenery or a small bush held on high.

While they waited for pennies in the hat, they chanted:

The wran, the wran the king of all birds,
St Stephen's Day he was caught in the furze.
Up with the kettle and down with the pan,
Give us our answer and let us be gone.

It was late afternoon now, but a straggling singing group, here and there, still appeared and vanished. The gaslighters would soon be on their rounds. The blue, high-collared uniforms of the Gardaí in their flat peaked caps shone out from the crowd. At the County Club, where a string of cars was parked, light from windows and hallway shone out on the pillared and pedimented approach.

Arnie and Edward were silent. The job that lay ahead, an act of mercy, had need neither for words nor discourse. It had been decided.

Passing the Club, Arnie said, "I've never been inside its doors."

Edward waited.

"It was built," Arnie rambled on, "by the landlord class for the landlord class. The Bennetts were tradespeople. Times change."

Edward remained silent.

"Years ago, after the war, there was an invitation from one of their lordships. I didn't reply. Landlords ravaged this country. It'll take the rest of a century to find its feet."

"We still have lordships," Edward said, "but getting thin on the ground. A few of them will survive. The Irish ones."

Arnie drove across the bridge and into Clare and the countryside. Arnie offered cigarettes and they smoked.

"Four or five years ago," he said, "Harry was drinking at that club. I had him in the business, paid him well. I bought him a car. He might show up in the office once in a week. He wasn't interested in anything much except drinking and whoring." Arnie paused and was silent for a little while. "Eleven years ago," he said, "he was thirteen. I didn't know it, but he was drinking then. There was always drink in the house, and if it was short he ordered it in his mother's name. Ethel wasn't good at house management. I was always busy, too damn busy: meetings, travelling, always on the move. He was a randy tearaway. I used to think about it and laugh! He was big and strong. They'd serve him in hotels and boat clubs, too. He was just a runaway horse. He screwed every whore on the docks. Lived with some of them. He's just a corpse now, covered in gleeted sores. His brain is rotted. That's the end."

"Yes."

"You can't touch him. They've strapped him to his bed."

Edward said, "I know. I've seen him."

After a long silence, Arnie said, "Thank you for coming. I needed help. It won't be easy, will it?"

"No, but it must be done. We can do it."

"Yes."

Light in windows brought life to the first early dusk of December, shining against the rising fertile ground and shelves of stone above it. An occasional motor-car full of laughing young people passed them on its way to the city, to Georgian hall doors, lighted hallways decked with holly and mistletoe, fruit bowls, sparkling wine, food on sideboards and buffets, and servants. Edward was glad he had married Lillian; she knew the good life was a privilege. And the imprisoned poor, imprisoned in their own hopelessness, were always in her mind. They must have work and pay, forget the awful humility of dogma, have pride in possessions. There would always be a residue, ill-equipped, who would need help. A hand should be held out to them. She had a simple faith in mankind. Edward, without faith, envied her.

Arnie said, "Another fifteen minutes should bring us there. I've been meaning to speak to you, Edward," he said. They were in a narrow, rutted country lane now, of spiky hedges and creeping grass verges. "The Bennett business is strong. It will get better. It will grow with this new state."

Edward nodded in agreement. "A host of merchants and men of business have gone back across the water. And to Ulster."

Arnie brought the car to a halt, and left it ticking over. "I need a partner, Edward," he said. "I need a partner in business. I'd like you to consider it. You'd be very good for Bennett's. I don't have any doubts. I don't want an answer now. Just think about it."

"All right," Edward said.

Arnie drove on. The usually locked gates were opened, and he drove between the trees and shrubs to the main entrance of the nursing home. The supervisor came to meet them and took them to her office.

"You will find his condition disturbing," she said. "The restraints on his bed are necessary. I'm sorry, Mr Bennett, Mr Burke. We do everything possible."

Arnie said, "Of course. We understand."

She rang for a porter who led them across the sweep of forecourt to these outbuildings of isolation. He rang for admittance, and a nurse escorted them to the ward door. She said, "Don't make physical contact. That's important. Ring when you are ready to leave. The door will be locked."

Harry Bennett was a grotesque frame. Arms, legs and body had been strapped down and he heaved against the shackles. His ulcerated eyes were glazed with blindness. The warm room smelt of ordure. There were no bedclothes; they had wrapped him in a heavy sleeping suit that had been pulled awry in these awful spasms of rigor. He was a suppurating skin of decay.

"This is a visit," Edward said. "We must wait ten, fifteen minutes."

"I can't look at him," Arnie said. "There isn't even a window in this room. God, what a way to die! What a place to die!"

Edward found him a chair, which Arnie turned away from the bed before he seated himself. Edward looked at his watch and lit cigarettes for them both. The smell of decay was the smell of death.

Edward said to him, "You have a flask, haven't you?"

"Not a time for a flask," Arnie whispered towards the floor. "I must be sober, Edward. You'll understand that, I know."

"Yes."

"I'm glad you came. I couldn't have sat here alone."

"No."

"He's twenty-four. I was twenty-three when he was born. Ethel was twenty-two. I couldn't wait to marry Ethel. My God, she was a looker, bowled me over. Now they've all gone."

Minutes wasted away with only the noise of Harry's struggle. Edward stood and watched. He thought of his mother in her house of spirits, of her disdain, her bitterness, her bloodied uniform and her beloved son; the awful dark house and blazing coal fire; the open silent piano with the unplayed sheet music. He had always called at Christmas in previous years, even to stand on the threshold, to leave his seasonal wish with her. This Christmas had been a time of grief.

He looked at his watch; eleven minutes had passed. He said to Arnie, "It's time now. What did Thaddeus give you?"

Arnie pushed himself erect. His face was calm now, composed. He took a slender, corked phial, hardly two inches high, of colourless liquid from his waistcoat pocket.

"Thaddeus said it would kill pain for ever in a few instants. I didn't ask him what it was. I didn't want to know." He looked at Edward. "Now?"

"Yes."

There was no protective screen now; Harry was shackled, oblivious.

They walked across to the bedside. The body stiffened for long moments, slumped and stiffened again, the teeth clenching and loosening. Arnie's hand was unsteady.

"Wait," Edward said. He slipped off his topcoat and held it on his arm. "Don't touch him. Wait for an open mouth." He gripped Arnie's hand. "Wait."

When the time came they spilled the contents into the gaping throat. Edward pushed Arnie aside and clamped the overcoat over Harry's mouth and nostrils and held it there for some seconds till there was no movement. Then he dropped the topcoat on the floor and laid a chair on top of it.

"Time to go, is it?" Arnie asked. He didn't look at the bed.

"Yes. He's still. It's over now."

Arnie rang the bell. When the nurse came, Edward said without explanation, "The topcoat is infected."

"And you, sir?"

"I'm all right. Untouched."

They heard the clang of the gateway behind them as they drove out of the grounds. They drove the journey back in silence to gaslights that had a new brilliance after miles of growing darkness. The city had come to life for this holiday at least. The New Year was approaching. The George Hotel was like a great lighted ship at sea. Arnie parked at the kerb. The bar was in carnival.

Arnie brought two gills of whiskey from the counter in tall glasses. He hadn't spoken since the nurse had locked the door at Harry's ward. Now he said, "Let him rest in peace."

They raised glasses and drank.

Edward said, "To Harry."

They drank again.

"Thaddeus, you and I and Lillian: no one else need know. He was dying and he's dead. The supervisor will ring. She'll have him coffined tonight. A hearse will collect him, and tomorrow he and Matilda will be buried. I'll arrange it."

CHAPTER EIGHTEEN

DEATH AND BEREAVEMENT pass smoothly over a few days, and the gathering of family and the mild confusion it brings seem to accelerate the pace of time. Routine, lying beneath the surface of even wildly eccentric lives, is distorted. Days and nights are unreal spaces of time.

The ritual of prayer and burial carried the Bennetts and Edward Burke in its inexorable stream. There was a family vault in the cathedral churchyard, a deep well-constructed resting place with niches and shelving for twenty coffins. Steps descended to the door of chased skilled ironmongery, beyond which the Bennett ancestors slept. John Benjamin Bennett, died 1822, the pioneer, had been a man of confidence and resolution to envisage the survival of his line.

The family had watched the pall-bearers carry the coffins of Matilda and Harry out of sight to their entombment. Even Alexandra and Lillian had attended, and Abigail. There had been quiet dignity and sadness.

Ten days had passed. John and Alexandra had returned to the Hermitage; Thaddeus was at work again; Abigail had a house to put in order. Arnie felt only that a great weight had been lifted from him, that even the sharp loneliness of his house was blunted.

Although Lillian and Edward had returned quickly to their normal life, Edward was unsettled, filled with unease. They had been sitting in the warmth of their own drawing-room on the afternoon of one of the first days of the New Year when Edward surrendered to it.

The enormity, the suddenness of his thoughts, had shocked him; what had been flimsy imaginings took shape. The first barb of doubt had come at Harry's deathbed when he was remembering unwelcomed Christmas visits to his own threshold. A place of darkness, of incantations and shadows of spiritism.

He remembered feeling the unseen presence of his elder brother in his torn bloodied uniform. But when he reached the street the image was more distant than a dream. What had come to the surface of his thoughts now was the secrecy of his mother's bedroom. He could never remember his father entering it. She scarcely spoke to him. Then, suddenly, after years of celibacy, she was pregnant.

He said to Lillian, "I must talk to you."

Lillian, listening, sat facing him.

"I had two older brothers . . .," Edward paused.

"Who are dead," Lillian said. "Don't let family histories or bereavements pull you down. Or Harry's death."

"I'm glad Harry is out of pain," he said. "My brothers were born in 1883 and 1885."

"Yes?"

"Twelve, fourteen years of a gap."

"Oh Edward, that can happen."

"I don't think my father had shared my mother's bed in all that time."

"Edward, of course he did. An arrangement is made, but arrangements are broken. Maybe only once."

Hannah arrived with tea. Outside, the sky was low above the rooftops, the light pushing greyness through its filter. A steady silky drizzle fell, polishing the world. Hannah laid the tray before them at the sofa and replenished the fire.

"I brought strips of toast and potted veal and ham," she said.

"Thank you, Hannah."

Edward nodded at her and smiled.

"The curtains and the light, ma'am?"

"Yes, Hannah."

With a taper Hannah lighted two ornate pendant gas lanterns and a majestic oil lamp that stood on the sideboard. She drew the curtains. The light gently flowed about and settled. Hannah left. They took tea and ate a little.

Lillian said, "Marriage and fertility play all kinds of tricks, Edward. Some people grow cold and then become warm again. People share a room and have separate beds. People have separate beds in separate rooms. Lapses of child-bearing are commonplace."

"My eldest brother shared my mother's room and bed from birth till his school-days were over," he said. "I had another brother, remember, who grew up observing it. He told me."

Lillian moved close to Edward and smiled. "Michael? He remembered when she was pregnant with you?"

"I don't know. I was a child. He didn't talk very much. But I remember my father's bedroom. I used to sit there and talk to him."

"Why are you troubled?" she asked. "Do you remember something?"

"I thought about it only days ago. A thought suddenly surfaced into light. He shared her bed. Michael and I knew that. She was besotted with him."

"Your father. . . ."

"In my memory she was hardly aware of him." Edward stood. "I'm going to see her. Fifteen or twenty minutes walk in the drizzle will bring a little calm. I'll talk to her."

Lillian stood and faced him. "Yes, talk to her, Edward.

Find out what you have to live with. But remember, whoever you are, that I love you."

Edward took her in his arms and felt her close to him. He said, "I'll remember it."

In the hallway Hannah handed him a lined mackintosh, hat, gloves and umbrella, and held open the door. "It's a bad day for walking, Mr Edward."

"An overdue visit," he said. "I didn't do justice to the veal and ham, but thank you. Tomorrow perhaps."

The lamplighters were busy, and under the glowing and spreading orbs of light, the drizzle became visible brittle threads. When Edward turned downhill towards the church of St Michael and stood at his mother's door, the house was a black lifeless mass.

He rapped with the heavy cast-iron knocker and waited; he would rap for an hour, two hours, however long it took. He had knocked a half dozen times before there were sounds in the hallway.

She opened the door and appraised him. "Yes?"

"I'm coming in," he said. "I must talk to you."

"You don't cross my threshold."

As he moved she swung her hand to strike him, but he pushed her, stumbling, into the darkness. He moved from the hallway into the crepuscular gloom of her drawing-room where only firelight sent out little spears of light.

Her private "chaplain" was there, half risen in fear from his chair. He was a grey, emaciated man more than seventy years of age, his face caught in uncertainty now. A haunted fugitive man, Edward thought. Edward passed him, stood beyond the fireplace and watched the door.

Catherine Burke didn't have to assume histrionics, but she displayed them, held them in perfect control. She stood in the doorway in a long black gown of expensive fabric, her hair tied back, a pendant gold crucifix shining at her breast. The pallor of her face and hands might have been a painted skin of grease-paint.

She said to the cleric, "We will begin now."

Edward might have been something insubstantial, or not present.

The cleric was unsteady on his feet. Edward saw that a table had been arranged close to the warmth of the fire. A gleaming linen cloth covered it, and there was a chalice and pyx and beautiful chased candlesticks, all with the purity of white matt silver. Moving with slow dignity, Catherine Burke brought a taper from the fireside and lighted the candles.

She knelt, head bowed, hands joined, a poor penitent.

The cleric, at his altar, stood facing her. He took an unblessed host, a small disc of unleavened bread, from the pyx and held it aloft with his hands. He prayed aloud:

> This offering, do thou, O God, vouchsafe in all things to bless, consecrate, approve; that it may become for us the Body and Blood of thy most beloved son, our Lord Jesus Christ. For this is my Body.

He rested the host in the open pyx. He raised up the chalice with both hands and prayed again:

> For this is the Chalice of my Blood, of the New and Eternal Testament; the mystery of faith; which shall be shed for you and for many unto the remission of sins.

He broke the host in two and put one half on her tongue. Behind the altar again, he took the remainder of the host himself and stood bowed in prayer. His hands were trembling. He reached for the chalice and raised it again, then quickly held it to his lips and drank. In the warm room, a smell of whiskey was wafted. Hands clasped, the cleric was kneeling now. Edward felt no anger for him. He needed the life-saving, life-destroying whiskey. The church's wine for the daily miracle of transubstantiation had its alcohol, too, Edward thought; content hardly mattered.

As Edward watched, they both stood, and the cleric made a blessing sign with his hand.

"You can go now," she dismissed him. "Put the table and its cloth away. And the chalice and candlesticks."

The cleric put the little pyx in his pocket and turned to remove the table and silver. Edward could see that he was distressed, breathless. The makeshift altar was put aside.

"A drink?"

"Yes, yes, you know where to find it. And hurry."

The cleric took a bottle and a glass from the sideboard, poured himself an overflowing measure and drained it in a single gulp. He put on his black hat and an overcoat to cover the surplice and stole that he had worn.

She handed him a banknote. "See yourself out," she told him. "And close the doors as you leave."

He hurried away, and they listened to the snap of the outer door. She arranged herself in her chair by the fire and sat in silence. Edward looked at her face that was bled of emotion, that seemed to create illusions for others, seemed to conjure a dead son from his grave and groan out her passion with him. An illusion? And the tottering old priest who was at her beck and call, the ritual of body and blood here at her own fireside: was it all a great design of blasphemy?

He broke the silence. "Am I my father's son?" he asked.

"I had always thought so."

"He hadn't been in your bed for years before my birth. You couldn't bear to touch him, could you?"

"How could you know? You hadn't been born."

"My brother."

"Not your eldest brother?"

Edward looked at her, at the restful placid face. "No, not from him. He was yours, wasn't he? He shared your bedroom and your bed. You let him penetrate your life of witchery, didn't you? I think he wanted to die, but you call him back up from his grave."

She was standing up suddenly, in rage.

"You took him into your body, didn't you?"

She sat and held her hands loosely on her knees, softened

into a calm self-possession again. She sat in silence.

"You fornicated with him."

He could rouse no anger. She looked past him towards her bedroom, but he felt he was being watched. This house, this awful place of darkness and shadows. Once, when it had brightness and daylight, he had run about its rooms and stairway, gazed from its windows. He had found the adventures of a lonely child. Her bedroom door had always been locked.

She was calm now, her hands clasped loosely, her head poised. "Yes," she said, "I love him. We love each other."

All her movements were practised and balanced; this was her stage. She rose and walked to the sideboard, poured pale golden sherry from a decanter, sipped a little and brought it back to her seat.

He saw her settling into silence again. His anger was rising.

He spoke very softly to her, "Who am I?"

"I'm tiring of this," she told him. "It's time for you to go now."

"It's time for words now."

She drank a little sherry and appraised him. "Who are you, you ask me."

"Yes."

"Are you your brother's child?"

"Yes."

She stood and faced him. "I wonder." She held open the door to the dark hallway. "Go," she said. "You only stir anger and loathing when you come. I should bring evil down on you, but you are worthless."

"My brother's love-child, his bastard?"

"Don't come here again," she said. "Ever. Remember that."

Edward walked through the hallway, stood on the pavement and pulled the door shut. He heard the bolts being fastened.

He stood and looked up at the façade of the house. He looked at its dark silent windows, at the high wall that had enclosed the work yard and storage sheds, the arched cutstone of the entrance and the solid oak-panelled gates.

He was standing in the dim light between gas-lamps, growing accustomed to the gloom, when he saw movement in the shadows. A figure stood in the gateway. It was the cleric. Outside the security of the darkened room and its coal fire, he seemed a mere wisp.

Edward walked to him. "Were you waiting?"

"Yes."

"For me?"

"Yes, Mr Burke. You see me as a renegade priest. I can tell. You see me with bread and whiskey, wearing a surplice and stole, intoning the words of the mass. A mockery? For her perhaps. For me, nothing. I am a drunkard. The Church discreetly tries to hide us. In very bad times, it locks us away. I am a priest, I have the powers of a priest, but I lost my faith. The Church silenced me, I can no longer perform sacred duties. I drink and I never reach drunkenness."

Edward, looking back at the bulk of the church of his parish, asked, "Is this your church?"

"My church is a long walk from here, a long walk for failing legs. They call me a lay brother now. I do what menial work I can. I have a bed and food. I have no money."

"You bring her the Host, the Body of Christ?"

"The convent nuns make little discs of bread. They come to churches in cardboard boxes. Only at a certain moment in the mass, when sacred words are said, do they become the Body of Christ. If you believe it, Mr Burke. I bring to your mother's house a disc of bread once a month, that's all, a disc of bread. For wine in my chalice she gives me whiskey. I play out my little charade. I get whiskey. And money for days ahead. It is her ritual."

"Her ritual?"

"The ritual that she prescribed. She is an evil star, Mr Burke." Edward Burke looked into his face: the worn flesh, the eyes dull and veined, the smell of whiskey. A renegade, a drunkard, caught in the awful trap of avowed obedience, but he was an honest man.

"Have you known her long?"

"Since she has had an empty house."

"Do you remember my family?"

"I have spent forty years in this city, Mr Burke. Priests hear even the smallest whispers. They trickle down even to lay brothers. She was an incestuous woman who took your brother to her bed." He caught Edward's gloved hand in his. His still strong fingers tightened. "Forget that woman," he said. "She is nothing to you."

The wind was rising a little, blowing the thin drizzle before it. It would be coming from the south-west, blowing in from the tails of an Atlantic storm across the estuary and the river, from barren rockland to fields of grass and sheltering cattle: sixty miles of rain-swept world. It glistened on this narrow street and put the gas flames in a splutter of noise, in breathless gusts.

This old wasted man was rambling; he said to him, "You waited to tell me she is nothing."

"Yes," the cleric said. The rain glistened on his face and the perished nap of his topcoat. "I knew your father. Every month he came into the darkness of my church and waited until I came down the empty aisle. He gave me a sovereign. He knew what loneliness was."

"His marriage?"

"He had four years of marriage before she banished him."

"And she raised my brother to be her lover?"

"Yes," the cleric said. "Remember there has always been incest. Leviticus laid down an ordinance against it." After a pause, he said, "But your father found some happiness. She was a person of character and beauty, too. From the north, of farming stock, a rebel, a fighter, a Land-Leaguer. They were lovers for seven years. She died giving you birth. 1897. She was twenty-nine."

Edward was still; the rain gathered and dripped from his face.

"Her family came for her body. They came a long journey.

Your father travelled with her to the burial, somewhere in the north. I don't know where. Or where you were born."

"Her name?"

"I don't know. They were troubled times, harder than now. Armed soldiers, police, battering-rams, evictions, murders. You didn't carry your name on a banner. They were times of bloodshed."

"Yes," Edward said.

"But he brought you back into his own house. He wouldn't lose that battle. And he brought a wet nurse to care for you."

"I wasn't born in this house?"

"No," the cleric said. "I waited to tell you. You are your father's son and the son of the woman he loved. On the birth certificate you are the son of the woman who discarded him, to give you legitimacy. That was important."

Edward looked along the rain-swept street. He knew that he was close to tears. He took money from his pocket.

"No," the cleric said, brushing it aside. "Remember, never enter that house again." He pulled his coat about him and walked, steady with whiskey now, downhill to the corner and out of sight.

Edward dried the rain from his face, suddenly remembering the umbrella in his gloved hand. He opened it and walked slowly uphill towards the brighter lights and the traffic. He thought of his father's affection. How do you repay gratitude to the dead? This night, in the rain, he had been born again, five years after he stood at his father's graveside. He walked away from the empty house.

He reached the highroad feeling cleansed, lightened. His father had loved and been loved; he had been loved for seven years.

Edward took a horse cab through George's Street, past the patriot statue, to his doorstep. A light shone from the marquise, and the warmth of the hallway glowed in the stained-glass side panels of the door.

Before he could knock or reach for a key, Hannah had swung open the door.

"Mr Edward!"

"I'm fine, Hannah."

"You're soaked."

"It's nothing."

She guided him up the staircase to his dressing-room. "Change, Mr Edward. There are warm towels. You know how this city is for colds and illness." She paused.

"Yes, Hannah."

"I'll tell Madam you've arrived."

Edward towelled and put on fresh warm clothing. The day had brought happiness. Wearing a house jacket, he went downstairs to Lillian, who was waiting at the door of their drawing-room.

Hannah called out, "Dinner in an hour, ma'am."

Edward and Lillian hugged in the doorway; it was good to be home. She guided him to the sofa at the fire and seated him; stood, finger to lip for silence, then brought him a drink from the sideboard.

She sat on a stool facing him. "When you left you looked unhappy, Edward."

"I was." He knew she had been in tears.

"And now?"

Edward took her hands and raised her up. "I love you, Lillian," he said.

"I love you, Edward."

"You wept for me?"

"Oh, yes."

Edward raised his glass and smiled. "I am my father's son," he said. "My mother was his lover. You could call her a rebel." He looked at her. "You're crying again."

"Happiness, Edward. I'm glad he found happiness."

"There's sadness, too. She died a long time ago, at my birth. She was twenty-nine. It's a long story."

"Tell it," she said.

At half past ten, Hannah came to say good-night. "The rain is gone, Mr Edward. You caught the worst of it. That wind is drying the streets."

"Edward," Lillian said when Hannah was gone, "we could go to the coast one day soon, spend a few days together in our special village. The hotel, the fire, so much beauty everywhere. We could wrap up and walk in the wind. Or sit in the warmth and watch the sea pounding against cliffs. Just the two of us."

"Yes," he said, "I'd like that."

"Wet or dry, storm or calm, we'll enjoy it."

"Yes."

She went to the window and looked beyond the rooftops at broken cloud sailing on the wind.

There were two trains, a great snorting one for twenty miles and then a little puffing one that wandered from place to place until the end of the line. "The journey is an adventure, too."

Edward laughed. "There's a song about it," he said.

CHAPTER NINETEEN

MULVEY HAD KEPT Carmody in his sights: he watched him hire and fire on the dockside; he saw him, spick and span, as he walked home at dusk; followed him to the sports club which he used as a headquarters of his citizen army; he saw him at the presbytery door. He watched the contributions of coal that were made to his premises.

At night-time Barrett walked the crowded streets of Irishtown. He took a drink and sat in pubs, talked, listened, and enjoyed the bar-room singers. He heard names that were greeted with approval or condemnation, gathered scraps of information. He bought his round.

"Still driving the bank manager, Barrie?"

"He's an inspector. He's all right."

"The money's fair?"

"And steady. No fixed hours of course. . . ."

The picture took shape. Carmody was looking up at high places. He would be a man of business, a city councillor. That was the stepping stone. From there, with time, he could make it to the top.

"A hard man, a stevedore," Barrett would say.

"Dangerous. But everyone can take a fall."

"Dangerous?"

"Yes, he's dangerous."

Barrett would nod, push it aside as unimportant. He enjoyed his company and his drinks and let conversation flow about him. He drank his stout and listened.

"A big confraternity man, too, wearing white gloves and carrying the canopy like an Ulster procession."

"He calls to the priests' house on the hill."

"Dr Cafferey opens his door for him."

"Confraternity business?"

"It might be."

Barrett stored away his information for Mulvey.

Mulvey asked, "What about his dead son?"

"Left sick in his bed for more than a week with diphtheria. He was dying when they took him to the workhouse."

"He was a loving father, wasn't he?" Mulvey asked.

"A tyrant, a drill-sergeant, is the story. The boy was afraid of him, they say."

"His wife?"

"She lives with it. A decent enough woman, clever too. She turns him out well. She'll shape him for the future."

"You think he's plotting now?"

"Oh yes."

"We can wait," Mulvey said.

Christmas passed and the Bennett funerals, which had been private.

Mulvey had joined the bank staff at Christmas midday for a couple of glasses of malt. Weak drinks were for clerical staff, sherry for wives. It was an hour of chatter and muted laughter in the manager's drawing-room, soft in politeness.

Mulvey moved on to the George Hotel where he had booked an overnight room. He enjoyed his Christmas food, drink, casual company, cheerful women. Chinese women, Mulvey thought, were painted attractive dolls, skilled in pleasure. He missed them.

It was late evening, almost night-time, more than a week later. It had been drizzling since morning and people and traffic were thin on the streets, but now a breeze had swept in to clear it. Mulvey had spent a couple of hours in his chair by the fire.

Now he was dressed in a dark grey felt hat and mackintosh, and he carried a hand-gun and a heavy cane. On the stroke of midnight, Barrett drew up to the door with the brougham.

On the pavement, he asked Barrett, "Can we stay out of sight?"

Barrett said, "I've arranged it."

They drove down to where the fringes of the new city joined with Irishtown. These were four-storey brick houses, fallen into the decrepitude of neglect, let out in rooms to tallymen for storage, or to bone-setters, faith-healers, occasional prostitutes and pimps – people in movement. It had been a street of reasonable quality once. Now it was empty in dim gaslight.

Barrett drove down to what had once been a service road entrance to coach-houses and stabling behind the dwellings. It had been bricked across to a height of twenty feet and a broad coach-way with heavy wooden gates installed. The fascia board, framed and once stylishly sign-written, had been painted and smudged, faded to a peeling palimpsest. It said "Horse Repository".

Once minor gentry and rising landowners, wealthy Catholics, from the surrounding countryside, arriving to spend a day in town, had left their coaches and horses here for the vehicles to be polished and the horses watered and groomed. The motor-car had ruined business.

The gates were closed and chained now. Barrett stepped down and, with a bolt cropper, cut across the link of the chain. Calm and unhurried, he surveyed the almost dark street, its neglected doors and windows, and then pushed open the gates. The passageway had been trussed and roofed with corrugated iron. It was black as pitch. He pulled the brougham in out of sight.

Mulvey had alighted when Barrett stepped down to join him. Pointing at what might be a derelict dwelling, he said, "The second floor. The hall door is pulled shut but not latched. There's a lighter door at the end of the hallway. A cross door. Ten seconds with a lever or a tommy bar. It's a tenement."

"The second floor is Carmody's target?"

"The office of a Mr Flanagan. He comes from Dublin once a week to do his business. Flanagan, of course, isn't his name. He is a foreigner who deals in short term loans. A pound for a week costs half a crown."

Mulvey said, "Twelve and a half percent. A pound for a year would be six pounds ten shillings. Six hundred and fifty per cent."

They stood in darkness and silence for a long time. This passageway had been carpeted in straw: easy on carriage wheels, and a wrapping for horse dung. It had been a place of good business once. And a little farther on, tucked away out of sight, had been the meeting house of the Society of Friends, the Quakers, friends of the poor in the best of times and the worst of times.

Barrett remembered this street during his youth when doors and windows were painted, fresh curtains on display and doorsteps and pavements clean. There had been a doctor and a dentist, civil servants, drapers, solicitors' clerks. A licensed premises had the strange name of "Mannix" above its door. You could look downhill a couple of blocks, past the General Post Office, and see the sweep of the river not far from the bridge.

Barrett said, "This has become a ragged place."

Mulvey nodded. "Too near the laneways and the sound and smell of the bacon factory."

There was noise on the street now, faint footfalls. Four men arrived, a pair from each end of the street. In moments they had pushed in the hall door of the house and vanished from sight.

Mulvey said, "Carmody is there?"

"Yes, he's there."

"We'll give them time to do their work and scatter. I want Carmody."

In a few minutes the group was on the steps again; cautious, fast-moving men. A moment to survey the street and they had dispersed.

Mulvey and Barrett crossed the street and entered the house. They closed the hall door behind them and moved in darkness. The cross door had been forced. They climbed two flights of stairs to Flanagan's office. The door was open.

"An open door?" Barrett said.

"Part of the ritual. A warning. People must see."

It was a front room, its two windows looking out on the street. The glass had a skin of permanent dirt, but gaslight from the world outside filtered in. The room and its few items of furniture had been devastated. Flanagan wouldn't keep records, Mulvey thought. A string had been tied across the end of the room, and a curtain hung from it. Mulvey pulled it aside.

Flanagan was stretched on a camp-bed, bloody and semiconscious. He had taken a beating. He was a fleshy balding man in his fifties. He had come from Dublin to spend a day and a night in the city. In the morning he would be on the move again. Flanagan wouldn't waste money on boarding houses. Fully dressed, he kipped here for a single night. His face was a bleeding swollen mass; one arm hung limply down from the narrow bed. Mulvey searched his pockets, coat and trousers. Nothing. Not even small change or a rail ticket.

"His arm?" Barrett said.

"Broken. He needs help."

"Telephone? A hospital?"

"Exchange operators need the caller's number. We might make trouble for ourselves. You go back and have the brougham ready to move."

Barrett left. Mulvey had seen a bucket in a corner. That would be Flanagan's personal midden. It held a day's urine that Mulvey tipped over with his feet. There was no gas-fitting in the room, only a cheap oil lamp with a glass shade. Mulvey filled the bucket with broken wood and poured paraffin from the lamp over it.

He lit the drained lamp and left it standing in the open doorway; the saturated wick would keep it alight for a while. On the doorstep to the street, he lit his bucket brazier with a match and a piece of torn wallpaper. The paraffin on dry wood caught the flame at once. It would be the money-lender's cry for help.

Mulvey ran across the street to the repository; the brougham door was open, Barrett high on his seat ready to move. Before they were out of sight, Mulvey looked back and saw the flames from the bucket rising up in the darkness.

"Drive along the quays," he called up to Barrett. "There are dark enough places there to stand. We need to talk."

The winter river was a great streak of ink; spaced gaslights sent out shivering pillars of reflection; river buoys dragged in the current. On board the berthed coal boats, lights still burned and a faint sound of music and singing reached them. The holiday lingered on. In the near distance was the clock tower by the harbour office, and the swivel bridge that waited for tides before it gave escape or access. The scarlet women, the "harbour lights", had gone back to the Windmill and other places, and sleep was muffling the city. Barrett halted in the shadows and climbed down.

Mulvey was waiting. "They wore dungarees?" he asked.

"Workmen's dungarees, stained and patched. Mufflers and caps. A poor man's rig-out, weekdays or Sundays."

"They aren't poor."

"No."

"A kind of battle-dress?"

"Yes."

"Where do they change? The club?"

Barrett nodded. "Wives wouldn't be included in their important work."

"Good. That gives us some time," Mulvey said.

Mulvey gave his instructions, and Barrett, moving at a fair pace, drove across the city, down the Mall and turned into Irishtown. He reached the big corner that was Carmody's and drove a little past it. The street was empty. He looked carefully over the roadway, the footpaths, the houses.

A big double gate led to Carmody's coal yard, with a wicket gate fitted in it. Barrett forced away the screws that held the bolts in place and levered it open. He nodded to Mulvey.

Mulvey said, "Wait for me out of sight, and watch." He stepped on to the pavement. He had left his mackintosh, and now his clothing was dark and he wore a cloth cap. He handed his gun to Barrett.

Barrett said, "Carmody might carry a gun."

"I don't want to kill him," Mulvey said. "I want to beat him to his knees. I want him to know what fear is." He was wearing skin-tight gloves. "You move," he said. "There isn't much time."

Mulvey stepped inside the wicket gate and left it hanging three inches open. The coal yard was blacker than the night. In less than ten minutes he heard sharp footsteps approaching outside. He crouched down on all fours beside a piled heap of slack.

The footsteps halted. Carmody would have seen his wicket gate forced open. Suddenly the gate was flung back to its extremity. It crashed, wood against wood. Cagey. Someone waiting behind the wicket wouldn't catch Carmody on the hop. He hung his topcoat and jacket on cleats on the main gate and stood in shirt-sleeves: the executioner. He was silhouetted for moments against the pale spread of the streetlights. He closed the wicket. He was gazing into the depths of the yard, waiting to accustom himself to the darkness. He moved a few steps.

Mulvey could see the dull image of a gun in his hand. He judged the distance – three, four paces – and let his body-weight rest on his feet. His gloved hands were free. In the space of a second he was behind Carmody. He struck him at the base of his spine, felt the thud of his fist against bone. Carmody was in rigor, blinded with an explosion of pain. The gun fell from his hand. With his fists Mulvey hammered the track of bone to his neck. He held him on his feet, rested him against the wall and a table-mounted weighing scale, half seated him. Carmody's mouth was agape, his head tilted back. Mulvey beat him until he was limp. Then he broke his arms. Carmody's mouth was open in a silent scream. Mulvey pulled him like a rag-doll across the ground, across the raised threshold of the wicket. He surveyed the street, signalled into the darkness for Barrett. He threw Carmody on his own doorstep and knocked hard on Carmody's door.

In moments he was in his seat in the brougham, out of sight, driving past the church of St Michael. He mopped the sweat from his face, exchanged his headgear and pulled the warmth of his mackintosh about him. Not a single cab or motor-car broke the night-time's sleep.

They reached home.

"Are you all right?" Barrett asked.

"Yes."

"Do you know where the bishop's palace is?"

"Yes," Barrett said.

"Tomorrow. Midday. Here."

Mulvey climbed the stairs to his rooms, still warm from exertion. A sudden end would have been too gentle for Carmody. He would let Barrett leak a story of the money-lender's retribution. Watchdogs even here in the city. There were weeks in hospital ahead for Carmody. Shame would corrode his mind. He would see always in his wife's eyes her knowledge of his weakness.

Mulvey poured himself whiskey and sat in his easy chair. He thought of his father: in policeman's uniform, growing old in occupation-days, the small burned out retirement home. The Mulvey family had been scattered: Boston, Toronto, Chicago, Shanghai. Scattered and swallowed up. He thought of the teeming streets of Shanghai and the Woosung Docks, the towering ships and cranes; the barges on mud banks and coolies laden with shoulder-poles trotting a single plank to shore, sure-footed as animals; the magnificence of shops and hotels, the affluence; the gambling palaces, the thousand clubs of food and drink and pleasure.

Families were lost there and never sought. A whole world of birth and death, riches and poverty, surrounded by five miles of city wall. Beyond the walls, elegant European suburbs took you in an instant to London or Paris or Lisbon. English, French, Portuguese, Dutch, Germans, Spanish, Greeks, Turks: all feeding there.

He poured himself another whiskey and drank it back. To hard times. To good people. He lay in a bath for half an hour, dried and went to his bedroom. Outside the city was soundless.

The Church's very considerable parochial and diocesan monies and the wealth of a rising Catholic middle class were in the care of the bank. Catholics were aware of the preponderance of Protestantism and Masonry that flourished from governor and directors to even maturing junior clerks, but strangely found in that an additional reassurance of integrity. The operation of the Church's account was in the hands of the incumbent diocesan bishop, who was among the special clients on Mulvey's list.

Mulvey had slept well and was looking out on a bright fresh morning. It was half past ten, and he had lit his first cigarette and opened his morning paper when his house-telephone rang.

He lifted the receiver.

"I've arranged that, Mulvey," the manager said from his

spacious office on the ground floor. "His Lordship will see you at half past twelve. He's an exact old fellow. Try not to be late, he stressed. I think he has a lunch appointment."

"Fine," Mulvey said. He laid down the telephone.

Barrett arrived at midday. "A half an hour to get to the bishop's palace," Mulvey said. "Can we make it?"

"Yes."

Barrett moved off at a nice trotting pace. He drove across two bridges and the toe of the island on to the northern bank, left a boathouse behind and passed an isolated pub en route. The gates of the bishop's palace were opened, and they drove up to the porticoed entrance. Barrett opened the brougham door and Mulvey alighted.

A workman told Barrett, "Take your cab and horse around to the back outhouses. I'll leave you a shovel and a barrow in case there are droppings."

Barrett nodded.

He drove off. Mulvey stood on the steps and looked at the garden, the shrubs, the careful beds for flowers. There were tall beech trees, too. It was a very desirable palace.

Behind him, a precise authoritative voice said, "Perhaps you weren't informed. His Lordship has a luncheon appointment."

Mulvey turned.

This plump young man was excellently groomed in his fine dark cloth. Mulvey said, "Yes, I was informed. I was admiring everything."

"His Lordship is a very busy man."

"I understand."

The round, pink face took shape for Mulvey now: the flawless skin, the eyes, the tilt of chin. The hair was smoothed, not a rib out of place. This was Carmody's patron who had stood with him on the doorstep of the church presbytery on the city hill. He spoke with a great importance.

"I am Dr Cafferey."

"You are the bishop's administrator?" Mulvey asked politely.

"No, but I am his very close colleague in Jesus Christ."

Mulvey removed his hat, looked at the winter sky. "It's quite cold, isn't it? An early sharpness."

Dr Cafferey said, "You are a messenger from the bank? Are you carrying a letter from some one in authority?"

Mulvey was still smiling, but his voice had hardened. "Could we step inside out of the weather?"

Dr Cafferey reappraised him. "Yes, if you wish. If it's necessary. His Lordship's time is very precious."

"You mentioned that he had a lunch appointment."

In a moment or two Dr Cafferey moved and Mulvey followed; the progress came to halt in the reception foyer.

Dr Cafferey said, "What was the message?"

Mulvey introduced himself. "My name is Mulvey," he said. "An appointment has been made for me to meet the bishop."

Dr Cafferey was incredulous. "An audience with His Lordship?"

"A conversation," Mulvey said. "The time mentioned was twelve thirty. It's close to it now. If there is an appointments book, I think you should consult it. My time is precious, too."

Dr Cafferey examined him from head to toe: good footwear, good clothes, good linen. The face was undisturbed but tight skinned, the eyes hard. A bank messenger? Dr Cafferey showed his impatience at the impossibility of it all; he said "Wait" and moved away out of sight.

Mulvey waited in the stillness and polish: polished woodblock floors, polished windows, everything polished. At the end of a corridor a black-robed figure of a nun, a shadow, soundlessly floated in and out of vision.

Dr Cafferey returned, still authoritative, magisterial, and stood some distance from Mulvey. "Come," he said.

Mulvey followed him into the fine comfortable study of the bishop, with its great glowing fire, its french windows looking on to a loggia, and beyond it a vista of gardens. The bishop, informal in his cassock, sat in his easy chair. A man aware of his importance, Mulvey thought. There was a faint smell of sherry in the air.

Dr Cafferey said, "This man is Mulvey from the bank, Your Lordship."

The bishop said, "Yes, there was a telephone call, but it slipped my mind. You have a message, Dr Cafferey says."

"I came to have a conversation," Mulvey said and felt a shock of silence. "You could call me a messenger, I suppose. All arrivals are messengers. My name, as you know, is Mulvey. I am the Regional Inspector of Bank Security and Procedure. The bank is my address." Mulvey looked at Dr Cafferey and back to the bishop. "My business is usually confidential. Should we be alone?"

The bishop was stung from his posture of repose. "Dr Cafferey is a friend and confidante!"

"Then I'll take a seat. I'll try not to keep you too late for your lunch."

The bishop held up a restraining hand to Dr Cafferey, whose temper was at a fine edge. "Get your business over as quickly as possible," he said.

Mulvey said, "My duties cover the whole field of security. Bank premises, their cash holdings and contents. Procedures and confidentiality. In the aftermath of a rebellion and a civil war, we live in troubled times. A government in power and an opposition still at war. Crime is an everyday occurrence. There is arson, even murder. That is the climate I work in . . . ."

The bishop said, "I think we are conversant with the political situation, Mr Mulvey."

"I'm sure. Your dealings with the bank are held in high esteem. You are on a list of clients who receive special security."

"Hardly necessary. I could leave my gates and doors open."

"I don't doubt it, but serious criminal behaviour by others could bring the Church into disrepute. The good name of the Church must also be secured."

Dr Cafferey said in disbelief, "Criminal activity?"

"By devout vigilantes. Confraternity, sodality members. Gangs of fire-raisers who don't stop at beatings and thuggery."

The bishop was suddenly dismissive. "You have proof of this?" he asked.

"The business of proof doesn't arise. I am not the law of the Church or the land. It is my duty to advise you that your good name is endangered. So I make the journey to see you this morning."

Dr Cafferey said, "Who are these people?"

"I had thought that perhaps with your associations and friendships in the city, you might have been of help. You have a great relationship with your flock. I sometimes see you talking to them on your doorstep. They could probably help you with names. They have confidence in you. Of course, finally, it would be a matter for the Garda force."

"Arson, beatings . . .," Dr Cafferey began.

"Arising from bigotry. The property of merchants, professional men, persons of repute, families who have spent more than a hundred years among us. Most of them are good people. They are being hounded."

The bishop was a little less confident, a little puzzled. "Bishops are isolated, become isolated," he said, "administering to the management of a diocese."

He paused and looked at Dr Cafferey.

Dr Cafferey said, "Of late there have been a few incidents in the city. I didn't want to burden you."

"Serious incidents?"

"One or two. I have spoken to my confraternity prefects about them. They feel the situation has blown over."

"Has it?"

"I would think so."

"Keep me informed." He looked at Mulvey. "I will telephone my administrator. All parish priests will be advised to instruct their congregations. Thank you, Mr Mulvey."

Dr Cafferey said, "Yes, thank you."

Mulvey paused, then he said, "There was a further incident last night. Serious bodily injury and destruction of property. The victim was of little prominence or importance, I suppose. He was a money-lender. But there is what is thought to have been an aftermath. A man, Carmody, took a severe beating and injuries. These money-lenders don't travel alone. They make deals and enforce them."

Mulvey stood in silence.

The bishop spoke very quietly. "This lawlessness must cease. It must be extirpated."

Dr Cafferey said, "I will address my confraternity personally."

Mulvey took his leave. Dr Cafferey escorted him to the portico, ordered his brougham, and watched him drive down the shaded avenue out of sight.

CHAPTER TWENTY

JANUARY IS THE month of shortest days and long, sometimes cold, bitter and wet evenings and nights. Beyond the lighted cluster of the city, even small farmhouse windows are bright as single stars. But it crawls slowly past, and February comes with moments of spring in its occasional days of bright skies.

This was the second week of February, bringing brightness from a sky of ragged cloud and momentary pale washes of sunshine. In the People's Park across from Thaddeus' drawing-room windows flowers were beginning to show and a fresh greenness had brushed against everything. The library building was sharp and clean.

The city was more at peace, too. The awful plague of diphtheria had passed, although there were the perennial visitations of bronchitis and influenza that were the day-to-day stuff of medicine. Tuberculosis, of course, was a resident.

Violence had all but ceased. Political marches, soapbox rallies and occasional brawls and bloodshed were spasmodic.

The Bennetts were gathered together again, beneath Thaddeus' roof: John and Alexandra from the Hermitage, their sons, their daughter, a grand-daughter, a son-in-law.

Old John Bennett said, "This is a fine reunion. I'm glad to see so many of us together again."

He raised his glass and they drank.

Thaddeus, at the head of the table, was moved by it all. Abigail, beside him, took his hand.

"Arnie will say a few words for me and himself," said Taddy. "He's good with words. He looks after us."

Brigid and her maids had gone; she had left the linen tablecloth, a centrepiece of flowers, ashtrays and glasses. The men smoked, the grey wisps making patterns in the stillness. It was the clear, fresh weather of a vanishing winter. Arnie was already speaking as he pushed back his chair and raised himself upright.

"It has been a long winter," he said. "It has passed and we have survived. Some have not. They are in our thoughts." He drank from his glass. "There has been fire-raising and thuggery, the loose ends of insurrection and civil war. I can tell you now that it, too, has passed. It's time to be at work again.

"We don't sit down together at lunch very often, but this is Thaddeus' birthday." Arnie was smiling. "Brigid said this morning that she was glad to see him growing just a little older and more sensible. He still has his boyhood figure, though, she said. Happy birthday from us all, Taddy."

They raised glasses.

Thaddeus said, "There's wisdom there, I can tell you. But my boyhood figure? I'm afraid age alters."

Arnie tapped his tight waistband. "Yes, it does," he said. "Transforms might be more accurate. Thaddeus assures me that he is cutting his workload. Occasional surgery, fewer patients. Abigail will be staying at home with us. She is going to Maggie Norris to join the Barrington's staff."

Abigail waved to John and Alexandra.

Arnie drank a little wine and smiled at his audience. "I,

too, will be spreading my load. Edward has accepted a partnership in Bennett and Company, I'm pleased to say. Edward and Lillian deserve each other," he said.

Old John Bennett stood again to say, "We'll drink to all the people and all the changes. And to those who have passed on."

Thaddeus nodded.

Arnie said, "Yes, to the absent ones.

"We must go soon. Edward and Lillian are going to spend a few days by the sea, and I'm driving them to the station. There isn't a lot of time left."

Lillian stood and held out her arms as if to embrace them all. "I must change," she said. "Fifteen minutes." She hurried away to Abigail's bedroom.

Thaddeus led them into the drawing-room. He stood in the embrasure of a tall window watching sunshine make long shadows by the library and the railings.

Arnie joined Edward and brought two whiskies. "There's time, Ed. A drink for the journey."

Edward took it, smiled, drank. "I'm glad Abigail will be at home," he said. "She'll brighten Taddy's house again."

Arnie laughed. "She'll make him toe the line," he said.

"She'll be able to visit the Hermitage more, too. She likes the house by the river, doesn't she?"

Arnie thought of the petrol cans and the rifle shot, the bloodied gardener; it seemed a long time ago. "We saved it," he said, nodding to Edward. "Carmody is out and about, discharged from the infirmary. He had a close call, the story goes, but he'll work again, make a living, maybe become a coal merchant. But warfare days are over. Who wants him? His wife sat at his hospital bed every day. No one visited. Not even his clergy."

"Money-lenders' men are savage crews," Edward said, waiting.

Arnie said, "Mulvey punished Carmody. He was settling an old score."

"Where is Mulvey now?"

"On a P & O liner somewhere, en route to old haunts on the other side of the world. Mulvey has His Majesty's pension, and I looked after him well. He likes the life out there. Clubs, food, women. He'll do a little trading up the Great River, as he calls it. Dope, I suppose. He's no angel, but he was a good soldier."

Edward agreed.

Arnie heard sounds and movement on the landing. "That's Lillian," he said. "Almost time. There was a letter from the bishop yesterday offering sympathy and concern for our loss of goods and property. And gratitude, of course, for our contributions to the parochial fund. Violence will be condemned from the altars."

"A good man on our side," Edward laughed. "Mulvey was clever."

Arnie glanced at him.

Lillian was in the doorway. Edward crossed to her. She was wearing a loose calf-length tweed coat with a tie belt, a jacquard scarf, a dainty cloche hat and shoes button-strapped at the instep. She was smart and attractive. She took Edward's hand. "We're only going for a break, a few days, so no hugging and farewells." She blew them a kiss. "Love to you all."

Brigid had brought topcoats and hats for Edward and Arnold from the hallway. In moments they were on the pavement. Arnie's driver, a tall, sturdy fellow, held open the door for them. Brigid waved.

They turned right and followed the park railings. The station was five minutes drive from Georgian elegance, through a mishmash of shops and small dwellings that masked hard times and poverty.

Edward turned to Arnie. "You've engaged a driver?"

"Yes. Barrett. He used to be Mulvey's man. Learned his driving in the army. A very useful fellow."

Edward smiled.

Barrett parked close to the station forecourt and opened

the doors. A porter took their trunks on a push-trolley. Lillian and Edward and Arnold climbed the stone steps to the entrance and talked for a few moments.

Lillian looked along the narrow street leading towards Irishtown. "There's so much work to be done," she said.

Edward said, "It's an ancient city. It can fight battles for style and dignity, too."

Arnie waved from his car as Barrett drove down to the clock tower near the church and turned left, out of sight. Edward and Lillian walked along the stone platform. The city station was a terminus with great buffers. At the door of the guard's van, a uniformed man consulted his watch. A well-fed man of importance in steady employment, he was removed from the travelling vulgus, but he made a slight movement of deference to Edward and Lillian. The bulk of travellers were farming men in Sunday best, or commercial-travellers in perennial suits and hats and overcoats. Carriage doors were open, luggage and freight was loaded. The monster engine stood in a cloud of steam, its driving wheels and piston rods gleaming from oil rags. Its nameplate was polished brass.

Lillian said, "I love all this movement, the smell of steam and oil and fire. And look ahead, Edward. A maze of silver tracks."

Edward took her arm and helped her from the wooden step to the corridor. The carriage had warmth and comfort, and they were alone. They sat at the window seats, facing each other. The carriage was decked in timeless upholstery, antimacassars without stain, luggage racks and framed pictures of landscapes, seascapes, streets with imposing buildings.

"Trains remind me of the ends and beginnings of school terms," Lillian said. "Home again to all its comforts, then back to dormitories and refectories." She looked at Edward. "You walked along the pavements to school. You were lucky. Always at home." She reached out and took his hand. "Were you happy then?"

Edward smiled. "Happy enough," he said, "but empty, too."

On the platform there were shouts, the slamming of doors, the blowing of whistles; the train stirred and stretched its couplings. They were moving, first in great gasps of effort, then steadily with a rhythmic tapping against rail-joints. They crossed the river to its northern bank in another county and paused along the way at small platforms or halts on the permanent way to the county town.

"Western passengers, all change," they heard.

Lillian and Edward crossed the platform to the small train on a small track that would puff and groan its way to the north and west, before turning south along the coastline to journey's end. The frantic downhill rushes and laboured climbs at hardly walking pace, the changing rhythms on the track, had made it a kind of mythical pilgrimage for holiday people and an act of penance for regular passengers.

Lillian said, "Percy French."

"And as you're waiting for the train," Edward said, "you'll hear the guard sing this refrain . . ."

Lillian recited it for him:

Are ye right there, Michael, are ye right?
Do you think we'll be there before the night?
'Tis all dependin' whether
The ould engine holds together,
And it might now, Michael, so it might!

Edward crossed and sat beside her and they sat close together down the last twenty miles of the track.

"I'm glad you thought of this," Edward said.

"So am I."

It was a small, neat station-house with three chimneys, a dwelling-house for the stationmaster and his family and waiting-rooms and some facilities for passengers. The canopy of slate and wood over the platform was mounted on iron stanchions; decorative woodwork fringed it and the gable end of the house. Only a few passengers alighted. In the early days of a year, summer holidays were still far off. A man in an oil-skin coat and a cap with shining peak approached. A polished brass badge on his cap announced him.

"Victoria Hotel," he called.

Lillian said, "That crotchety old queen lives on in a thousand specks of what was her empire."

They were moving in the hotel brougham through a small village: a few streets, a square, a strand-line promenade that was a horseshoe enclosing the bay.

As they reached the hotel, cliffs and bay spread out their colour, and the great power of ocean broke on the reef close to them. Back in the village, an oil lamp flickered here and there.

Lillian and Edward, from their bedroom, looked out at the arrival of night-time and drew the curtains. They changed from travelling clothes. It was a large bedroom with a fire and easy chairs. A maid arrived with a menu and to turn up the oil lamps. Lillian ordered. "You'll call us?" she asked.

"Yes, ma'am."

"But bring a whiskey for Mr Burke while we are waiting." When she had gone she said, "Bennetts have been coming here for years."

They sat at the fire.

Lillian said, "Sometime, would you like to go north and look for her grave?"

Edward thought about it. "I don't know her name or where she came from. Anyway, it was their secret love," he said. "They're together somewhere. I wouldn't intrude."

She smiled, nodded. The maid arrived with his drink and adjusted the lamp wicks. The wind had grown stronger, and it pushed against the windows. He raised his glass.

Lillian said, "I'm so glad you've joined forces with Arnie."

"Arnie is a strong man," Edward said, "clever and strong, but he has too much work. I can help."

"He needs help."

"Yes."

"In time, Thaddeus will be better, too."

She pulled her chair closer to his and he took her hand. They sat in silence for a long time. The sea was coming across the strand now, breaking on the fringe of stone. They could hear the hoarse drag of the ebb. The wind came in sweeping gusts.

"Edward," Lillian said.

"Yes?"

"I have news."

A few moments of silence focused his attention.

"News?"

"I am pregnant."

Edward stood and looked down at her; she gazed up at his face.

"Pregnant?"

"Yes, Edward, I am pregnant. You look as if you might topple over."

He drained back the whiskey, raised her up and embraced her. "I'm finding my feet," he said. "When?"

"September."

He could hear her laughing as she crossed the hallway to their bathroom. He remembered the dark house down near the church and the markets, the strange prayers and responses, the bloodied uniform, the silent piano, the awful grinding of love and the illusion of a dead son who could never rest. He would never enter that house again. No drop of her blood was in his veins.

Lillian was back.

"You were miles away," she said.

"Yes," he said. "I have just arrived. Today is my birthday." He embraced her again.

The maid knocked at the door and announced dinner.

"Yes, we're coming." Lillian took Edward's arm. "There are a lot of good thoughts," she said. "The lovers who made you. And what we have made."

At the doorway they stood and looked back at the bedroom: the fire, the lamplight, the polished gleaming woodwork. From the landing the village windows were little spots of glimmer in the darkness.

SOME OTHER FICTION
from
MOUNT EAGLE

Steve MacDonogh (ed) / *The Brandon Book of Irish Short Stories*

"Ranges hugely in setting, style and tone. The confident internationalism of these mostly young writers reflects something of the spirit of the new Ireland but it is grounded in an undeceived realism. . . On the evidence here, the future of Irish fiction is in good hands." *Observer*

"This unusual collection of work by some of Ireland's more recent exponents (poets, playwrights and novelists included) shows how slight a grip the familiar Irish themes – faith, superstition, hunger, oppression, heroism – now exercise on a radically altered national consciousness.

"Many locations are unspecified; others are refreshingly unfamiliar. . . And the concerns. . . are primarily with relationships. . .

"Religion and politics do slip in, but only in three of the twenty-four stories, and even then in unusual guises. . .

"All of this offers a consciousness far removed from conventional Irish concerns but typical of the range and eclecticism of this impressive collection." *Times Literary Supplement*

"This anthology has stories illuminating experiences and emotions that are universal and instantly familiar. . . Almost all are good, some are excellent . . . The book is also excellent value for money." *Examiner*

288 pages; ISBN 0 86322 237 4; Brandon original paperback £6.99

BRANDON is an imprint of Mount Eagle Publications

David M. Thomas / *Anger's Violin*

"There are many settings in which to base a novel and this has got to be one of the most original ideas. . . *Anger's Violin* is not an ordinary book. It is something different altogether – that rare commodity in these days of mass publishing, a good book with a good story and good characters. . . Thomas has genuine talent and his career as a writer should know no bounds. . . He writes with power and grit, yet maintains a soft touch." *The Irish World*

"Interwoven with stories of European myth as well as its rich history, which work especially well mixed in with the narrative. . . Most satisfyingly, its lead character and narrator finish up with a new outlook on life, conveyed by an author whose perspective is singular and refreshing." *Irish Post*

"The writing here is intelligent, erudite, witty, entertaining and rewarding. Even though one would normally regard a thin premise as a plot, and a denouement which is explained rather than discovered as being weaknesses, both are easily forgiven and forgotten such is the quality of the prose throughout this 'European' novel." *Examiner*

256 pages; ISBN 1 902011 04 X; Mount Eagle original paperback £7.99

Liam Nolan / *In and Out of the Shadow*

"Nolan is vivid in his total recall of a close-knit and loving family life and the eccentricities and characters that seem to belong peculiarly to the Cork environment. But his memories have an edge. Perhaps more than anywhere else in Ireland, Cobh, with its seafaring traditions, was aware of the Second World War. U-boat sinkings and tragedies at sea linked the people of Haulbowline, Spike Island and the Holy Ground with the outside world. . . But it is a local tragedy that first leads the young Nolan to melancholy and trauma. . . The effects of this disaster on the local community and on the psyche of a small boy form the core of this touching contribution to the ever-growing library of Irish reminiscence." *Irish Independent*

288 pages; ISBN 1 902011 05 8; Mount Eagle original paperback £7.99

Alice Taylor / *The Woman of the House*

"It is a story of love for the land. . . People read Alice Taylor's books, people crave Alice Taylor's company because they want to find peace. They find it in the leaves of her books and the folds of her laughter. . . She has rare things in a policed, anaesthetised world – a sense of place and a sense of person." *Ireland on Sunday*

"Love of the land is handed down from generation to generation, but Alice Taylor has skilfully shown that that love can cause jealousy between neighbours, which can turn to violence. For the urban dweller too, this book will prove something of an eye-opener, and give endless pleasure." *RTE Guide*

320 pages; ISBN 1 902011 00 7; Mount Eagle original paperback £9.99

Tom Phelan / *Iscariot*

"A novel about religion, families, sex, guilt and joy – with a 'whodunnit' narrative that keeps you reading to the last page. It is written by a writer who understands the concept of craft." *Examiner*

"Tom Phelan's second novel, leaves us in no doubt about his talents as a keen, indeed harsh, observer of humanity. . . By weaving a litany of characters rendered in a composite of opposites he mirrors the balancing of argument that is his peculiar horn of a dilemma. One on which sex predominantly features. But ultimately one on which Tom Phelan's world view is tempered with a warm, forgiving, humanity with the exception, that is, of the Catholic Church." *Sunday Tribune*

288 pages; ISBN 0 86322 246 3; Brandon paperback £6.99

Peter Tremayne / *Aisling and other Irish Tales of Terror*

"A superb series of stories." *Examiner*

"Deliberately calculated to give nightmares to anyone whose veins contain one drop of Irish blood." *Times Literary Supplement*

"The telling of each eerie legend is sure-footed and convincing, with Tremayne clearly enjoying his role as a curator of arcane knowledge." *Time Out*

"Somewhere at the core of legend lies a grain of fact, a sliver of history. It's this dimension that makes Peter Tremayne's *Aisling* such compelling reading." *Irish News*

"Peter Tremayne is a master of the genre." *Irish Post*

256 pages; ISBN 0 86322 247 1; Brandon paperback £6.99

Books by Walter Macken

The Grass of the People

This new collection from one of the most popular masters of the Irish short story includes twelve previously unpublished stories. Marked by Macken's own distinctive style, they present a rural world teeming with characters and life.

256 pages; ISBN 0 86322 248 X; Brandon hardback £12.99

City of the Tribes

"A vivid evocation of Galway and 'the plain people' of that city in the forties, full of insight and humour but free of romanticism, as they fight against the sea, poverty and political conservatism." *Irish Post*

256 pages; ISBN 0 86322 228 5; Brandon hardback £12.99

Brown Lord of the Mountain

"Walter Macken's dramatic, almost mystical tale, with full-blown romantic hero, reveals his theatrical background. Macken knows his people and his places and his love of them shines through; this final work is a fitting tribute to them." *Examiner*

284 pages; ISBN 0 86322 201 3; paperback £5.95

God Made Sunday

"The charm of Walter Macken's leisurely, lyrical tales is real but deceptive. . . Macken's scene is a western Eden, moments after the Fall – a setting of ecstatic beauty for a life of tribulation and toil." *The Scotsman*

222 pages; ISBN 0 86322 217 X; paperback £5.95

Green Hills

"More valuable than sociological studies, [these stories] show the skill of the dramatist . . . Brandon's uniform series of reprints is modest but dignified: just right." *Books Ireland*

220 pages; ISBN 0 86322 216 1; paperback £5.95

Quench the Moon

"Where the writer knows and loves his country as Walter Macken does, there is warmth and life." *Times Literary Supplement*

413 pages; ISBN 0 86322 202 1; paperback £5.95

Rain on the Wind

"It is a raw, savage story full of passion and drama set amongst the Galway fishing community . . . It is the story of romantic passion, a constant struggle with the sea, with poverty and with the political conservatism of post-independence Ireland." *Irish Independent*

320 pages; ISBN 0 86322 185 8; paperback £5.95